Good Housekeeping's
Best Book of
Adventure Stories

Good Housekeeping's
Best Book of
Adventure Stories

Edited by
PAULINE RUSH EVANS

Illustrated by
DAN NOONAN

GOOD HOUSEKEEPING MAGAZINE

BOOK DIVISION
250 West 55th St., New York 19, N. Y.

Acknowledgements

Thanks are due to the following authors, publishers, publications and agents for permission to use the material indicated.

Boys' Life for "Two Chests of Treasure" by Merritt Allen. Reprinted by permission of the author and *Boys' Life*, published by the Boy Scouts of America. Doubleday & Company, Inc. for "An Unqualified Pilot" from LAND AND SEA TALES FOR SCOUTS AND SCOUTMASTERS by Rudyard Kipling. Reprinted by permission of Doubleday & Company, Inc., The Macmillan Company of Canada, Ltd. and Mrs. George Bambridge. E. P. Dutton & Co., Inc. for "Four Generals" from SHEN OF THE SEA by Arthur B. Chrisman. Copyright, 1925, by E. P. Dutton & Co., Inc. Renewal, 1953, by Arthur B. Chrisman. Reprinted by permission of the publishers; "The Summit" by Sir Edmund Hillary from THE CONQUEST OF EVEREST by Sir John Hunt. Copyright, 1954, by Sir John Hunt. Reprinted by permission of the publishers. Mrs. Charles J. Finger for "A Brace of Cowards" by Charles J. Finger. Harper & Brothers for selections from LIFE ON THE MISSISSIPPI and THE ADVENTURES OF TOM SAWYER by Mark Twain. Hodder & Stoughton, Ltd. for "The Summit" by Sir Edmund Hillary from THE ASCENT OF EVEREST (The Conquest of Everest) by Sir John Hunt, based on the original dispatches from Brigadier Sir John Hunt and other members of the Everest Expedition to *The Times*. The selections from JOHNNY TREMAIN by Esther Forbes, copyright 1943, are reprinted by permission of and arrangement with Houghton Mifflin Company, the authorized publishers. Little, Brown & Company for "One Alaska Night" from ALASKA HOLIDAY by Barrett Willoughby. Copyright 1936, 1937, 1939, 1940 by Barrett Willoughby. Reprinted by permission of the publishers. The Macmillan Company for selections from CALL IT COURAGE by Armstrong Sperry. Copyright 1940 by The Macmillan Company. Reprinted by permission of the publishers. Charles Scribner's Sons for "A Narrow Escape" by Will James. Copyright 1927, 1955 by Charles Scribner's Sons. Reprinted from ALL IN A DAY'S RIDING by permission of the publishers. *Story Parade* for "The Terrible Stranger" by Robert M. Hyatt. Copyright, 1936, by Story Parade, Inc. Reprinted by permission.

The editor and publisher have made diligent efforts to trace the ownership of all copyrighted material in this volume, and believe that all necessary permissions have been secured. If any errors have inadvertently been made, proper corrections will gladly be made in future editions.

Introduction

There is adventure in everything—and adventure stories have been popular since time began. The oldest tales that have come down to us are about the adventures of legendary heroes and ever since the greatest stories seem always to have been about some adventure.

Not that these stories are in any sense all alike. They aren't. Like those in this book, they can be about almost anything—about a gay and light-hearted outlaw like Robin Hood who tricks the sheriff or about a boy like Mark Twain who gets the greatest job in the world; about a girl slave in Arabia who outwits a gang of thieves or an Australian school teacher who was the first man ever to stand on the top of the highest mountain in the world. A good adventure story can be true or made up, but it does have to *seem* real and it does have to make the person who is reading it feel that he has actually taken part in an exciting experience.

The kind of adventure you like keeps changing, of course. Today you may enjoy reading about Sir Lancelot, and tomorrow prefer to go with Jim Hawkins to hunt for pirate gold on Treasure Island. And a few years from now you will probably find the best adventure in the story of how a scientist discovered a new element or a miraculous cure. But of this you can be sure—you will like adventure stories now, and you will continue to enjoy adventures of some sort as long as you read.

Here, then, are more than twenty of the best and most famous adventure stories. There are all kinds, from the magical tales of long ago to the real adventures of yesterday. Some are complete stories in themselves and some have been taken from famous books. But in at least one way they are alike—they all make it possible for you to share an experience that you will never forget.

P. R. E.

Danbury, Conn.

Contents

Good Housekeeping's
Best Book of
Adventure Stories

RUDYARD KIPLING

An Unqualified Pilot

Almost any pilot will tell you that his work is much
more difficult than you imagine; but the Pilots of the
Hugli know that they have one hundred miles of the most
dangerous river on earth running through their hands—the
Hugli between Calcutta and the Bay of Bengal—and they
say nothing. Their service is picked and sifted as carefully
as the bench of the Supreme Court, for a judge can only
hang the wrong man, or pass a bad law; but a careless pilot
can lose a ten-thousand-ton ship with crew and cargo in
less time than it takes to reverse her engines.

There is very little chance of anything getting off again
when once she touches in the furious Hugli current,
loaded with all the fat silt of the fields of Bengal, where the
soundings change two feet between tides, and new channels make and unmake themselves in one rainy season. Men
have fought the Hugli for two hundred years, till now the
river owns a huge building, with drawing, survey, and telegraph departments, devoted to its private service, as well
as a body of wardens, who are called the Port Commis-
sioners.

They and their officers govern everything that floats from the Hugli Bridge to the last buoy at Pilots Ridge, one hundred and forty miles away, far out in the Bay of Bengal, where the steamers first pick up the pilots from the pilot brig.

A Hugli pilot does not kindly bring papers aboard for the passengers, or scramble up the ship's side by wet, swaying rope-ladders. He arrives in his best clothes, with a native servant or an assistant pilot to wait on him, and he behaves as a man should who can earn two or three thousand pounds a year after twenty years' apprenticeship. He has beautiful rooms in the Port Office at Calcutta, and generally keeps himself to the society of his own profession, for though the telegraph reports the more important soundings of the river daily, there is much to be learned from brother pilots between each trip.

Some million tons of shipping must find their way to and from Calcutta each twelve-month, and unless the Hugli were watched as closely as his keeper watches an elephant, there is a fear that it might silt up, as it has silted up round the old Dutch and Portuguese ports twenty and thirty miles behind Calcutta.

So the Port Office sounds and scours and dredges the river, and builds spurs and devices for coaxing currents, and labels all the buoys with their proper letters, and attends to the semaphores and the lights and the drum, ball and cone storm signals; and the pilots of the Hugli do the rest; but, in spite of all care and the very best attention, the Hugli swallows her ship or two every year. Even the coming of wireless telegraphy does not spoil her appetite.

When Martin Trevor had waited on the river from his boyhood; when he had risen to be a Senior Pilot entitled to bring up to Calcutta the very biggest ships; when he had thought and talked of nothing but Hugli pilotage all his life to nobody except Hugli pilots, he was exceedingly surprised and indignant that his only son should decide to follow his father's profession. Mrs. Trevor had died when the boy was a child, and as he grew older, Trevor, in the intervals of his business, noticed that the lad was very often by the river-side—no place, he said, for a nice boy. But, as he was not often at home, and as the aunt who looked after Jim naturally could not follow him to his chosen haunts, and as Jim had not the faintest intention of giving up old friends there, nothing but ineffectual growls came of the remark. Later, when Trevor once asked him if he could make anything out of the shipping on the water, Jim replied by reeling off the list of all the house-flags in sight at the moorings, together with supplementary information about their tonnage and captains.

"You'll come to a bad end, Jim," said Trevor. "Boys of your age haven't any business to waste their time on these things."

"Oh, Pedro at the Sailors' Home says you can't begin too early."

"At what, please?"

"Piloting. I'm nearly fourteen now, and—and I know where most of the shipping in the river is, and I know what there was yesterday over the Mayapur Bar, and I've been down to Diamond Harbour—oh, a hundred times already, and I've—"

"You'll go to school, son, and learn what they teach you, and you'll turn out something better than a pilot," said his father, who wanted Jim to enter the Subordinate Civil Service, but he might just as well have told a shovel-nosed porpoise of the river to come ashore and begin life as a hen. Jim held his tongue; he noticed that all the best pilots in the Port Office did that; and devoted his young attention and all his spare time to the river he loved. He had seen the nice young gentlemen in the Subordinate Civil Service, and he called them a rude native name for "clerks."

He became as well known as the Banks-hall itself; and the Port Police let him inspect their launches, and the tug-boat captains had always a place for him at their tables, and the mates of the big steam dredgers used to show him how the machinery worked, and there were certain native row-boats which Jim practically owned; and he extended his patronage to the railway that runs to Diamond Harbour, forty miles down the river. In the old days nearly all the East India Company's ships used to discharge at Diamond Harbour, on account of the shoals above, but now ships go straight up to Calcutta, and they have only some moorings for vessels in distress there, and a telegraph service, and a harbour-master, who was one of Jim's most intimate friends.

He would sit in the Office listening to the soundings of the shoals as they were reported every day, and attending

to the movements of the steamers up and down (Jim
always felt he had lost something irretrievable if a boat got
in or out of the river without his knowing of it) , and when
the big liners with their rows of blazing portholes tied up
in Diamond Harbour for the night, Jim would row from
one ship to the other through the sticky hot air and the
buzzing mosquitoes and listen respectfully as the pilots
conferred together about the habits of steamers.

Once, for a treat, his father took him down clear out to
the Sandheads and the pilot brig there, and Jim was
happily sea-sick as she tossed and pitched in the Bay. The
cream of life, though, was coming up in a tug or a police
boat from Diamond Harbour to Calcutta, over the "James
and Mary," those terrible sands christened after a royal
ship that they sunk two hundred years before. They are
made by two rivers that enter the Hugli six miles apart and
throw their own silt across the silt of the main stream, so
that with each turn of weather and tide the sands shift
and change under water like clouds in the sky. It was here
(the tales sound much worse when they are told in the
rush and growl of the muddy waters) that the *Countess of
Stirling*, fifteen hundred tons, touched and capsized in ten
minutes, and a two-thousand-ton steamer in two, and a
pilgrim ship in five, and another steamer literally in one
instant, holding down her men with the masts and shrouds
as she lashed over. When a ship touches on the "James and
Mary," the river knocks her down and buries her, and the
sands quiver all around her and reach out under water and
take new shapes over the corpse.

Young Jim would lie up in the bows of the tug and watch the straining buoys kick and choke in the coffee-coloured current, while the semaphores and flags signalled from the bank how much water there was in the channel, till he learned that men who deal with men can afford to be careless, on the chance of their fellows being like them; but men who deal with things dare not relax for an instant. "And that's the very reason," old McEwan said to him once, "that the 'James and Mary' is the safest part of the river," and he shoved the big black *Bandoorah*, that draws twenty-five feet, through the Eastern Gat, with a turban of white foam wrapped round her forefoot and her screw beating as steadily as his own heart.

If Jim could not get away to the river there was always the big, cool Port Office, where the soundings were worked out and the maps drawn; or the Pilots' room, where he could lie in a long chair and listen quietly to the talk about the Hugli; and there was the library, where if you had money you could buy charts and books of directions against the time that you would actually have to steam over the places themselves. It was exceedingly hard for Jim to hold the list of Jewish Kings in his head, and he was more than uncertain as to the end of the verb *audio* if you followed it far enough down the page, but he could keep the soundings of three channels distinct in his head, and, what is more confusing, the changes in the buoys from "Garden Reach" down to Saugor, as well as the greater part of the *Calcutta Telegraph*, the only paper he ever read.

Unluckily, you cannot peruse about the Hugli without money, even though you are the son of the best-known pilot on the river, and as soon as Trevor understood how his son was spending his time, he cut down his pocket money, of which Jim had a very generous allowance. In his extremity he took counsel with Pedro, the plum-coloured mulatto at the Sailors' Home, and Pedro was a bad, designing man. He introduced Jim to a Chinaman in Muchuatollah, an unpleasing place in itself, and the Chinaman, who answered to the name of Erh-Tze, talked business in pigeon-English to Jim for an hour. Every bit of that business from first to last was flying in the face of every law on the river, but it interested Jim.

"S'pose you takee. Can do?" Erh-Tze said at last.

Jim considered his chances. A junk, he knew, would draw about eleven feet and the regular fee for a qualified pilot, outward to the Sandheads, would be two hundred rupees. On the one hand he was not qualified, so he dared not ask more than half. *But*, on the other hand, he was fully certain of the thrashing of his life from his father for piloting without license, let alone what the Port Authorities might do to him. So he asked one hundred and seventy-five rupees, and Erh-Tze beat him down to a hundred and twenty. The cargo of his junk was worth anything from seventy to a hundred and fifty thousand rupees, some of which he was getting as enormous freight on the coffins of thirty or forty dead Chinamen, whom he was taking to be buried in their native country.

Rich Chinamen will pay fancy prices for this service,

and they have a superstition that the iron of steamships is bad for the spiritual health of their dead. Erh-Tze's junk had crept up from Singapore, *via* Penang and Rangoon, to Calcutta, where Erh-Tze had been staggered by the Pilot dues. This time he was going out at a reduction with Jim, who, as Pedro kept telling him, was just as good as a pilot, and a heap cheaper.

Jim knew something of the manners of junks, but he was not prepared, when he went down that night with his charts, for the confusion of cargo and coolies and coffins and clay-cooking places, and other things that littered her decks. He had sense enough to haul the rudder up a few feet, for he knew that a junk's rudder goes far below the bottom, and he allowed a foot extra to Erh-Tze's estimate of the junk's depth. Then they staggered out into midstream very early, and never had the city of his birth looked so beautiful as when he feared he would not come back to see it. Going down "Garden Reach" he discovered that the junk would answer to her helm if you put it over far enough, and that she had a fair, though Chinese, notion of sailing. He took charge of the tiller by stationing three Chinese on each side of it, and standing a little forward, gathered their pigtails into his hands, three right and three left, as though they had been the yoke lines of a row-boat. Erh-Tze almost smiled at this; he felt he was getting good care for his money and took a neat little polished bamboo to keep the men attentive, for he said this was no time to teach the crew pigeon-English. The more way they could get on the junk the better would she steer, and as soon as he felt a little confidence in her, Jim ordered the stiff, rustling sails to be hauled up tighter and tighter. He did not know their names—at least any name that would be likely to interest a Chinaman—but Erh-Tze had not banged about the waters of the Malay Archipelago all his life for nothing. He rolled forward with his bamboo, and the things rose like Eastern incantations.

Early as they were on the river, a big American oil (but they called it kerosene in those days) ship was ahead of them in tow, and when Jim saw her through the lifted mist he was thankful. She would draw all of seventeen feet, and if he could steer by her they would be safe. It is easier to scurry up and down the "James and Mary" in a police-boat that someone else is handling than to cram a hard-mouthed old junk across the same sands alone, with the certainty of a thrashing if you come out alive.

Jim glued his eyes to the American, and saw that at Ful-tah she dropped her tug and stood down the river under sail. He all but whooped aloud, for he knew that the num-ber of pilots who preferred to work a ship through the "James and Mary" was strictly limited. "If it isn't Father, it's Dearsley," said Jim, "and Dearsley went down yester-day with the *Bancoora,* so it's Father. If I'd gone home last night instead of going to Pedro, I'd have met him. He must have got his ship quick, but—Father *is* a very quick man." Then Jim reflected that they kept a piece of knotted rope on the pilot brig that stung like a wasp; but this thought he dismissed as beneath the dignity of an offici-ating pilot, who needed only to nod his head to set Erh-

Tze's bamboo to work.

As the American came round, just before the Fultah
Sands, Jim raked her with his spy-glass and saw his father
on the poop, an unlighted cigar between his teeth. That
cigar, Jim knew, would be smoked on the other side of the
"James and Mary," and Jim felt so entirely safe and happy
that he lit a cigar on his own account. This kind of piloting was child's play. His father could not make a mistake
if he tried; and Jim, with his six obedient pigtails in his
two hands, had leisure to admire the perfect style in which
the American was handled—how she would point her
bowsprit jeeringly at a hidden bank, as much as to say,
"Not to-day, thank you, dear," and bow down lovingly to
a buoy as much as to say, "*You're* a gentleman, at any
rate," and come round sharp on her heel with a flutter
and a rustle, and a slow, steady swing something like a
well-dressed woman staring all round the theatre through
opera-glasses.

It was hard work to keep the junk near her, though Erh-
Tze set everything that was by any means settable, and
used his bamboo most generously. When they were nearly
under her counter, and a little to her left, Jim, hidden behind a sail, would feel warm and happy all over, thinking
of the thousand nautical and piloting things that he knew.
When they fell more than half a mile behind, he was cold
and miserable thinking of all the million things he did not
know or was not quite sure of. And so they went down,
Jim steering by his father, turn for turn, over the Mayapur
Bar, with the semaphores on each bank duly signalling the

depth of water, through the Western Gat, and round Ma-koaputti Lumps, and in and out of twenty places, each more exciting than the last, and Jim nearly pulled the six pigtails out for pure joy when the last of the "James and Mary" had gone astern, and they were walking through Diamond Harbour.

From there to the mouth of the Hugli things are not so bad—at least, that was what Jim thought, and held on till the swell from the Bay of Bengal made the old junk heave and snort, and the river broadened into the inland sea, with islands only a foot or two high scattered about it. The American walked away from the junk as soon as they were beyond Kedgeree, and the night came on and the river looked very big and desolate, so Jim promptly anchored somewhere in grey water, with the Saugor Light away off toward the east. He had a great respect for the Hugli to the last yard of her, and had no desire whatever to find himself on the Gasper Sand or any other little shoal. Erh-Tze and the crew highly approved of this piece of seaman-ship. They set no watch, lit no lights, and at once went to sleep.

Jim lay down between a red-and-black lacquer coffin and a little live pig in a basket. As soon as it was light he be-gan studying his chart of the Hugli mouth, and trying to find out where in the river he might be. He decided to be on the safe side and wait for another sailing-ship and fol-low her out. So he made an enormous breakfast of rice and boiled fish, while Erh-Tze lit firecrackers and burned gilt paper to the Joss who had saved them so far. Then they heaved up their rough-and-tumble anchor, and made after a big, fat, iron four-masted sailing-ship, heavy as a hay-wain.

The junk, which was really a very weatherly boat, and might have begun life as a private pirate in Annam forty years before, followed under easy sail; for the four-master would run no risks. She was in old McEwan's hands, and she waddled about like a broody hen, giving each shoal wide allowances. All this happened near the outer Floating Light, some hundred and twenty miles from Calcutta, and apparently in the open sea.

Jim knew old McEwan's appetite, and often heard him pride himself on getting his ship to the pilot brig close upon meal hours, so he argued that if the pilot brig was get-at-able (and Jim himself had not the ghost of a notion where she would lie), McEwan would find her before one o'clock.

It was a blazing hot day, and McEwan fidgeted the four-master down to "Pilots Ridge" with what little wind remained, and sure enough there lay the pilot brig, and Jim felt shivers up his back as Erh-Tze paid him his hundred and twenty rupees and he went overside in the junk's one crazy dinghy. McEwan was leaving the four-master in a long, slashing whale-boat that looked very spruce and pretty, and Jim could see that there was a certain amount of excitement among the pilots on the brig. There was his father too. The ragged Chinese boatmen gave way in a most ragged fashion, and Jim felt very unwashen and disreputable when he heard the click of McEwan's oars

alongside, and McEwan saying, "James Trevor, I'll trouble you to lay alongside me."

Jim obeyed, and from the corner of one eye watched McEwan's angry whiskers stand up all round his face, which turned purple.

"An' how is it you break the regulations o' the Porrt o' Calcutta? Are ye aware o' the penalties and impreesonments ye've laid yourself open to?" McEwan began.

Jim said nothing. There was not very much to say just then; and McEwan roared aloud: "Man, ye've perrsonated a Hugli pilot, an' that 's as much as to say ye've perrsonated *ME!* What did yon heathen give ye for honorarium?"

" 'Hundred and twenty," said Jim.

"An' by what manner o' means did ye get through the 'James and Mary'?"

"Father," was the answer. "He went down the same tide and I—we—steered by him."

McEwan whistled and choked, perhaps it was with anger. "Ye've made a stalkin'-horse o' your father, then? Jim, laddie, he'll make an example o' you."

The boat hooked on to the brig's chains, and McEwan said, as he set foot on deck before Jim could speak, "Yon's an enterprising cub o' yours, Trevor. Ye'd better enter him in the regular business, or one o' these fine days he'll be acting as pilot before he's qualified, and sinkin' junks in the Fairway. He fetched yon junk down last night. If ye've no other designs I'm thinkin' I'll take him as my cub, for there's no denying he's a resourceful lad—for all he's an unlicked whelp."

"That," said Trevor, reaching for Jim's left ear, "is something we can remedy," and he led him below.

The little knotted rope that they keep for general purposes on the pilot-brig did its duty, but when it was all over Jim was unlicked no longer. He was McEwan's property to be registered under the laws of the Port of Calcutta, and a week later, when the *Ellora* came along, he bundled over the pilot brig's side with McEwan's enamelled leather hand-bag and a roll of charts and a little bag of his own, and he dropped into the sternsheets of the pilot gig with a very creditable imitation of McEwan's slow, swaying sit-down and hump of the shoulders.

from MARK TWAIN'S

The Adventures of Tom Sawyer

If Tom Sawyer liked anything more than an adventure it was a mystery—and when he started looking for it, he usually found it. Tom and Huck Finn had decided to hunt for buried treasure and had spent a whole day digging under the limbs of dead trees, but with no luck. So they decided to try the next most likely place—a haunted house. And this time they got more than they bargained for.

THE HAUNTED HOUSE

About noon the next day the boys arrived at the dead tree; they had come for their tools. Tom was impatient to go to the haunted house; Huck was measurably so, also—but suddenly said—

"Lookyhere, Tom, do you know what day it is?"

Tom mentally ran over the days of the week, and then quickly lifted his eyes with a startled look in them—

"My! I never once thought of it, Huck!"

"Well I didn't neither, but all at once it popped onto me that it was Friday."

"Blame it, a body can't be too careful, Huck. We might a got into an awful scrape, tackling such a thing on a Friday."

"*Might!* Better say we *would!* There's some lucky days, maybe, but Friday ain't."

"Any fool knows that. I don't reckon *you* was the first that found it out, Huck."

"Well, I never said I was, did I? And Friday ain't all, neither. I had a rotten bad dream last night—dreamt about rats."

"No! Sure sign of trouble. Did they fight?"

"No."

"Well, that's good, Huck. When they don't fight it's only a sign that there's trouble around, you know. All we got to do is to look mighty sharp and keep out of it. We'll drop this thing for to-day, and play. Do you know Robin Hood, Huck?"

"No. Who's Robin Hood?"

"Why he was one of the greatest men that was ever in England—and the best. He was a robber."

"Cracky, I wisht I was. Who did he rob?"

"Only sheriffs and bishops and rich people and kings, and such like. But he never bothered the poor. He loved 'em. He always divided up with 'em perfectly square."

"Well, he must 'a' been a brick."

"I bet you he was, Huck. Oh, he was the noblest man that ever was. They ain't any such men, now, I can tell you. He could lick any man in England, with one hand tied behind him; and he could take his yew bow and plug a ten-cent piece every time, a mile and a half."

"What's a *yew* bow?"

"I don't know. It's some kind of a bow, of course. And if he hit that dime only on the edge he would set down and cry—and curse. But we'll play Robin Hood—it's noble fun. I'll learn you."

"I'm agreed."

So they played Robin Hood all the afternoon, now and then casting a yearning eye down upon the haunted house and passing a remark about the morrow's prospects and possibilities there. As the sun began to sink into the west they took their way homeward athwart the long shadows of the trees and soon were buried from sight in the forests of Cardiff Hill.

On Saturday, shortly after noon, the boys were at the dead tree again. They had a smoke and a chat in the shade, and then dug a little in their last hole, not with great hope, but merely because Tom said there were so many cases where people had given up a treasure after getting down within six inches of it, and then somebody else had come along and turned it up with a single thrust of a shovel. The thing failed this time, however, so the boys shouldered their tools and went away feeling that they had not trifled with fortune but had fulfilled all the requirements that belong to the business of treasure-hunting.

When they reached the haunted house there was something so weird and grisly about the dead silence that reigned there under the baking sun, and something so depressing about the loneliness and desolation of the place, that they were afraid, for a moment, to venture in. Then they crept to the door and took a trembling peep. They saw a weed-grown, floorless room, unplastered, an ancient fireplace, vacant windows, a ruinous staircase; and here, there, and everywhere, hung ragged and abandoned cobwebs. They presently entered, softly, with quickened pulses, talking in whispers, ears alert to catch the slightest sound, and muscles tense and ready for instant retreat.

In a little while familiarity modified their fears and they gave the place a critical and interested examination, rather admiring their own boldness, and wondering at it, too.

Next they wanted to look up stairs. This was something like cutting off retreat, but they got to daring each other, and of course there could be but one result—they threw their tools into a corner and made the ascent. Up there were the same signs of decay. In one corner they found a closet that promised mystery, but the promise was a fraud —there was nothing in it. Their courage was up now and well in hand. They were about to go down and begin work when—

"Sh!" said Tom.

"What is it?" whispered Huck, blanching with fright.

"Sh! . . . There! . . . Hear it?"

"Yes! . . . O, my! Let's run!"

"Keep still! Don't you budge! They're coming right toward the door."

The boys stretched themselves upon the floor with their eyes to knot holes in the planking, and lay waiting, in a misery of fear.

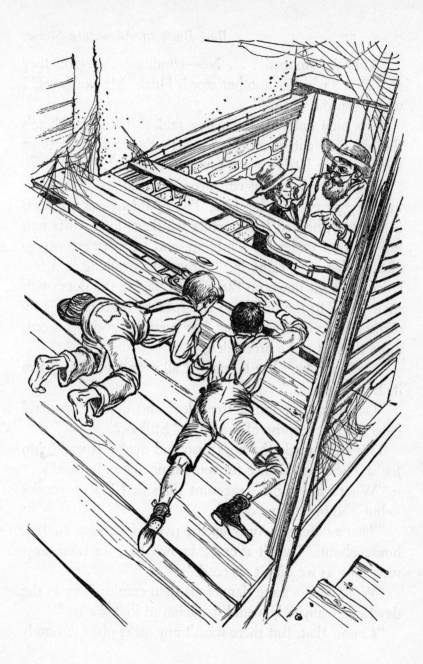

"They've stopped . . . No—coming . . . Here they are. Don't whisper another word, Huck. My goodness, I wish I was out of this!"

Two men entered. Each boy said to himself: There's the old deaf and dumb Spaniard that's been about town once or twice lately—never saw t'other man before."

"T'other" was a ragged, unkempt creature, with nothing very pleasant in his face. The Spaniard was wrapped in a *serape*; he had bushy white whiskers; long white hair flowed from under his sombrero, and he wore green goggles. When they came in, "t'other" was talking in a low voice; they sat down on the ground, facing the door, with their backs to the wall, and the speaker continued his remarks. His manner became less guarded and his words more distinct as he proceeded;

"No," said he, "I've thought it all over, and I don't like it. It's dangerous."

"Dangerous!" grunted the "deaf and dumb" Spaniard —to the vast surprise of the boys. "Milksop!"

This voice made the boys gasp and quake. It was Injun Joe's! There was silence for some time. Then Joe said:

"What's any more dangerous than that job up yonder —but nothing's come of it."

"That's different. Away up the river so, and not another house about. 'Twon't ever be known that we tried, anyway, long as we didn't succeed."

"Well, what's more dangerous than coming here in the day time!—anybody would suspicion us that saw us."

"I know that. But there warn't any other place as handy

after that fool of a job. I want to quit this shanty. I wanted to yesterday, only it warn't any use trying to stir out of here, with those infernal boys playing over there on the hill right in full view."

"Those infernal boys" quaked again under the inspiration of this remark, and thought how lucky it was that they had remembered it was Friday and concluded to wait a day. They wished in their hearts they had waited a year.

The two men got out some food and made a luncheon. After a long and thoughtful silence, Injun Joe said:

"Look here, lad—you go back up the river where you belong. Wait there till you hear from me. I'll take the chances on dropping into this town just once more, for a look. We'll do that 'dangerous' job after I've spied around a little and think things look well for it. Then for Texas! We'll leg it together!"

This was satisfactory. Both men presently fell to yawning, and Injun Joe said:

"I'm dead for sleep! It's your turn to watch."

He curled down in the weeds and soon began to snore. His comrade stirred him once or twice and he became quiet. Presently the watcher began to nod; his head drooped lower and lower, both men began to snore now.

The boys drew a long, grateful breath. Tom whispered—

"Now's our chance—come!"

Huck said:

"I can't—I'd die if they was to wake."

Tom urged—Huck held back. At last Tom rose slowly and softly, and started alone. But the first step he made wrung such a hideous creak from the crazy floor that he sank down almost dead with fright. He never made a second attempt. The boys lay there counting the dragging moments till it seemed to them that time must be done and eternity growing gray; and then they were grateful to note that at last the sun was setting.

Now one snore ceased. Injun Joe sat up, stared around —smiled grimly upon his comrade, whose head was drooping upon his knees—stirred him up with his foot and said—

"Here! *You're* a watchman, ain't you? All right, though —nothing's happened."

"My! have I been asleep?"

"Oh, partly, partly. Nearly time for us to be moving, pard. What'll we do with what little swag we've got left?"

"I don't know—leave it here as we've always done, I reckon. No use to take it away till we start south. Six hundred and fifty in silver's something to carry."

"Well—all right—it won't matter to come here once more."

"No—but I'd say come in the night as we used to do— it's better."

"Yes; but look here; it may be a good while before I get the right chance at that job; accidents might happen; 'tain't in such a very good place; we'll just regularly bury it—and bury it deep."

"Good idea," said the comrade, who walked across the room, knelt down, raised one of the rearward hearthstones and took out a bag that jingled pleasantly. He subtracted from it twenty or thirty dollars for himself and as much for Injun Joe and passed the bag to the latter, who was on his knees in the corner, now, digging with his bowie knife.

The boys forgot all their fears, all their miseries in an instant. With gloating eyes they watched every movement. Luck!—the splendor of it was beyond all imagination! Six hundred dollars was money enough to make half a dozen boys rich! Here was treasure-hunting under the happiest auspices—there would not be any bothersome uncertainty as to where to dig. They nudged each other every moment —eloquent nudges and easily understood, for they simply meant—"O, but ain't you glad *now* we're here!"

Joe's knife struck upon something.

"Hello!" he said.

"What is it?" said his comrade.

"Half-rotten plank—no it's a box, I believe. Here—bear a hand and we'll see what it's here for. Never mind, I've broke a hole."

He reached his hand in and drew it out—

"Man, it's money!"

The two men examined the handful of coins. They were gold. The boys above were as excited as themselves, and as delighted.

Joe's comrade said—

"We'll make quick work of this. There's an old rusty pick over amongst the weeds in the corner the other side of the fireplace—I saw it a minute ago."

He ran and brought the boys' pick and shovel. Injun Joe took the pick, looked it over critically, shook his head, muttered something to himself, and then began to use it. The box was soon unearthed. It was not very large; it was iron bound and had been very strong before the slow years had injured it. The men contemplated the treasure a while in blissful silence.

"Pard, there's thousands of dollars here," said Injun Joe.

" 'Twas always said that Murrel's gang cruised around here one summer," the stranger observed.

"I know it," said Injun Joe; "and this looks like it, I should say."

"*Now* you won't need to do that job."

The half-breed frowned. Said he—

"You don't know me. Least you don't know all about that thing. 'Tain't robbery altogether—it's *revenge!*" and a wicked light flamed in his eyes. "I'll need your help in it. When it's finished—then Texas. Go home to your Nance and your kids, and stand by till you hear from me."

"Well—if you say so, what'll we do with this—bury it again?"

"Yes. [Ravishing delight overhead.] *No!* by the great Sachem, no! [Profound distress overhead.] I'd nearly forgot. That pick had fresh earth on it. [The boys were sick with terror in a moment.] What business has a pick and a shovel here? What business with fresh earth on them? Who brought them here—and where are they gone? Have you heard anybody?—seen anybody? What! bury it again and leave them to come and see the ground disturbed? Not exactly—not exactly. We'll take it to my den."

"Why of course! Might have thought of that before. You mean Number One?"

"No—Number Two—under the cross. The other place is bad—too common."

"All right. It's nearly dark enough to start."

Injun Joe got up and went about from window to window cautiously peeping out. Presently he said:

"Who could have brought those tools here? Do you reckon they can be up-stairs?"

The boys' breath forsook them. Injun Joe put his hand on his knife, halted a moment, undecided, and then turned toward the stairway. The boys thought of the closet, but their strength was gone. The steps came creaking up the stairs—the intolerable distress of the situation woke the stricken resolution of the lads—they were about to spring for the closet, when there was a crash of rotten timbers and Injun Joe landed on the ground amid the *débris* of the ruined stairway. He gathered himself up cursing, and his comrade said:

"Now what the use of all that? If it's anybody, and they're up there, let them *stay* there—who cares? If they want to jump down, now, and get into trouble, who objects? It will be dark in fifteen minutes—and then let them follow us if they want to. I'm willing. In my opinion, whoever hove those things in here caught a sight of us and took us for ghosts or devils or something. I'll bet they're running yet."

Joe grumbled a while; then he agreed with his friend that what daylight was left ought to be economized in

getting things ready for leaving. Shortly afterward they
slipped out of the house in the deepening twilight, and
moved toward the river with their precious box.

Tom and Huck rose up, weak but vastly relieved, and
stared after them through the chinks between the logs of
the house. Follow? Not they. They were content to reach
ground again without broken necks, and take the town-
ward track over the hill. They did not talk much. They
were too much absorbed in hating themselves—hating the
ill luck that made them take the spade and the pick there.
But for that, Injun Joe never would have suspected. He
would have hidden the silver with the gold to wait there
till his "revenge" was satisfied, and then he would have
had the misfortune to find that money turn up missing.
Bitter, bitter luck that the tools were ever brought there!

They resolved to keep a lookout for that Spaniard when
he should come to town spying out for chances to do his
revengeful job, and follow him to "Number Two," wherever that might be. Then a ghastly thought occurred to
Tom:

"Revenge? What if he means *us*, Huck?"

"O, don't!" said Huck, nearly fainting.

They talked it all over, and as they entered town they
agreed to believe that he might possibly mean somebody
else—at least that he might at least mean nobody but
Tom, since only Tom had testified.

Very, very small comfort it was to Tom to be alone in
danger! Company would be a palpable improvement, he
thought.

THE YOUNG DETECTIVES

The adventure of the day mightily tormented Tom's dreams that night. Four times he had his hands on that rich treasure, and four times it wasted to nothingness in his fingers as sleep forsook him and wakefulness brought back the hard reality of his misfortune. As he lay in the early morning recalling the incidents of his great adventure; he noticed that they seemed curiously subdued and far away—somewhat as if they had happened in another world, or in a time long gone by. Then it occurred to him that the great adventure itself must be a dream! There was one very strong argument in favor of this idea—namely, that the quantity of coin he had seen was too vast to be real. He had never seen as much as fifty dollars in one mass before, and he was like all boys of his age and station in life, in that he imagined that all references to "hundreds" and "thousands" were mere fanciful forms of speech, and that no such sums really existed in the world. He never had supposed for a moment that so large a sum as a hundred dollars was to be found in actual money in any one's possession. If his notions of hidden treasure had been analyzed, they would have been found to consist of a handful of real dimes and a bushel of vague, splendid, ungraspable dollars.

But the incidents of his adventure grew sensibly sharper and clearer under the attrition of thinking them over, and so he presently found himself leaning to the impression that the thing might not have been a dream, after all. This uncertainty must be swept away. He would snatch a hurried breakfast and go and find Huck.

Huck was sitting on the gunwale of a flatboat, listlessly dangling his feet in the water and looking very melancholy. Tom concluded to let Huck lead up to the subject. If he did not do it, then the adventure would be proved to have been only a dream.

"Hello, Huck!"

"Hello, yourself."

Silence, for a minute.

"Tom, if we'd a left the blame tools at the dead tree, w'd 'a got the money. O, ain't it awful!"

" 'Tain't a dream, then, 'tain't a dream! Somehow I most wish it was. Dog'd if I don't, Huck."

"What ain't a dream?"

"Oh, that thing yesterday. I been half thinking it was."

"Dream! If them stairs hadn't broke down you'd 'a' seen how much dream it was! I've had dreams enough all night—with that patch-eyed Spanish devil going for me all through 'em—rot him!"

"No, not rot him. *Find* him! Track the money!"

"Tom, we'll never find him. A feller don't have only one chance for such a pile—and that one's lost. I'd feel mighty shaky if I was to see him, anyway."

"Well, so'd I; but I'd like to see him, anyway—and track him out—to his Number Two."

"Number Two—yes, that's it. I ben thinking 'bout that. But I can't make nothing out of it. What do you reckon it is?"

"I dono. It's too deep. Say, Huck—maybe it's the number of a house!"

"Goody! . . . No, Tom, that ain't it. If it is, it ain't in this one-horse town. They ain't no numbers here."

"Well, that's so. Lemme think a minute. Here—it's the number of a room—in a tavern, you know!"

"O, that's the trick! They ain't only two taverns. We can find out quick."

"You stay here, Huck, till I come."

Tom was off at once. He did not care to have Huck's company in public places. He was gone half an hour. He found that in the best tavern, No. 2 had long been occupied by a young lawyer, and was still so occupied. In the less ostentatious house No. 2 was a mystery. The tavern-keeper's young son said it was kept locked all the time, and he never saw anybody go into it or come out of it except at night; he did not know any particular reason for this state of things; had had some little curiosity, but it was rather feeble; had made the most of the mystery by entertaining himself with the idea that the room was "ha'nted"; had noticed that there was a light in there the night before.

"That's what I've found out, Huck. I reckon that's the very No. 2 we're after."

"I reckon it is, Tom. Now what you going to do?"

"Lemme think."

Tom thought a long time. Then he said:

"I'll tell you. The back door of that No. 2 is the door that comes out into that little close alley between the tavern and the old rattle-trap of a brick store. Now you get hold of all the doorkeys you can find, and I'll nip all of Auntie's and the first dark night we'll go there and try 'em. And mind you keep a lookout for Injun Joe, because he said he was going to drop into town and spy around once more for a chance to get his revenge. If you see him, you just follow him; and if he don't go to that No. 2, that ain't the place."

"Lordy, I don't want to foller him by myself."

"Why it'll be night, sure. He mightn't ever see you—and if he did, maybe he'd never think anything."

"Well, if it's pretty dark I reckon I'll track him. I dono—I dono. I'll try."

"You bet *I'll* follow him, if it's dark, Huck. Why he might 'a' found out he couldn't get his revenge, and be going right after that money."

"It's so, Tom, it's so. I'll foller him; I will, by jingoes!"

"Now you're *talking!* Don't you ever weaken, Huck, and I won't."

HUCK MOUNTS GUARD

That night Tom and Huck were ready for their adventure. They hung about the neighborhood of the tavern until after nine, one watching the alley at a distance and the other the tavern door. Nobody entered the alley or left it; nobody resembling the Spaniard entered or left the tavern door. The night promised to be a fair one; so Tom went home with the understanding that if a considerable degree of darkness came on, Huck was to come and "meow," whereupon he would slip out and try the keys. But the night remained clear, and Huck closed his watch and retired to bed in an empty sugar hogshead about twelve.

Tuesday the boys had the same ill-luck. Also Wednesday. But Thursday night promised better. Tom slipped out in good season with his aunt's old tin lantern, and a large towel to blindfold it with. He hid the lantern in Huck's sugar hogshead and the watch began. An hour before midnight the tavern closed up and its lights (the only ones thereabouts) were put out. No Spaniard had been seen. Nobody had entered or left the alley. Everything was auspicious. The blackness of darkness reigned, the perfect stillness was interrupted only by occasional mutterings of distant thunder.

Tom got his lantern, lit it in the hogshead, wrapped it closely in the towel, and the two adventurers crept in the gloom toward the tavern. Huck stood sentry and Tom felt his way into the alley. Then there was a season of waiting anxiety that weighed upon Huck's spirits like a mountain. He began to wish he could see a flash from the lantern— it would frighten him, but it would at least tell him that Tom was alive yet. It seemed hours since Tom had disappeared. Surely he must have fainted; maybe he was dead; maybe his heart had burst under terror and excitement. In his uneasiness Huck found himself drawing closer and closer to the alley; fearing all sorts of dreadful things, and momentarily expecting some catastrophe to happen that

would take away his breath. There was not much to take
away, for he seemed only able to inhale it by thimblesful,
and his heart would soon wear itself out, the way it was
beating. Suddenly there was a flash of light and Tom came
tearing by him:

"Run!" said he; "run, for your life!"

He needn't have repeated it; once was enough; Huck
was making thirty or forty miles an hour before the repetition was uttered. The boys never stopped till they reached
the shed of a deserted slaughter-house at the lower end of
the village. Just as they got within its shelter the storm
burst and the rain poured down. As soon as Tom got his
breath he said:

"Huck, it was awful! I tried two of the keys, just as soft as I could; but they seemed to make such a power of racket that I couldn't hardly get my breath I was so scared. They wouldn't turn in the lock, either. Well, without noticing what I was doing, I took hold of the knob, and open comes the door! It warn't locked! I hopped in, and shook off the towel, and, *great Caesar's ghost!*"

"What—what'd you see, Tom!"

"Huck, I most stepped onto Injun Joe's hand!"

SEUMAS MacMANUS

Rory the Robber

Rory was the greatest robber in that whole country, and there was a great gentleman lived there who owned a great estate in a distant part of the country. But he never got any good of the estate, for whoever he sent to lift the rents was always sure to be robbed by Rory in the mountains coming home again, and maybe killed into the bargain. So the gentleman found it was no use trying to lift the rents, and for the past five years he gave up lifting them altogether. Then there was a boy named Billy come to the gentleman looking to be hired, and the gentleman axed what he could do; and Billy said he could do anything, and then the gentleman engaged him. And when that time of year came, says Billy, says he, to his masther, "Masther," says he, "are ye sendin' no one to lift your rents this year?" "No, Billy," says the masther, "for it is no use. Rory would only rob them, and maybe murder them into the bargain on the way back." Says Billy, says he, "I'll try." Well and good the masther consinted, and told Billy to harness the best horse in the stable, so that he might have a chance of escaping from Rory. "No," says

Billy, "but give me the very worst horse." And the worst
horse Billy saddled, and went off. And when he was going
through the mountains he enquired for Rory, and finding
him out, he told him, says he, "I'm Billy, the masther's
boy, and I'm going to such a place" (mentioning the name
of where the estate was), says he, "to collect his rents;
and if you're here when I'm coming back, I'll hand the
money over to you." Rory thanked him for nothing, and
said he would be there right enough to take the rents from
him.

So, when Billy got to the estate and collected the rents
in gold and notes, he had it all sewed into the lining of
his coat, all except ten pounds that he changed into coppers and tied up in a bag, and put on the saddle before
him. And when he reached the mountains on his way back,
there he met Rory waiting for him.

Then, says Billy, "I want to purtend to my masther that
I made a hard fight before I gev up the money, so do you,"
says he, holding out his coat, "shoot your pistols through
that coat, that I can be able to show him the marks." Then
Rory shot all his pistols through Billy's coat, making a
number of holes in it. Then Billy threw the bag of coppers
on the road, and says he, "There's the rints," and when
Rory got down off his horse to lift the bag, Billy jumped
up on it, and away off, and it was one of the swiftest horses
in the country, so that Rory couldn't overtake him, and he
couldn't fire after him, because Billy was so cute as to
make him empty all his pistols into his coat.

When Billy got home to his masther, and gev him up

the rints, and told him the whole story of how he had tricked Rory, his masther was proud of him, and couldn't make too much of him. "But then," says the masther, "it was a bad thing to take his horse, for he'll never rest contented now till he's revenged on me." They agreed it was best to leave back the horse with Rory, and so Billy started, and when he fell in with the robber and gev him up his horse, Rory said he was a clever fellow and no mistake, and he would like Billy would join his band. Billy said well and good, he would.

Off they went, then, to the cave in the mountains where the robbers had their den, and when they came there Rory introduced Billy to his brother robbers, and they proposed to welcome him with a big supper. So one of their cleverest hands was sent away to steal a sheep that they might make a fine roast. He was a long time away and they begun to chat about what was keeping him. "I'll bet you fifty pounds," says Billy to Rory, "that I steal the sheep from him." "Done," says Rory.

Then Billy started away, and taking off a pair of splendid big top boots he had on him, he dropped one of them about a mile from the cave in the path the robber would take coming home with the sheep, and then travelling on about half a mile further he dropped the other, after rubbing it well with soft mud to make it right dirty. Then, when, not long after, the robber comes along with the sheep, and comes up to this boot, he looks at it and says, "It's a fine top boot, but, bad luck to it," says he, "it's too dirty entirely to carry, and where's the use of it anyhow when I haven't its fellow?" On he went then himself and the sheep till he come to the next boot, and when he seen it, "Bad scran to me," says he, "but there is its fellow, and I was unlucky I didn't take it." So he took and tied the sheep to a stump of a bush that was by, and started away back to get the other top boot. In the meantime Billy loosed the sheep and took it to the cave, and got his bet from Rory. Soon the robber come then to the cave with the pair of top boots in his hand, and told how he tied the sheep to the stump of a bush till he'd go back and look for the other top boot, and how, when he come back, the sheep was broke away, and he couldn't get her.

Then Rory ordered him to go back and steal another sheep; "And now," says he to Billy, when he was gone, "I'll hold ye a hundred pound ye don't steal this sheep from him." "Done," says Billy, and started off after him. When Billy got to the place he had stole the first sheep he hid close by, and waited till the robber come up with the next; and when he come up Billy commenced bleatin' like a sheep and "Bad luck be off me," says the robber, says he, "but there's the sheep I lost." And with that he tied the sheep he had with him now to the very same tree stump, and went over the ditches looking for the other sheep. Billy stole round, and loosed the sheep, and away to the cave with it, and won that hundred pounds too.

Rory had to confess that Billy was by far the cleverest thief he ever met, and even cleverer than himself. "I'll tell you what," says he to Billy, "there's one thing I want stolen, and I have been after it for the last five years and couldn't succeed—but maybe you'd come better speed than me; it's the King of Connaught's black mare, the grandest and swiftest in the world, that never was beaten yet, or never will be beaten; if I only had her, I would defy the whole country, for none could catch me. I'll give you, Billy," says he, "four hundred pounds in goold if ye can succeed in stealing her for me. But it's a very difficult job," says he, "for there's always a guard of soldiers on the stable, and a man sitting on the back of the black mare, night and day, for fear of me stealing her." "Well," says Billy, "if I had only a good harper to come with me I'd steal her." "Well," says Rory, "you have that here, for I'm reckoned a first class player on the harp, and my father before me was harper to the Chieftain of Knockree."

Well and good, then, Billy made him disguise as a blind harper, and they both of them set off, and the harp with them, for the King of Connaught's castle, and Billy put Rory to play the harp before the castle windows where there was a lot of high-up folk being entertained. And when the King of Connaught saw the blind harper he made him be brought in to amuse the company, and then, of course, a dance was started, and every one was taken up with the fun, the captain of the guards along with every one else. Then, when Billy found the spree at its height, he went and got a jar of whiskey and drugged it with sleeping drops, and then went into the courtyard and lay down, close by the stables, like a drunken man fallen asleep, with the drugged jar beside him. The guards soon saw the jar, and smelled it, and saying to themselves that there was no

watch over them this night, when everybody was too taken on with the fun, and that it would be no harm to taste just a little of it, they passed the jar round, and every man of them fell fast asleep; and the man that was on the horse's back dropped off it, asleep with the drink, too; and Billy got up and went into the stable, and taking out the black mare, started off with her to the mountains.

And when Rory arrived he was a proud man to find the King of Connaught's black mare there before him. He counted down to Billy four hundred yellow, shining sovereigns, and Billy went home with his five hundred and fifty pounds, and lived an honest and happy man ever after.

MERRITT P. ALLEN

Two Chests of Treasure

Twilight was on the Caribbean and so magically did it blend all things it touched that no one could mark the spot where sea and sky met. Sky and sea—they seemed to comprise the whole world except one tiny speck of land that lay like a grain of sand on the rounded face of the ocean. There was no life on the island above that of insects unless a migrating bird chanced to rest there for an hour or a turtle crawled up the rocks to bask in the sand. To find a man in such a place would have been startling, but to find a boy there, alone, was nigh amazing. Yet a boy was sleeping on the sand; a lad perhaps sixteen years old was curled up in the shadows of the rocks.

He slept as the evening deepened, then at a sound he sat up suddenly, as one does who has been on the alert for days and nights together. He had a harried look, his blue eyes were weary, his hair, worn in a short queue, was unkempt and his linen shirt, velvet breeches, silk hose and silver-buckled shoes were stained with salt water and wrinkled.

Again came the sound, the crackling of a sail in the wind. He leaped to his feet and ran to the edge of the rocks. Yes, there was a ship, an English ship by the build of her, standing off the island in the gloom. A weakness seized the boy so that before he could hail the stranger he must lean against the rocks, giddy with joy. And then, as he filled his lungs to shout, he suddenly caught his breath and remained silent.

What he saw was a small boat on the beach and at the moment two negroes were coming ashore from it, each carrying a heavy chest on his shoulder and a spade in his hand. Behind them walked a man bearing a ship's lantern, whose light played on the brass bindings of the chests. A pirate captain come to bury his treasure! Even in that day, it was the year 1680, such a sight was enough to strike any boy dumb.

The three men came up the slope silently and pitched over into the little valley in the center of the island.

"Here!" The captain indicated a spot on the sand. "Sink a hole half a fathom and be quick, ye black heathen."

The slaves put down the chests and fell to work with their spades in the manner of men who fear their master with good cause. The captain set his lantern on the ground and by its light the boy saw that he was short and powerfully built, with the dress of a sailor save for a plumed hat such as cavaliers wore. His face was shaded by the wide brim of this hat but doubtless it matched his character. He stepped back, his feet wide apart as though standing on a deck, and when he folded his arms across his chest there was a pistol in each hand. The boy watched, spell-bound, forgetful of all else, for this was no sailor's yarn such as he had heard on the docks at home, but a living reality.

"Lay off!" the captain snapped.

The negroes dropped their spades.

"Heave 'em in."

They placed the chests in the hole.

"Bury 'em."

The negroes resumed their spades and the lantern-light flickered on their naked, sweating backs. The captain watched them silently as the sand filled the hole, making a swishing, ghostly sound. In the shadow of the rocks the boy's brain had run ahead of his eyes and was rapidly seeking the best way to discover himself to the captain. He must make himself known, for this chance ship was his heaven-sent means of escape, but to reveal himself as a witness of the planting of the treasure would be to run after death. Better to wait until the men were re-embarking, then shout as though just sighting them. After that, events must guide him as they appeared. He had already passed through enough to have faith in the future. To be sure, he had never before met pirates on the open sea, though he had seen plenty of them in Port Royal, but such fellows were human, with instincts and sympathies common to other men.

This comforting thought was shattered in a moment. The hole was full and as the slaves stooped to smooth the sand above it the captain stepped close behind them, his arms unfolded, and fire leaped simultaneously from his hands. The negroes sank upon the sand and, pocketing his pistols and picking up the lantern, their master left them where they fell. They would tell no tales.

Shivering with horror, the boy watched the captain climb the slope. On the crest, he stopped in his tracks, a volley of curses rolled from his lips, and he swung the lantern around his head with the frenzy of a maniac. Looking past him the boy saw the cause—the ship that had been standing by was now bearing away to sea under full sail in a good breeze, abandoning him! The captain dropped his lantern and went in great leaps toward the beach and there he halted, for the small boat was gone.

"Ahoy, sir!" the boy shouted. There was now a bond between himself and the man that made him throw away discretion.

"Who's that?" The captain wheeled and drew his pistols, searching for the source of the voice.

"Don't shoot. I'm a castaway like yourself. I have a boat. Shall we follow them?"

"A boat?"

"A small open craft with a sail."

"A fine match for my ship! The scoundrels have foxed me, but I ain't struck my flag yet. Who are ye, lad?" he asked, walking slowly back from the water.

The boy picked up the lighted lantern and went to meet him, boldly. "I'm Roger Wilkes from Port Royal," he said.

"What ye doing on this beast's thumb o' rock?"

"Shipwrecked and drifting eight days in a boat. I landed here at midday to feel the earth again."

"Alone?"

"Yes, sir. When our ship foundered we were making ready the boats, but we were too late and all went down with her. When I came up I saw a boat floating and climbed into it, but I never sighted one of our crew."

"Your boat was provisioned?"

"Partly. There is still some water and boucan left. And the mate had put his navigating instruments aboard. I don't know how to use them, but mayhap you do."

"Aye, I'm a navigator." The captain's small eyes glinted uneasily in the lantern light. "Show me the craft."

"She lies the other side of the island," Roger said and led the way.

The captain inspected the little boat with a glance that saw everything.

"Seaworthy if handled right," he muttered. "These instruments are good. I could circle the world with 'em."

"Then we can get away from here," Roger cried. "It is providential for both of us."

"This all the water aboard?" The captain kicked a cask.

"Yes. And there is not a drop on the island. Are we far from fresh water?"

"No," he said, for he knew it was hundreds of leagues.

"Let's start now. This is a—a horrible place."

"Easy, lad. We'll give the ship leeway. If they sighted us at daylight they'd send us to the bottom to be rid o' me."

"They mutinied against you, sir?"

"The jellyfish lack the sand to mutiny." The captain sat down on the cask and removed his hat, revealing an egg-shaped skull set on a thick, brutish neck. "I reckon ye see'd what happened here tonight," he added.

"I did," Roger answered evenly. "But circumstances have made us shipmates and closed my mouth."

"Spoke like a gentleman! I reckon ye *be* a gentleman," the captain said. He was becoming more friendly all the while and his tone was now that of a fisherman who wanted to swap yarns for an idle hour. And Roger, who had been alone on the ocean staring death in the eye for days, found relief in talking.

"My father was captain of a ship running between Port Royal and London," he explained, answering the hint in the other's words. "She was a mail ship, the *Rose of Jamaica.*"

"That was her as went down with ye aboard?" The captain replaced his hat so that its shadow masked his face.

"Oh, no. I was on another one bound to trade with the Dutch at Darien. My father's ship has been missing a year past."

"Missing, ye say?"

"Strangely missing. She was a stout craft with a full crew, there were no great storms at the time and no hostilities that we know of."

"Queer things happen at sea, lad."

"But I'll not believe what some say happened," Roger cried passionately.

"To the *Rose of Jamaica?*" The captain waited expect-
antly.

"Yes, sir. You see, she carried secret messages from the
governor of Jamaica to the King as about the Spaniards
in Hispaniola. It's being whispered that she went over to
the Dons and sold the papers for gold."

"They accuse your father of treason, eh?"

"No! Not him nor his officers. But they say the crew
was bought in port and mutinied on the sea. It's a disgrace to a captain to be unable to handle his crew. My
father's name is not as fair as it was. You know what rumor
will do. I would give my life to clear my father's reputa-
tion."

The captain's teeth flashed in the starlight as he bit off
a quid of tobacco. "So it's a disgrace, eh, to let the crew
get the upper hand?"

Roger went cold at his own clumsy wit, but he would
not retreat. "I've said it and I'll not deny it," he answered.

"Yours is a bold tongue, cockerel, and a bold heart,
too. For that I'll tell ye something. Shamed I may be for
being left here like a puppy, but the jest is on the crew.
For weeks past they've been a-muttering and I know'd
they was smelling the treasure in my cabin. My own treasure it was, too, my fair share of the purchases we'd made."

"And they wanted it?"

"Aye. They'd wasted their own and hankered for mine.
So I hid it under my cabin floor, square in front o' the
door where they don't expect it to be. I was a ship's carpenter once and I did the job myself. Then I filled them

two chests with sand from the ballast and come ashore here to bury my treasure. 'Twas necessary to finish the blacks to put the stamp o' reality on the business. Aye, lad, them chests yonder is full o' sand from the beach o' Tortuga." He threw back his head and laughed.

"But you have lost your treasure," Roger pointed out.

"I'll find it again. I'll find my ship, for I know this old Spanish Main as a merchant knows his pocket."

"You've no doubt we can escape from a place like this?"

"Didn't I say I could sail this craft round the world?"

"Then let's be going. The wind is favorable. Your ship will be far out of sight by morning and we'll be safe from it."

For a full minute the captain gazed at the stars, which blazed like diamonds on a velvet cloak. Then, "We'll waste no more time," he said. "Is all aboard?"

"Everything," Roger answered eagerly. And well he might be excited as well as devoutly thankful to be thus provided with a skilled navigator when all had seemed lost.

By the light of the lantern the captain examined the oars, the sail, everything.

"She floats here?"

"Yes, sir. She's moored to that rock."

"Cast off and shove her out. I'll steer with an oar past the point."

Roger waded in, pushing the boat, until the water lapped his armpits, then he started to climb aboard.

"Stand off!" The captain's voice cut like a knife.

The boy looked past the lantern, which was on a boat

seat, and saw a pistol pointed at his head.

"What are you doing?" His voice was high-pitched with fear and he sank back in the water.

"It's me or you," the captain said, unmoved, "and having the upper hand, it's me that gets away."

"You're going to leave me here!"

"Aye. There's water enough for only one. I'll leave ye here or shoot ye where ye stand. 'Twill help none to whimper."

"I'm not whimpering!" The boy's eyes blazed as he looked over the gunwale. "I'll not whimper for a coward like you."

"Lad," the captain said in a voice that was a bit less hard, "I've fancied the spirit o' ye from the start. I'd take ye if I could, but 'twould be death for the both o' us."

"I gave you all I had. I trusted you—you pirate!"

"I don't deny it, but I'm a man as wants to live. Ye may be took off."

"You know a ship never comes near this island. I'll die of thirst."

"Likely enough. But I'll give ye a crumb o' comfort. 'Twas I as sunk the *Rose of Jamaica*."

"You murdered my father!"

"He died fighting like a man."

"Thank you for that—if it is true."

" 'Tis true. We needed supplies, so when we sighted a ship we run up distress signals and when she hove to we boarded her."

"You brute! And now you taunt me with it."

"Listen, lad. I took the captain's papers, for they might be handy in a pinch. Many a time I've saved my skin by knowing what was in a ship's papers. Among them was the secret dispatches ye spoke of. They meant nothing to me but I kept 'em, for it's things like that as saves a man's neck sometimes. They're in my cabin now and when I regain my ship—and I *will* regain her!—I'll send them papers to the governor o' Jamaica with a word that'll take the blot from yer father's name. That'll be the price o' this boat I'm taking from ye. Now, will ye take a bullet or will ye go ashore?"

Roger went ashore, for human nature fights for life to the last. Slowly the captain rowed away from land, then raised the sail and disappeared in the darkness.

There was nothing to do, that was one of the terrible aspects of the situation, nothing to do but watch the horizon and wait. And in that unfrequented part of the ocean there was nothing to wait for but death. When daylight came Roger buried the two negroes. Poor wretches, he thought, but he knew that before it was finished he would envy them the merciful suddenness of their going. Toward night, in order to occupy his mind, he dug up the chests and found that truly they were full of sand. There was no disappointment in that for if they had held diamonds he could not have bartered them for a tinful of water. Sand was as good as gold in that place where nothing of value could be bought.

Before the second morning his tormenting thirst had become an obsession and he was powerless to relieve it. The endless lapping of the salt waves drove the agony deeper and deeper into his brain like blows from a hammer. He sucked a pebble until his swollen tongue no longer made room for it in his mouth. He prayed for a storm that might bring rain or drive a ship his way, but the sky was serene and he knew there would be no rain for months. So overshadowing was thirst that hunger was forgotten, which was one mercy. And gradually, toward the close of the fourth day, everything began to be forgotten. Half delirious, he had drunk sea water, knowing and not caring that such an act was the signal of surrender. Crawling on his hands and knees, fainting, reviving and crawling on in some subconscious hope of finding help, he reached his lookout on the rocks. It was sunset and, raising himself on one elbow, he took a final look around the horizon. It was merely mechanical action, some sort of last involuntary gesture against death, for his brain was too weak to register what his eyes saw. Whether that was a sail or a seabird in the southwest made no difference to him.

While he lay there, still breathing, the ship bore in and anchored off the island in the darkness. She knew the place well for she had left her commander there four days before and was now returning for his treasure which the crew had not dared to fight for then. The old tiger would have downed a dozen of them before they could have landed and finished him, but now, even if he were alive, he would be too weak to resist.

At dawn they saw the prostrate form on the rocks and came ashore, jeering at the Old Man they had outwitted.

"Saint's blood!" cried the one who reached him first. "This is a lad!"

"The fiend's work!" another gasped, as he tried to remember how to cross himself. "The Old Man has changed his form!"

"Fools! He's some castaway," the mate said.

"Then where's the Old Man?"

"Search the island."

"We can see it all from here and he ain't on it."

"I tell ye, he's changed hisself into a bird and flew away."

"There's the treasure chests!" They rushed upon them.

"Full o' sand!" They formed a ring and stared.

"He's changed the gold to sand," persisted the one who

believed in miracles.

"The castaway done it. He's dug up the gold."

"But where's the Old Man?"

"Got away somehow."

"Then 'e took the gold. I knows 'im."

"I tell ye, it's the fiend's work. Git back to the ship."

"Fools!" the mate roared again. "The castaway holds the key to this."

" 'E's dead."

"He ain't."

" 'E's good as dead."

"Heave him to the sharks!" another cried in disappointment.

"Ye'll do nothin' like that." The mate drew his pistols. "Ye'll take him aboard and ye'll nurse him back to life like he was yer own mother's son. It's him and him alone that can give us the treasure."

There was sense in that and they saw it, so they bore Roger to the ship and with all their skill, which was considerable, they drew him back into the world he had so nearly left. And when he was finally in the land of the living once more, with the deck of the old pirate craft rolling under his feet and the island to starboard bringing him memories of torment, he said wearily to the mate, "It was all done for treasure! The thought sickens me."

"But where is the treasure?" the mate asked, and the pirates pressed close for the answer.

"I know where it is." Roger felt a thrill at the power he had over them.

"We'll give ye a share," the mate promised.

"You will not." The boy shuddered. "It's blood money a thousand times over."

"Ye'd best tell where it is." A threatening buzz arose.

"I'll bargain with you first. In the captain's cabin on this ship are papers taken from the *Rose of Jamaica*. When you set me ashore in Jamaica with those papers in my possession, I will tell you where the treasure is. I give you my word that every penny of it shall be yours. Kill me here and you will lose it all." He looked into the fierce eyes about him.

He had the cards and his hand could not be forced. There were curses and threats, but eventually on a dark night he was rowed ashore at a point where the hills of Jamaica meet the sea. There he completed his story to the mate and told where the treasure lay under the cabin floor. Then he turned and ran toward the town where the lights of home twinkled peacefully.

from MARY MACLEOD'S

King Arthur and His Noble Knights

The stories of King Arthur and his knights of the Round Table are not truly fact, but also are not completely fiction. There was a King Arthur who lived in Wales in the 6th century whose court was renowned for its chivalry in that uncivilized time. The knights of King Arthur's court rode out in search of adventure, and to perform acts of daring, of courtesy and of charity. The bravest and biggest and handsomest of all these knights was Sir Lancelot of the Lake. Here Sir Lancelot goes searching for adventure —and he finds it.

SIR LANCELOT AND THE STRONG KNIGHT OF THE FOREST

At the Court of King Arthur were many valiant knights, and some among them increased so in arms and worship that they surpassed all their fellows in prowess and noble deeds. But chief among them all was Sir Lancelot of the Lake, for in all tournaments and jousts and deeds of arms, both for life and death, he excelled all other knights, and never at any time was he overcome, unless it were by treason or enchantment.

Because of this, Queen Guinevere held him in higher favour than all other knights, and Sir Lancelot for his part loved the Queen above all other ladies and damsels all his life; and for her he did many deeds of arms, and more than once saved her from death by his noble chivalry.

When King Arthur returned to England from Rome all the Knights of the Round Table resorted to him, and many jousts and tournaments were held. Sir Lancelot rested himself for some time with sport and play, but at last he longed again to make trial of himself in strange adventures. Therefore, bidding his nephew Sir Lionel make ready, they mounted their horses, armed at all points, and rode into a deep forest, and so on to a wide plain.

About noon the weather was very hot, and Sir Lancelot felt sleepy. Then Sir Lionel espied a great apple-tree that stood by a hedge, and he said:

"Brother, yonder is a fair shadow; there we may rest ourselves and our horses."

"It is well said," answered Sir Lancelot; "for this seven years I have not been so sleepy as I am now."

So they alighted there, and tied their horses to a tree, and Lancelot lay down, and put his helm under his head, and fell very fast asleep. But Lionel kept awake.

In the meanwhile came three knights riding, fleeing as fast as ever they could ride, and these three were followed by one knight. When Sir Lionel saw him he thought he had never seen so great a knight, nor so well faring a man, nor one so well apparelled. In a little while this strong knight overtook one of the three, and smote him to the cold earth, so that he lay still. Then he rode to the second knight, and smote him so that both man and horse fell down. Then he rode straight at the third knight and smote him a spear's length behind his horse's tail. Then he alighted, and bound all the three knights fast with the reins of their own bridles.

When Sir Lionel saw him do thus he thought he would assay him, so making ready he took his horse very quietly in order not to awake Sir Lancelot. He soon overtook the strong knight, and bade him turn, but the latter smote Sir Lionel so hard that he bore horse and man to the earth. Then he alighted and bound him fast, and threw him and the three other knights each across his own horse, and rode with them away to his Castle. When he got there he took away their armour, and beat them with thorns, and put them into a deep dungeon, where there were many more knights who made much lamentation.

Sir Ector de Maris in the meanwhile, finding that Sir Lancelot had left the Court to seek adventures, was angry with himself, and made ready to go in search of him. Riding through a great forest he met a man who looked like a forester, and he asked this man if he knew of any adventures near at hand. The forester replied that within a mile was a strong manor, with a moat all round it; and near the manor on the left hand was a ford for horses to drink from. At the ford grew a beautiful tree on which hung many fair shields that had once belonged to gallant knights. On the tree hung also a basin of brass and copper, and the forester bade Sir Ector strike thrice on the basin with the butt of his spear, and he would soon hear new tidings, unless he had the greatest luck of any knight who had passed through that forest for many a year.

Thanking the man Sir Ector departed, and soon came to the tree, where he found many fair shields; among them he saw his brother's shield, Sir Lionel, and many more that he knew were his fellows of the Round Table, which grieved his heart, and he promised to revenge his brother.

He beat at once on the basin, as if he were mad, and then he gave his horse drink at the ford. There came a knight behind him, and bade him come out of the water and make him ready. Sir Ector turned sharply, and cast his spear, and smote the other knight a great buffet, so that his horse reeled twice round.

"That was well done," said the strong knight, "and knightly hast thou stricken me"; and therewith he rushed his horse on Sir Ector, and catching him under his right arm, he bore him clean out of the saddle and rode with him away into his own hall, where he threw him down in the middle of the floor.

The name of this knight was Sir Turquine.

"Because thou hast done this day more unto me than any knight did these twelve years," said he to Sir Ector, "now will I grant thee thy life, if thou wilt swear to be my prisoner all the days of thy life."

"Nay," said Sir Ector, "that I will never promise thee."

"I am sorry for that," said Sir Turquine.

Then he took Sir Ector's armour away, and beat him with thorns, and put him down in a deep dungeon, where he found many companions whom he knew. But when he saw Sir Lionel there he made great sorrow. "Alas," he said, "where is my brother Sir Lancelot?"

"I left him asleep, under an apple-tree, when I went from him," said Lionel, "and what is become of him I cannot tell you."

"Alas," said the knights, "unless Sir Lancelot help us we shall never be delivered, for we know now no knight that is able to match our master Turquine."

In the midst of a highway in the same forest where he had lain sleeping, Sir Lancelot met a damsel riding a white palfrey, and they each saluted the other.

"Fair damsel," said Sir Lancelot, "know ye in this country any adventures?"

"Sir Knight," said the damsel, "here are adventures near at hand, if thou darest prove them."

"Why should I not prove adventures?" said Sir Lancelot, "for that cause came I into the country."

"Well," said she, "thou seemest indeed to be a good knight, and if thou dare meet with a good knight I will bring thee where is the best and the mightiest that ever thou found, so thou wilt tell me what is thy name, and what knight thou art."

"To tell thee my name I am quite ready, truly it is Sir

Lancelot of the Lake."

"Sir, thou art a well-seeming knight; here are adventures to suit thee. For hereby dwelleth a knight that will not be over-matched by any one I know, unless ye over-match him; his name is Sir Turquine. And, as I understand, he hath in his prison three score and four good knights of Arthur's Court, whom he hath won with his own hands. But when ye have done this day's work ye shall promise me as ye are a true knight to go with me and help me and other damsels that are distressed daily with a false knight."

"I will fulfill all your desire, damsel, so that you bring me to this knight."

So she brought him to the ford and to the tree where hung the basin.

Sir Lancelot let his horse drink, and then he beat with all his might on the basin with the butt of his spear, till at last the bottom fell out, but he saw nothing. He rode up and down in front of the gates of that manor for nearly half-an-hour; then he was aware of a great knight coming who drove a horse before him, and across the horse lay an armed knight, bound. As they came nearer and nearer Sir Lancelot thought he should know him, and then he saw it was Sir Gaheris, Gawaine's brother, a Knight of the Round Table.

By that time Sir Turquine had seen Lancelot, and they both gripped their spears.

"Now, fair knight," said Lancelot, "put that wounded knight off the horse, and let him rest awhile, and let us two prove our strength. For, as I am told, thou dost, and

hast done, great despite and shame unto Knights of the Round Table; therefore, now defend thee!"

"If thou be of the Round Table I defy thee and all thy fellowship," said Sir Turquine.

"That is saying overmuch," said Sir Lancelot.

Then they put their spears in rest, and came together with their horses as fast as they could run, and each smote the other in the midst of their shields, so that the two horses' backs were broken. Both knights were astonished, and as soon as they could get clear of the horses they flung their shields in front of them, and drew their swords, and rushed together eagerly, so that neither shields nor armour could withstand their strokes. Within a little while they had both grim wounds, and thus it fared for two hours or more. Then at the last they were both breathless, and stood leaning on their swords.

"Now, fellow," said Sir Turquine, "hold thy hand awhile and tell me what I shall ask thee."

"Say on," said Lancelot.

"Thou art the biggest man that ever I met withal, and the most skilled, and like one knight that I hate above all other knights. If so be that thou art not he then I will willingly agree with thee, and for thy love I will deliver all the prisoners I have, who are three score and four, so thou wilt tell me thy name. And thou and I will be friends together and never fail, as long as I live."

"Well said," answered Sir Lancelot, "but since I may have thy friendship, what knight is he whom thou so hatest above all others?"

"Faithfully he is Sir Lancelot of the Lake, for he slew my brother at the Dolorous Tower, who was one of the best knights living. Therefore him I except, for may I once meet with him, the one of us shall make an end of the other, I swear a vow. And for Sir Lancelot's sake I have slain a hundred good knights, and as many have I maimed, and many have died in prison, and still I have three score and four. But all shall be delivered if thou wilt tell me thy name, so it be that thou art not Sir Lancelot."

"Now see I well," said Sir Lancelot, "that I might be such a man that I might have peace, and I might be such a man that there should be deadly war betwixt us. And now, Sir Knight, at thy request I desire that thou learn and know that I am Lancelot of the Lake, King Ban's son, of Benwick, and true Knight of the Table Round. And now I defy thee, do thy best!"

"Ah, Lancelot," said Turquine, "thou art most welcome to me that ever was knight, for we shall never part till the one of us be dead."

Then they hustled together like two wild bulls, rashing and lashing with their shields and swords. Thus they fought still two hours and more, and never would have rest. And Sir Turquine gave Sir Lancelot many wounds, so that all the ground there where they fought was be-speckled with blood. Then at the last Sir Turquine waxed faint, and gave somewhat aback, and bore his shield low for weariness. Sir Lancelot espied this, and leaped upon him fiercely, and got him by the beaver of his helmet, and plucked him down on his knees. Then he quickly raised off his helm and smote his neck in sunder.

And when Sir Lancelot had done this, he went to the damsel, and said:

"Damsel, I am ready to go with you where you will have me, but I have no horse."

"Fair sir," said she, "take this wounded knight's horse, and send him to the Manor, and command him to deliver all the prisoners."

So Lancelot went to Gaheris, and prayed him not to be aggrieved at lending him his horse.

"Nay, fair lord," said Gaheris, "I will that ye take my horse at your own commandment, for ye have saved both me and my horse; and this day I say you are the best knight in the world, for you have slain here in my sight the mightiest man and the best knight, except you, that ever I saw. I pray you, sir, tell me your name."

"Sir, my name is Lancelot of the Lake, that ought to help you of right for King Arthur's sake, and in especial for my Lord Gawaine's sake, your own dear brother. And when you come within yonder Manor, I am sure you will find there many Knights of the Round Table, for I have seen many of their shields that I know on yonder tree. And among them are my two kinsmen's shields, Sir Ector de Maris, and Sir Lionel. Wherefore I pray you, greet them all from me, and say that I bid them take such treasure as they find in the Manor, and that in any case let my kinsmen go to the Court and wait till I come, for by the Feast of Pentecost I purpose to be there; for at this time I must ride with this damsel to keep my promise."

So Sir Lancelot departed, and Sir Gaheris went into the
Manor, and there he found a yeoman porter, keeping many
keys. Sir Gaheris quickly threw the porter to the ground,
and took the keys from him, and hastily he opened the
prison door, and let out all the prisoners; and every man
loosed each other's bonds.

When they saw Gaheris they all thanked him, for they
saw he was wounded.

"Not so," said Gaheris, "it was Lancelot that slew your
captor, I saw it with my own eyes. And he greeteth you
all well, and prayeth you to hasten to Court; and as for
Sir Lionel and Sir Ector de Maris, he prayeth you to wait
for him at Court."

"That shall we not do," said the brothers, "we will find
him, if we live."

"So shall I find him before I go to Court, as I am true knight," said Sir Kay.

Then all the knights sought the house where the armour was, and armed themselves, and every knight found his own horse, and all that belonged to him. And when this was done there came a forester with four horses laden with fat venison.

"Here is good meat for us for one meal," said Sir Kay, "for we have had no good repast for many a day."

So the venison was roasted, baked, and boiled, and after supper some of the knights abode there in the Manor all that night, but Sir Lionel and Sir Ector de Maris and Sir Kay rode after Sir Lancelot to find him if they could.

Sir Lancelot rode away with the damsel, as he had promised, to aid her against the wicked knight who robbed and
distressed all ladies and gentlewomen.

"He doth shame unto the order of knighthood and contrary unto his oath," he said; "it is pity that he liveth. But,
fair damsel, you shall ride on in front, and I will keep myself in covert, and if he trouble or distress you, I will rescue
you, and teach him to be ruled as a knight."

So the maid rode gently along the highway.

Soon out of the wood came the wicked knight on horseback, and his page with him, and he took the damsel from
her horse, and she cried out.

With that came Sir Lancelot as fast as he could.

"O thou false knight, and traitor unto knighthood!" he
said. "Who taught thee to distress ladies and gentlewomen?"

When the knight heard this rebuke he made no answer,
but drew his sword and rode at Sir Lancelot. Then Lancelot threw his spear from him, and drew out his sword, and
struck him such a buffet on the helmet that he clave his
head and neck to the throat.

"Now thou hast thy payment which thou hast long de-
served, and that is truth," said the damsel. "For as Sir
Turquine watched to destroy knights, so did this knight
wait to destroy and distress ladies, damsels, and gentlewomen; and his name was Sir Peris of Forest Savage."

"Now, damsel," said Sir Lancelot, "will ye any more
service of me?"

"Nay, sir, not at this time," she said, "but Christ preserve you wheresoever you ride or go! For the courtliest knight thou art, and meekest unto all ladies and gentlewomen that now liveth."

And so Sir Lancelot and she parted.

Two days before the Feast of Pentecost he went home, and the King and all the Court rejoiced greatly at his coming. And all his deeds were made known. So at that time Sir Lancelot had the greatest name of any knight of the world, and he was the most honoured, both by high and low.

ARTHUR B. CHRISMAN

Four Generals

Prince Chang petitioned his father, the King. "My Honored Parent, give me permission to make a journey throughout the kingdom. I would learn how the people live, and note wherein they are contented and discontented. Thus I shall be prepared against the time when I ascend the throne." The King nodded approval. "Your plan is good, my son. I shall immediately order that new gold tires be put upon the royal carriage, and summon ten troops of cavalry to guard you." But the prince would not listen to such arrangements. "Oh, no, sire, I mean to go alone and in disguise. Instead of the carriage, a stick will serve for my vehicle. Instead of the troops, that self-same stick will guard me."

Whereat, the King was greatly troubled, and the prince was put to much argument before he won his point. "Then do as you wish, my only and much beloved son," said the King, grudgingly. "But it behooves you to observe extreme care. Disorder is rife in all the provinces. Go, and may your stick be as strong as the magic mace of Sun How Erh."

"Farewell, my royal father."

"Farewell, my noble son."

Now it must be remembered that Prince Chang was no graybeard. In years he was nearing thirteen. Is it, after all, such a great wonder that homesickness caused his heels to drag, and his eyes to need the kerchief? He had walked all of twenty li. That, he began to imagine, was journey enough for the present. To the edge of Hu Pei Forest he continued. At the edge of the forest he stopped. The woodland was so dark . . . so dark. The wolves howled "Oo-o-o-o-o-wh—We starve." And such a futile little stick with which to enter the forest of Hu Pei. "Oo-o-o-o-owh." What wolves. . . .

The prince had turned his face toward home when a merry voice hailed him. "Ho. Brother, I'm glad you are come. Tell me if my fiddle be in tune." A comical fellow hopped down from a stump and chinned his fiddle while Prince Chang stared. "Eek. Eeek. Eeek." "How does it sound, little brother?" "I dare say it—" But the fiddler was not waiting for an answer. His bow arm fell to sawing while his legs and voice joined in the tune—"A beggar asked the King to dine." And that's a foolish song. Prince Chang thought he had never before heard or seen anything so funny by half. The more he laughed the greater his need for laughter. Such a comical beggar and how he could play and sing.

From one end of Hu Pei Forest to the other Prince Chang laughed while the beggar capered and fiddled. No wolves at all appeared. Homesickness was a thing of the past—forgotten. "Let me give you a copper cash, merry stranger," said Chang, when they came to a Y of the road. "Not now," said he of the fiddle and bow. "I judge you are poorer than I." "Indeed?" laughed the prince. "When I am King (he forgot himself there), I shall reward you handsomely." "Ho. Ho," shrieked the beggar. "When you are King. When you are King, I'll accept a reward. Make

me a general in your army." "It shall be done," said Chang. "What is your very nice name?" "My pitiful name is Tang—Tang, the fiddler. Farewell, my little King, who rides a bamboo horse." So, they parted, both merry.

Sad to relate, Prince Chang's merriment was to be of brief duration. A band of robbers sprang up from the road side and surrounded him, pummeling him without mercy

—all striking at one time. They took his stick and his clothing and the little bag of coins that hung from his neck. They left him in the road for dead. A sorry ending, that, to his journey. . . .

Shortly, another traveler chanced by, and he was a man of warm heart. He revived Prince Chang and took him on his shoulder, carrying him to a village. There he set out food and clothing and bade the prince ask for what more he desired. Chang was deeply thankful. "How can I ever repay you?" "*Ya ya pei* (Pish tush) ," said the man. "It is nothing. What is a bit of food? And what is a gift of clothing? Besides, you must know that I am a tailor and will charge my next customer double. 'A tailor—a rogue,' says the proverb." "I do not believe it," exclaimed Chang, "and when I become King—" (There he forgot himself again.)

"Ho. Ho. Ho," roared the tailor. "When you become King. Ho. Ho. When you are King, you may reward me. You may make me a general in your army." "It shall be done," declared Chang. "What is your honorable name?" "Wang is my miserable name. Wang, the tailor. Farewell, and good luck be with you, my future King." So they parted, merrily enough—each laughing at the excellent jest.

Prince Chang continued his journey. For three days he saw no man of flesh and bone, nor came upon a dwelling. At the end of the third day he was weak and unsteady from hunger. His stick broke beneath his weight and he lay beside the road, waiting for death to come. Instead of death, there came a shepherd with sheep and goats. The shepherd picked up Chang and saw that the boy was far spent. It

was quite plain that hunger had used him evilly. Promptly
the quick-witted fellow slung Chang on his shoulder and
carried him off to a cave. Milk in bottles of leather hung on
the cavern walls. Also, there were cheeses. Chang was made
to drink of the milk—a little at first—only enough to mois-
ten his throat. With the return of strength, he drank greed-
ily, completely emptying a goatskin. And the emptier the
bottle grew, the more he thanked the shepherd. "You have
done me a great service," said Chang. "If I had money
I—" "*Ya ya pei* (Pish tush)," said the shepherd. "It
is nothing. I fed you with no thought of reward." "Nevertheless," declared Chang, "when I am made King I—"
The shepherd was like to strain his throat with guffawing.
"Ho. Ho. Ho. When you are made King. What a merry
chap you seem to be. Very well, when you are King you
may reward me. Make me a general in your army. Ho. Ho.
Ho." "I shall. I shall." The prince was emphatic. "What is
your honorable name?" "My paltry name? Most folk call
me Mang—Mang, the shepherd. And here, you must carry
some food with you, for the nearest house is thirty li distant.
Take this cheese—and may good luck be your companion,
my King of the wandering road."

Burdened as he was, Prince Chang made slow work of
getting over the mountain. He had begun to think seriously
of dropping the cheese when a troop of soldiers clattered
up the road behind him. "How fortunate," said Chang.
"Here are my father's soldiers. They will take me on their
horses to the next village." But the soldiers halted with a
"Who are you, and what brings you here?" queried most

fiercely and with scowls. The prince stammered that he
was sometimes called Chun, a most unfortunate invention,
for Chun was the name of a local bandit. The soldiers'
frowns turned to pleased smiles (there was a reward offered), and the captain said: "So you are Chun, and you
have just robbed some poor person of a new suit and a
cheese. Off with his head, my braves." Chang now saw that
he was indeed in a tangle. A bold face seemed the only
escape. He put on a stern look, saying: "How dare you
execute men without a trial? Do you not know that I am
Prince Chang, son of your noble King?" The captain bowed
in mock humility. "Your Highness seems large for such a
tender age. I happen to know that King Yen Chi's eldest
son is only two years old. Let your swords drink, men."

The terrible truth was made plain to Chang. He had
wandered across the border of his father's kingdom. He
was in a neighboring and hostile country. . . .

The swords were lifted to strike, when—swish—came an
arrow. After it, quickly, another, and another. Each
found its mark. For each arrow a soldier crumpled. The
others dug heels in their horses galloping pell-mell for their
lives.

A stalwart youth stepped out from a pine. "You had
better go quickly," he said to Chang. "The border of
our own country lies a full mile back." "I thank you with
all my heart," declared Prince Chang, "and shall reward
you fittingly when—" "When you are King?" finished the
other. "I heard what you said to the soldiers, and wondered at your daring. Very well. Make me a general when

you become King, and that will be ample reward." "It shall be done," vowed the prince. "What brave name do you bear?" "Name? Oh, you may call me Lang. Lang, the very indifferent archer. And now you must go, for more soldiers will come, and my arrows are few."

Prince Chang was not long returned from his journey when the King passed away in an illness. Immediately the crown was placed on Chang's brow, and all the people burned much incense of *la ka* wood, crying "Hail." And almost with their next breath they shouted *"Kou chou* (The Enemy)*."* An enemy was marching upon Ku Hsueh. The new King had barely seated himself upon the heighty throne before he found it necessary to see about raising an army. There were two great troubles with the old army. It was dwarfish small and it boasted more generals than bowmen. Of course, the generals never fought. They did nothing but plan—usually what they'd have for dinner, and which sword they'd wear to the King's next reception. Yet, King Chang added more generals to the army.

The first complaint raised against King Chang by his people was that he had added four more generals to the army. His new generals were named Tang, Wang, Mang, and Lang—though doubtless, such information is hardly necessary. They were old friends of the King. The four arrived at the capital in time to see a huge army of hostiles encamp on the far side of the river that bordered the city. By great good fortune, the river was past fording, so holding the enemy in check. The King and his generals gazed across the river. Said he: "It is easily seen that the enemy has twenty men for every one we muster. What are your plans?" Of all his generals, only Wang seemed to have so much as the shadow of a plan. Wang said, "Give me all the tailors in the city, and all the cloth stored in the royal go-downs." "Take them," said King Chang. "If you don't, the enemy will."

Throughout the night General Wang and his tailors slaved needle and thread. The click of thimbles made a continuous humming sound. The hostiles on the farther shore heard, and wondered what strange warlike engines King Chang might be preparing.

With day's coming, Chang moved all his troops—he had only a thousand. The thousand men marched in parade along the river's brim. Their uniforms were old and dowdy. The words, "We are brave," that adorned their tattered jackets seemed a poor and weak boast. They were ragamuffins. They marched as if weary. The enemy jeered.

But, lo. The first thousand had no sooner disappeared than another thousand circled past the river—stepping smartly, smartly uniformed in cloth of gold, the words "Very brave" embroidered upon their fronts. The enemy was not so quick to jeer.

Following the second thousand came a thousand men in trim red uniforms. Upon their breasts were broidered "Extremely brave." They stepped it briskly, shouting dares across the river. The enemy replied with little heart.

Another thousand followed. Jade green uniforms clothed them. Rumbledumblededum sang their drums, and their steps kept perfect time. Upon their breasts were the words "Still braver," and upon their lips great threats. The enemy said little.

Now came men in crow's-wing black. Upon their breasts were the words "Braver by far." Their taunts were hard to bear. Yet, the enemy remained silent.

A thousand men in pink, the same number in blue. Came white-clad men and orange-clad men. Violet uniforms replaced uniforms of brown. . . . The enemy thought it hardly fair. King Chang, evidently, had a million soldiers. . . . How could they fight against a million? The tents came down and the enemy vanished.

General Wang continued to sew until the last hostile disappeared. He and his tailors were terribly tired. But the thousand soldiers were even more tired. All day long they had marched and changed uniforms, then marched again. They had changed from red to green, to black, to every color in the spectrum. They were color blind and weary. But King Chang married much and blessed the day that had sent him General Wang, the tailor.

In a month or so King Chang's happiness turned to gloom. The enemy had learned of Wang's clever trick, and resolved to march again. The army of Chang was scarcely larger than before. To come off victorious each man would have to whip a dozen of the enemy. There was no time to increase the royal army. And the enemy lay on the other side of Ku Hsueh River waiting for the waters to lower.

King Chang rode with his generals to the river. Said he: "There lies the enemy. The depth of the river lessens with each minute. Who has a plan?" Some of the generals stroked their beards. Others twisted their mustachios. All wrinkled their brows. Not one of them parted his lips. "Come. Come, my doughty generals. Have you no plan? General Tang?" Tang bowed his head the three times required by law and courtesy. "Sire, with your permission, I have a small scheme that may serve": *"Chen hao* (Very good) ; spare no expense. Draw on the treasury for whatever you may desire—silk, tailors, fans, or false faces—anything except more soldiers, for soldiers we have not." "Then, please, Your Majesty," said Tang, "may I ask you to sign an order on the treasury for one ounce of pine resin." Then the King thought Tang jesting. His first impulse was to strike off his head. Instead of doing so, however, he signed the order for two cents' worth of resin.

At night General Tang sat upon a crag that towered above the river. He fondled his precious violin. A little breeze sprang up at his back. Tang the general was no more, but Tang the musician lived and thrilled. Bow swept strings with a magic sweetly said. The breeze caught up the melody. The river was its sounding board. The soldiers on the farther shore turned in their blankets to listen. Than home there is no spot dearer—and the violin sang of home. More and more sad came the music. The musician wept. Across the river ten thousand eyes grew moist. The soldiers wept and were unashamed. Why had they left their warm hearthstones—to die in an alien land? Fierce resolve faded, and a longing took its stead, a longing for home and the loved ones it sheltered.

Morning saw the hostile camp deserted. Soldier after soldier had stolen away in the darkness, thinking only of home. Not one remained to threaten Ku Hsueh City.

King Chang assembled his generals and spoke high praise of Tang. Then he discussed the need of preparation for the future. He knew very well that the enemy would return. "Have any of you, my trusty generals, a plan for humbling the enemy in his next invasion?" General Mang, the former shepherd, voiced a plan. "I would suggest that all horses be replaced by lean sheep of the mountain." General Lang, the archer, said, "I would suggest that all cases at law be settled by trial with bow and arrow." "So be it," said the King, "I grant both requests."

The enemy soon marched upon Ku Hsueh in greater numbers than before. Grasshoppers in the August fields were never thicker. It was plain that only a miracle could save the city. All eyes were turned to General Mang, turned beseechingly, and rather doubtfully. Could a mountain shepherd save Ku Hsueh?

That night the question was answered. Mang herded his sheep in a tremendous body toward the enemy camp. At the proper moment he raised a great din and startled the animals into flight. Through the camp of the enemy they rushed, and instantly the camp was confusion. The soldiers had fared none too well on their march. They were hungry. And here was good food to be had for the catching. Away went sheep. Away went soldiers. Thoroughly frightened, the lean-limbed sheep sped their fastest. Thoroughly desirous, the hungry soldiers followed at their fastest.

While the camp was empty, Mang and a score of daring men darted from tent to tent. In their hands were torches. Behind them rose a flare of ever-spreading flames. "To roast their meat when they catch it," said Mang. The wind was a helpful friend, scattering brands with a will. The destruction was soon finished. What had been a white encampment became a red and rolling flame. The tents were burned, and the spears and the bows. Nothing was spared. A thoroughly discomfited enemy stole away from Ku Hsueh that night.

So far, General Lang had done nothing of a warlike nature—nothing at all—unless stepping upon the toes of a citizen be considered warlike. Lang had done that. Naturally, the citizen was incensed. He wished to see justice done and went to a court of law.

The judge said: "Take this bow and shoot five arrows in yonder target. He who shoots best has the right on his side." The young citizen shot first, and his marksmanship was poor to say the least. Whereupon, Lang drew the bow. Oddly enough, his aim was no better than that of the citizen. With that the judge declared the suit undecided and set a future date for its retrial. General Lang left court well pleased. The young citizen went home to spend many hours in practice with bow and arrow.

Thereafter the courts were flooded with lawsuits. From morn till night the bow strings twanged. It appeared that all the men of Ku Hsueh had grievances to be settled. And they who were wise spent much time in archery practice ere they went to court. Many became quite expert with the bow and arrow. . . .

King Chang impressed all of them into his army. At last he had a large force, a force that would give pause to any foe. Long the King waited for his enemy's return. But he waited in vain. Spies had watched the men of Ku Hsueh at practice with the bow. They sent messages that Ku Hsueh was prepared. So the country was troubled no more by alarms of hostile armies.

Thus, without loss of a man, was the kingdom saved for Chang, by Wang, Tang, Mang, and Lang—a thousand years ago all this, but very learned men still dispute as to which was the greatest, Lang, Mang, Tang, or Wang— which of the four generals.

from ARMSTRONG SPERRY'S

Call It Courage

This is the heroic story of a boy who was the son of a great chief in ancient Polynesia, but who was called by his people the Boy Who Was Afraid. When Mafatu was three years old, he had been almost drowned, and this left him with a great fear of the sea. He would not even join the other boys in the great sport of spear-fishing. The Polynesians worshipped courage above all, and at last Mafatu is driven from his native island of Hikueru by his own shame. All alone, except for his dog Uri, he sets out to face the sea and prove his courage. The first night out his canoe is smashed in a furious storm and he is cast ashore on an unknown island. Mafatu soon finds evidence that it is inhabited by cannibals, and he determines to build a new canoe and make his escape.

THE FIRST TEST

The very next morning Mafatu set about building his canoe. He had banked his fire the night before in the natural shelter of a cave and he resolved never to let the sparks die out. For it was altogether too difficult to make fire with the firestick, and it required too much time. In Hikueru, for that reason, the fires were always kept burning, and it was the special charge of the younger members

of a family to see that fuel was ever at hand. Woe unto
the small boy who let the family fires go out!

While his breakfast roasted in the coals, the boy cleared
the brush away from the base of the great *tamanu*. There
was no wood better for canoe-building than this. It was
tough, durable, yet buoyant in the water. Mafatu could
fell his tree by fire, and burn it out, too. Later he would
grind an adze out of basalt for the finished work. The adze
would take a long time, but he had made them often in
Hikueru and he knew just how to go about it. The boy
was beginning to realize that the hours he had spent fash-
ioning utensils were to stand him now in good stead. Nets
and knives and sharkline, implements and shell fishhooks
—he knew how to make them all. How he had hated those
tasks in Hikueru! He was quick and clever with his hands,
and now he was grateful for the skill which was his.

The fire crackled and snapped about the base of the
tamanu tree. When at length it had eaten well into the
trunk, Mafatu climbed aloft and crept cautiously out upon
a large branch that overhung the beach. Then taking firm
hold of the branches above his head, he began to jump up
and down. As the fire ate deeper into the trunk, the tree
began to lean under the boy's weight. With a snap and a
crash it fell across the sand. As it fell, Mafatu leaped free
of the branches, as nimbly as a cat.

"That's enough for today, Uri," he decided. "Tomorrow
we'll build our fires down the trunk and start burning it
out. When the eaters-of-men come, we will be ready!"

In the meantime there were many other things to do:

A fish trap of bamboo, a net of sennit, a fishhook, too, it only he could find some bone. And while the canoe was building, how could Mafatu get out to the distant reef to set his trap, unless first he made a raft of bamboo?

The boy decided that the raft was of first importance. He chose a score or more of fine bamboos as large around as his arm, felling them by fire; then he lashed them together with strips of *purau* bark, making a sturdy raft of two thicknesses. It would serve him well until his canoe should be finished.

As he worked, his mind returned again and again to the wild pig he was determined to kill. How could he go back to Hikueru without a boar's-tooth necklace? Why, that necklace was almost as important as a canoe! For by that token men would know his strength and courage. When the day came that he should leave this high island, he would sail to the north and east. Somewhere in that quarter lay the Cloud of Islands; the great Tuamotu Archipelago which extends across a thousand miles of ocean and ten degrees of latitude. Within those reef-spiked channels floated Hikueru, his homeland. . . . There was no doubt in his mind that he would find it; for Maui, who had led him safe to this shore, would some day guide him home again. But first, Mafatu knew, he must prove himself worthy. Men should never again call him Mafatu, the Boy Who Was Afraid. And Tavano Nui should say with pride: "Here is my son, come home from the sea."

Kivi, the albatross, came and went on his mysterious errands, emerging out of blue space, vanishing into it again. At sundown, regularly, the white bird came wheeling and circling, to alight clumsily on the beach almost at Mafatu's side, while Uri pranced about and greeted his friend after his own fashion. As for Uri, he was having the time of his life; for there were countless sea-birds nesting along the shore to be chased and put to rout; and wild goats and pigs in the mountains to make life exciting enough for any dog.

Mafatu had discovered a mulberry tree. He stripped off the bark and removed the inner white lining. Then he wet the fiber and laid it upon a flat stone and set about beating it with a stick of wood. The fiber spread and grew thinner under the persistent beating. The boy added another strip, wet it, and beat it into the first one; then another and another. Soon he had a yard of "cloth" to serve as a *pareu*. It was soft and white, and now at last he was clothed.

"Before I go home I will make a dye of *ava* and paint a fine design on my *pareu*," the boy promised himself. "I must not go back ill-clothed and empty-handed. Men must know that I have conquered the sea, and made the land serve me as well."

The days passed in a multitude of tasks that kept Mafatu busy from dawn till dark. His lean-to grew into a three-sided house with bamboo walls and a thatch of palm leaves. The fourth wall was open to the breezes of the lagoon. It was a trim little house and he was proud of it. A roll of woven mats lay on the floor; there was a shelf in the wall

with three bowls cut from coconut shells; bone fishhooks
dangled from a peg; there was a coil of tough sennit, many
feet long; an extra *pareu* of *tapa* waterproofed with gum of
the *artu* tree, for wet weather. All day long the wind played
through the openings in the bamboo walls and at night
lizards scurried through the thatch with soft rustlings.

One morning, wandering far down the beach, Mafatu
came upon a sheltered cove. His heart gave a leap of joy;
for there, white-gleaming in the sun, was all that remained
of the skeleton of a whale. It might not have meant very
much to you or to me; but to Mafatu it meant knives and
fishhooks galore, splintered bone for darts and spears, a
shoulder blade for an axe. It was a veritable treasure-trove.
The boy leaped up and down in his excitement. "Uri!" he
shouted. "We're rich! Come—help me drag these bones
home!"

His hands seemed all thumbs in his eagerness; he tied
as many bones as he could manage into two bundles. One
bundle he shouldered himself. The other Uri dragged behind him. And thus they returned to the camp site, weary,
but filled with elation. Even the dog seemed to have some
understanding of what this discovery meant; or if not, he
was at least infected with his master's high spirits. He
leaped about like a sportive puppy, yapping until he was
hoarse.

Now began the long process of grinding the knife and
the axe. Hour after long hour, squatting before a slab of
basalt, Mafatu worked and worked, until his hands were
raw and blistered and the sweat ran down into his eyes.

The knife emerged first, since that was the most imperative. Its blade was ten inches long, its handle a knob of
joint. It was sharp enough to cut the fronds of coconut
trees, to slice off the end of a green nut. Ai, but it was a
splendid knife! All Mafatu's skill went into it. It would be
a fine weapon as well, the boy thought grimly, as he
ground it down to a sharp point. Some sea-robber had
been breaking into his bamboo trap and he was going to
find out who the culprit was! Probably that old hammerhead shark who was always cruising around. . . . Just as
if he owned the lagoon!

Fishing with a line took too long when you were working against time. Mafatu could not afford to have his trap
robbed. Twice it had been broken into, the stout bamboos
crushed and the contents eaten. It was the work either of
a shark or of an octopus. That was certain. No other fish
was strong enough to snap the tough bamboo.

Mafatu's mouth was set in a grim line as he worked
away on his knife. That old hammerhead—undoubtedly
he was the thief! Mafatu had come to recognize him; for
every day, when the boy went out with his trap, that shark,
larger than all the others, was circling around, wary and
watchful. The other sharks seemed to treat the hammerhead with deference.

Hunger alone drove Mafatu out to the reef to set his
trap. He knew that if he was to maintain strength to accomplish all that lay ahead he must have fish to add to
his diet of fruit. But often as he set his trap far out by the
barrier-reef, the hammerhead would approach, roll over

slightly in passing, and the cold gleam of its eye filled Mafatu with dread and anger.

"Wait, you!" the boy threatened darkly, shaking his fist at the *ma'o*. "Wait until I have my knife! You will not be so brave then, *Ma'o*. You will run away when you see it flash."

But the morning that the knife was finished, Mafatu did not feel so brave as he would have liked. He hoped he would never see the hammerhead again. Paddling out to the distant reef, he glanced down from time to time at the long-bladed knife where it hung about his neck by a cord of sennit. It wasn't, after all, such a formidable weapon. It was only a knife made by a boy from a whale's rib.

Uri sat on the edge of the raft, sniffing at the wind.

Mafatu always took his dog along, for Uri howled unmercifully if he were left behind. And Mafatu had come to rely upon the companionship of the little yellow dog. The boy talked with the animal as if he were another person, consulting with him, arguing, playing when there was time for play. They were very close, these two.

This morning as they approached the spot where the fish trap was anchored, Mafatu saw the polished dorsal of the hated hammerhead circling slowly in the water. It was like a triangle of black basalt, making a little furrow in the water as it passed.

"*Aiá, Ma'o!*" the boy shouted roughly, trying to bolster up his courage. "I have my knife today, see! Coward who robs traps—catch your own fish!"

The hammerhead approached the raft in leisurely fashion; it rolled over slightly, and its gaping jaws seemed to curve in a yawning grin. Uri ran to the edge of the raft, barking furiously; the hair on the dog's neck stood up in a bristling ridge. The shark, unconcerned, moved away. Then with a whip of its powerful tail it rushed at the bamboo fish trap and seized it in its jaws. Mafatu was struck dumb. The hammerhead shook the trap as a terrier might shake a rat. The boy watched, fascinated, unable to make a move. He saw the muscles work in the fish's neck as the great tail thrashed the water to fury. The trap splintered into bits, while the fish within escaped only to vanish into the shark's mouth. Mafatu was filled with impotent rage. The hours he had spent making that trap — But all he could do was shout threats at his enemy.

Uri was running from one side of the raft to the other, furious with excitement. A large wave sheeted across the reef. At that second the dog's shift in weight tipped the raft at a perilous angle. With a helpless yelp, Uri slid off into the water. Mafatu sprang to catch him, but he was too late.

Instantly the hammerhead whipped about. The wave slewed the raft away. Uri, swimming frantically, tried to regain it. There was desperation in the brown eyes—the puzzled eyes so faithful and true. Mafatu strained forward. His dog. His companion. . . . The hammerhead was moving in slowly. A mighty rage stormed through the boy. He gripped his knife. Then he was over the side in a clean-curving dive.

Mafatu came up under his enemy. The shark spun about. Its rough hide scraped the flesh from the boy's shoulder. In that instant Mafatu stabbed. Deep, deep into the white belly. There was a terrific impact. Water lashed to foam. Stunned, gasping, the boy fought for life and air.

It seemed that he would never reach the surface. *Aué*, his lungs would burst! . . . At last his head broke water. Putting his face to the surface, he saw the great shark turn over, fathoms deep. Blood flowed from the wound in its belly. Instantly gray shapes rushed in—other sharks, tearing the wounded hammerhead to pieces.

Uri—where was he? Mafatu saw his dog then. Uri was trying to pull himself up on the raft. Mafatu seized him by the scruff and dragged him up to safety. Then he caught his dog to him and hugged him close, talking to

him foolishly. Uri yelped for joy and licked his master's cheek.

It wasn't until Mafatu reached shore that he realized what he had done. He had killed the *ma'o* with his own hand, with naught but a bone knife. He could never have done it for himself. Fear would have robbed his arm of all strength. He had done it for Uri, his dog. And he felt suddenly humble, with gratitude.

Ali Baba and the Forty Thieves

In a town in Persia, there lived two brothers, one named Cassim, the other Ali Baba. Their father left them scarcely anything; but Cassim married a wealthy wife and prospered in life, becoming a famous merchant. Ali Baba, on the other hand, married a woman as poor as himself, and lived by cutting wood, and bringing it upon three asses into the town to sell.

One day, when Ali Baba was in the forest, he saw at a distance a great cloud of dust, which seemed to be approaching. He observed it very attentively, and distinguished a body of horsemen.

Fearing that they might be robbers, he left his asses and climbed into a tree, from which place of concealment he could watch all that passed in safety.

The troop consisted of forty men, all well mounted, who, when they arrived, dismounted and tied up their horses and fed them. They then removed their saddlebags, which seemed heavy, and followed the captain, who approached a rock that stood near Ali Baba's hiding place. When he was come to it, he said, in a loud voice, "Open, Sesame!"

As soon as the captain had uttered these words, a door opened in the rock; and after he had made all his troop enter before him, he followed them, after which the door shut again of itself.

Although the robbers remained some time in the rock, Ali Baba did not dare to move until after they had filed out again, and were out of sight. Then, when he thought that all was safe, he descended, and going up to the door, said, "Open, Sesame!" as the captain had done, and instantly the door flew open.

Ali Baba, who expected a dark dismal cavern, was surprised to see it well lighted and spacious, receiving light from an opening at the top of the rock. He saw all sorts of provisions, rich bales of silk, brocades, and valuable carpeting, piled upon one another; gold and silver ingots in great heaps, and money in bags. The sight of all these riches made him suppose that this cave must have been occupied for ages by robbers, who had succeeded one another.

Ali Baba loaded his asses with gold coin, and then covering the bags with sticks he returned home. Having secured the door of his house, he emptied out the gold before his wife, who was dazzled by its brightness, and told her all, urging upon her the necessity of keeping the secret.

The wife rejoiced at their good fortune, and wished to count all the gold, piece by piece. "Wife," said Ali Baba, "you do not know what you undertake, when you pretend to count the money. You will never have done. I will dig a hole, and bury it. There is no time to be lost."

"You are right, husband," replied she; "but let us know, as nigh as possible, how much we have. I will borrow a small measure and measure it, while you dig the hole."

Away the wife ran to her brother-in-law Cassim, who lived just by, and addressing herself to his wife, desired her to lend her a measure for a little while. The sister-in-law did so, but as she knew Ali Baba's poverty, she was curious to know what sort of grain his wife wanted to measure, and artfully putting some suet at the bottom of the measure, brought it to her with an excuse, that she was sorry that she had made her stay so long, but that she could not find it sooner.

Ali Baba's wife went home and continued to fill the measure from the heap of gold and empty it till she had done: when she was very well satisfied to find the number of measures amounted to as many as they did, and went to tell her husband, who had almost finished digging the hole. While Ali Baba was burying the gold, his wife, to show her exactness and diligence to her sister-in-law, carried the measure back again, but without taking notice that a piece of gold had stuck to the bottom. "Sister," said she, giving it to her again, "you see that I have not kept your measure long. I am obliged to you for it, and return it with thanks."

As soon as Ali Baba's wife was gone, Cassim's wife looked at the bottom of the measure and was greatly surprised to find a piece of gold stuck to it. Envy immediately possessed her breast. "What!" said she, "has Ali Baba gold so plentiful that he has to measure it?" When Cassim came home, his wife said to him, "I know you think your-self rich, but you are much mistaken. Ali Baba is infinitely richer than you. He does not count his money, but meas-ures it." Cassim desired her to explain the riddle, which she did, by telling him the stratagem she had used to make the discovery, and showed him the piece of money, which was so old that they could not tell in what prince's reign it was coined.

Cassim was also envious when he heard this, and slept so badly that he rose early and went to his brother.

"Ali Baba," said he, "you pretend to be miserably poor, and yet you measure gold. My wife found this at the bot-tom of the measure you borrowed yesterday."

Ali Baba perceived that Cassim and his wife, through his own wife's folly, knew what they had so much reason to conceal. However, what was done could not be recalled. Therefore, without showing the least surprise or trouble, he confessed all, and offered him part of his treasure to keep the secret. "I expected as much," replied Cassim haughtily. "But I must know exactly where this treasure is, and how I may visit it myself when I choose. Otherwise I will go and inform against you, and then you will not only get no more, but will lose all you have, and I shall have a share for my information."

Ali Baba told him all he desired, and even the very words he was to use to gain admission into the cave.

Cassim rose the next morning, long before the sun, and set out for the forest with ten mules bearing great chests, which he planned to fill. He was not long before he

reached the rock, and found out the place by the tree and
other marks which his brother had given him. When he
reached the entrance of the cavern, he pronounced the
words, "Open, Sesame!" The door immediately opened,
and when he was in, closed upon him. He quickly entered,
and laid as many bags of gold as he could carry at the door
of the cavern, but his thoughts were so full of the great
riches he should possess, that he could not think of the
necessary word to make it open. Instead of Sesame, he
said, "Open, Barley!" and was much amazed to find that
the door remained fast shut. He named several sorts of
grain, but still the door would not open.

Cassim had never expected such an incident, and was so
alarmed at the danger he was in that the more he endeavored to remember the word "Sesame," the more his memory was confounded, and he had as much forgotten it as
if he had never heard it mentioned. He threw down the
bags he had loaded himself with, and walked distractedly
up and down the cave, without having the least regard for
the riches about him.

About noon the robbers chanced to visit their cave,
and at some distance from it saw Cassim's mules strag-
gling about the rock, with great chests on their backs.
Alarmed at this novelty, they galloped full speed to the
cave. Cassim, who heard the noise of the horses' feet from
the middle of the cave, never doubted of the arrival of the
robbers, and resolved to make one effort to escape from
them. To this end he rushed to the door, and no soonei
saw it open, than he ran out and struck down the leader,

but could not escape the other robbers, who with their sabers soon made an end of him.

The first care of the robbers after this was to examine the cave. They found all the bags which Cassim had brought to the door, to be ready to load his mules, and carried them again to their places, without missing what Ali Baba had taken away the previous day. Then holding a council, they agreed to cut Cassim's body into four quarters, to hang two on one side and two on the other, within the door of the cave, to terrify any person who should attempt the same thing. This done, they mounted their horses, went to beat the roads again, and to attack any caravans they might meet.

In the meantime, Cassim's wife was very uneasy when night came and her husband had not returned. She ran to Ali Baba in alarm, and said, "I believe, brother-in-law, that you know Cassim your brother is gone to the forest, and upon what account. It is now night and he is not returned. I am afraid some misfortune has happened to him." Ali Baba told her that she need not frighten herself, for that certainly Cassim would not think it proper to come into the town till late at night.

Cassim's wife passed a miserable night, and bitterly repented of her curiosity. As soon as daylight appeared, she went to Ali Baba, weeping profusely.

Ali Baba departed immediately with his three asses to seek for Cassim, begging of her first to cease her lamentations. He went to the forest, and when he came near the rock, having seen neither his brother nor the mules on his way, was seriously alarmed at finding some blood spilt near the door, which he took for an ill omen. But when he had pronounced the password, and the door had opened, he was struck with horror at the dismal sight of his brother's remains. He loaded one of his asses with them, and covered them over with wood. The other two asses he loaded with bags of gold, covering them with wood also as before; and then bidding the door shut, came away. But he took care to stop some time at the edge of the forest, so that he might not reach the town before night. When he came home, he drove the two asses loaded with gold into his little yard, and left the care of unloading them to his wife, while he led the other to his sister-in-law's house.

Ali Baba knocked at the door, which was opened by Morgiana, an intelligent slave, whose tact was to be relied upon. When he came into the court, he unloaded the ass, and taking Morgiana aside, said to her, "Mention what I say to no one. Your master's body is contained in these two bundles, and our business is to bury him as if he had died a natural death. I can trust you to manage this for me."

Ali Baba consoled the widow as best he could, and having deposited the body in the house returned home.

Morgiana went out at the same time to an apothecary, and asked for a sort of lozenge very efficacious in the most dangerous disorders. The apothecary inquired who was ill. She replied with a sigh, "My good master Cassim himself. He can neither eat nor speak." After these words Morgiana

carried the lozenges home with her, and the next morning
went to the same apothecary's again, and with tears in
her eyes, asked for an essence which they used to give to
sick people only when at the last extremity. "Alas!" said
she, "I am afraid that this remedy will have no better
effect than the lozenges; and that I shall lose my good
master."

On the other hand, as Ali Baba and his wife were often
seen to go between Cassim's and their own house all that
day, and to seem melancholy, nobody was surprised in the
evening to hear the lamentable shrieks and cries of Cassim's wife and Morgiana, who gave out everywhere that
her master was dead. The next morning Morgiana betook
herself early to the stall of a cobbler named Mustapha,
and bidding him good morrow, put a piece of gold into
his hand, saying, "Baba Mustapha, you must take your
sewing tackle, and come with me. But I must tell you, I
shall have to blindfold you when you come to the place."

Baba Mustapha hesitated a little at these words. "Oh!
oh!" replied he, "you would have me do something against
my conscience, or against my honor?"

"God forbid!" said Morgiana, putting another piece of
gold into his hand, "that I should ask anything that is
contrary to your honor. Only come along with me, and
fear nothing."

Baba Mustapha went with Morgiana, who, after she
had bound his eyes with a handkerchief, conveyed him to
her deceased master's house, and never unloosed his eyes
till he had entered the room, where she had put the corpse

together. "Baba Mustapha," said she, "you must make haste and sew these quarters together. And when you have done, I will give you another piece of gold."

After Baba Mustapha had finished his task, she once more blindfolded him, gave him the third piece of gold as she had promised, and recommending secrecy to him, conducted him back again to the place where she had first bound his eyes, pulled off the bandage, and let him go home, but watched him that he returned toward his shop, till he was quite out of sight, for fear that he should have the curiosity to return and follow her. She then went home.

The ceremony of washing and dressing the body was hastily performed by Morgiana and Ali Baba, after which it was sewed up ready to be placed in the mausoleum. While Ali Baba and the other members of the household followed the body, the women of the neighborhood came, according to custom, and joined their mourning with that of the widow, so that the whole quarter was filled with the sound of their weeping. Thus was Cassim's horrible death successfully concealed.

Three or four days after the funeral, Ali Baba removed his goods openly to the widow's house. But the money he had taken from the robbers he conveyed thither by night. When at length the robbers came again to their retreat in the forest, great was their surprise to find Cassim's body taken away, with some of their bags of gold. "We are certainly discovered," said the captain, "and if we do not find and kill the man who knows our secret, we shall gradually lose all the riches."

The robbers unanimously approved of the captain's speech.

"The only way in which this can be discovered," said the captain, "is by spying on the town. And, lest any treachery may be practiced, I suggest that whoever undertakes the task shall pay dearly if he fails—even with his life."

One of the robbers immediately started up, and said, "I submit to this condition, and think it an honor to expose my life to serve the troop."

The robber's courage was highly commended by the captain and his comrades, and when he had disguised himself so that nobody would know him, he went into the town and walked up and down, till accidentally he came to Baba Mustapha's shop.

Baba Mustapha was seated, with an awl beside him, on the bench, just starting to work. The robber saluted him, and perceiving that he was old, said, "Honest man, you begin to work very early. How is it possible that one of your age can see so well? I question, even if it were somewhat lighter, whether you could see to stitch."

"Why," replied Baba Mustapha, "I sewed a dead body together in a place where I had not so much light as I have now."

"A dead body!" cried the robber, with affected amazement.

"It is so," replied Baba Mustapha. "But I will tell you no more."

"Indeed," answered the robber, "I do not want to learn your secret, but I would fain to see the house in which this strange thing was done." To impress the cobbler he gave him a piece of gold.

"If I were disposed to do you that favor," replied Baba Mustapha, "I assure you I cannot, for I was led both to and from the house blindfolded."

"Well," replied the robber, "you may, however, remember a little of the way that you were led blindfolded. Come, let me bind your eyes at the same place. We will walk together; and as everybody ought to be paid for his trouble, there is another piece of gold for you. Gratify me in what I ask you."

The two pieces of gold were too great a temptation for Baba Mustapha, who said, "I am not sure that I remember the way exactly. But since you desire, I will see what I can do." At these words Baba Mustapha rose up, and led the robber to the place where Morgiana had bound his eyes. "It was here," said Baba Mustapha, "I was blindfolded; and I turned as you see me."

The robber, who had his handkerchief ready, tied it over his eyes, walked by him till he stopped, partly leading, and partly guided by him. "I think," said Baba Mustapha, "I went no farther." He had now stopped directly at Cassim's house, where Ali Baba then lived. The thief, before he pulled off the band, marked the door with a piece of chalk which he had already in his hand. Then he asked him if he knew whose house that was, to which Baba Mustapha replied, that, as he did not live in that neighborhood, he could not tell.

The robber, finding he could discover no more from Baba Mustapha, thanked him for the trouble he had taken, and left him to go back to his shop, while he, himself, returned to the forest, persuaded that he should be very well received.

Shortly after the robber and Baba Mustapha had parted, Morgiana went out of Ali Baba's house upon some errand, and upon her return, she saw the mark the robber had made and stopped to observe it. "What can be the meaning of this mark?" said she to herself. "Somebody intends my master no good. However, with whatever intention it was done, it is advisable to guard against the worst." Accordingly, she fetched a piece of chalk, and marked two or three doors on each side, in the same manner.

When the robber reached the camp, he reported the success of his expedition. It was at once decided that they should very quietly enter the city and watch for an opportunity of slaying their enemy. To the utter confusion of the guide, several of the neighboring doors were found to be marked in a similar manner. "Come," said the captain, "this will not do. We must return, and you must die." They returned to the camp, and the false guide was promptly slain.

Then another volunteer came forward, and he in like manner was led by Baba Mustapha to the spot. He cautiously marked the door with red chalk, in a place not likely to be seen. But the quick eye of Morgiana detected this likewise, and she repeated her previous action, with equal effectiveness, for when the robbers came they could not distinguish the house. Then the captain, in great anger, led his men back to the forest, where the second offender was immediately put to death.

The captain, dissatisfied by this waste of time and loss of men, decided to undertake the task himself. And so having been led to the spot by Baba Mustapha, he walked up and down before the house until it was impressed upon his mind. He then returned to the forest. When he came into the cave, where the troop waited for him, he said, "Now, comrades, nothing can prevent our full revenge." He then told them his contrivance. When they approved of it, he ordered them to go into the villages about, and buy nineteen mules, with thirty-eight large leather jars, one full of oil, and the others empty.

In two days all preparations were made, and the nineteen mules were loaded with thirty-seven robbers in jars, and the jar of oil. The captain, as their driver, set out with them, and reached the town by the dusk of the evening, as he had intended. He led them through the streets till he came to Ali Baba's, at whose door he planned to have knocked; but was prevented, as Ali Baba was sitting there after supper to take a little fresh air. He stopped his mules, and said, "I have brought some oil a great way, to sell at tomorrow's market, but it is now so late that I do not know where to lodge. Will you allow me to pass the night with you, and I shall be very much obliged for your hospitality."

Ali Baba, not recognizing the robber, bade him welcome, and gave directions for his entertainment, and after they had eaten he retired to rest.

The captain, pretending that he wished to see how his jars stood, slipped into the garden, and passing from one to the other he raised the lids of the jars and spoke: "As soon as I throw some stones out of my window, do not fail to come out, and I will immediately join you." After

this he retired to his chamber; and to avoid any suspicion, put the light out soon after, and laid himself down in his clothes, that he might be the more ready to rise.

While Morgiana was preparing the food for breakfast, the lamp went out, and there was no more oil in the house, nor were there any candles. What to do she did not know, for the broth must be made. Abdalla, seeing her very uneasy, said, "Do not fret, but go into the yard, and take some oil out of one of the jars."

Morgiana thanked Abdalla for his advice, took the oil pot, and went into the yard. As she came nigh the first jar, the robber within said softly, "Is it time?"

Morgiana naturally was much surprised at finding a man in a jar instead of the oil she wanted, but she at once made up her mind that no time was to be lost, if a great danger was to be averted, so she passed from jar to jar, answering at each, "Not yet, but presently."

At last she came to the oil jar, and made what haste she could to fill her oil pot, and returned into her kitchen. Here, as soon as she had lighted her lamp, she took a great kettle, went again to the oil jar, filled the kettle, set it on a large wood fire, and as soon as it boiled went and poured enough into every jar to stifle and destroy the robber within.

When this action, worthy of the courage of Morgiana, was executed without any noise, as she had planned, she returned to the kitchen with the empty kettle. She then put out the great fire which she had made to boil the oil. Leaving just enough to make the broth, she put out the lamp also, and remained silent; resolving not to go to rest till she had observed what might follow through a window of the kitchen, which opened into the yard.

She had not waited long before the captain gave his signal, by throwing the stones. Receiving no response, he repeated it several times, until becoming alarmed he descended into the yard and discovered that all the gang

were dead. And by the oil he missed out of the last jar
he guessed the means and manner of their death. Enraged
to despair at having failed in his design, he forced the
lock of a door that led from the yard to the garden, and
climbing over the walls, made his escape.

Morgiana then went to bed, happy at the success of her
plan.

Ali Baba rose before day, and followed by his slave,
went to the baths, entirely ignorant of the important events
which had taken place at home. When he returned from
the baths, the sun had risen. He was very much surprised
to see the oil jars, and that the merchant had not gone
with the mules. He asked Morgiana, who opened the door,
the reason of it. "My good master," answered she, "God
preserve you and all your family. You will be better in-
formed of what you wish to know when you have seen
what I have to show you, if you will but give yourself the
trouble to follow me."

Ali Baba following her, she requested him to look into
the first jar and see if there was any oil. Ali Baba did so,
and seeing a man, started back in alarm, and cried out.
"Do not be afraid," said Morgiana, "the man you see
there can neither do you nor anybody else any harm. He
is dead."

"Ah, Morgiana!" said Ali Baba, "what is it you show
me? Explain yourself."

"I will," replied Morgiana. "Moderate your astonishment, and do not excite the curiosity of your neighbors.
Look into all the jars."

Ali Baba examined all the other jars, one after another. And when he came to that which had been filled with oil, he found it almost empty. He stood for some time motionless, sometimes looking at the jars, and sometimes at Morgiana, without saying a word, so great was his surprise. At last, when he had recovered himself, he said, "And what is become of the merchant?"

"Merchant!" answered she, "he is as much a merchant as I am. I will tell you who he is, and what has become of him." She then told the whole story from beginning to end; from the marking of the house to the destruction of the robbers.

Ali Baba was overcome by this account, and he cried, "You have saved my life, and in return I give you your liberty—but this shall not be all."

Ali Baba and his slave Abdalla then dug a long deep trench at the farther end of the garden, in which the robbers were buried. Afterward the jars and weapons were hidden, and by degrees Ali Baba managed to sell the mules for which he had no use.

Meanwhile the captain, who had returned to the forest, found life very miserable. The cavern became too frightful to be endured. But, resolved to be revenged upon Ali Baba, he laid new plans, and having taken a shop which happened to be opposite Cassim's, where Ali Baba's son now lived, he transported many rich stuffs thither. And, disguised as a silk mercer, he set up in business, under the name of Cogia Houssain.

Having by chance discovered whose son his opposite

neighbor was, he often made him presents and invited him to dinner, and did everything to win his good opinion.

Ali Baba's son, who did not like to be indebted to any man, told his father that he desired to ask him to dinner in return, and requested him to do so. Ali Baba readily complied with his wishes, and it was arranged that on the following day he should bring Cogia Houssain with him to dinner.

At the appointed time Ali Baba's son conducted Cogia Houssain to his father's house. And strange to say, when the robber found himself at the door, he would have liked to withdraw, though he had now gained access to the very man he wanted to kill. But at that moment Ali Baba came forward to receive him and thank him for his goodness to his son. "And now," said Ali Baba, "you will do me the honor of dining with me."

"Sir," replied Cogia Houssain, "I would gladly, but that I have vowed to abstain from salt, and I scarcely like to sit at your table under such conditions."

"Trouble not yourself about that," answered Ali Baba, "I will go and bid the cook put no salt in the food."

When Ali Baba went to the kitchen to give this order, Morgiana was much surprised, and desired to see this strange man. Therefore she helped Abdalla to carry up the dishes, and directly she saw Cogia Houssain, she recognized him as the captain of the robbers.

Morgiana at once decided to rescue Ali Baba from this fresh danger, and resolved upon a very daring plan to frustrate the robber's designs; for she guessed that he intended no good. In order to carry out her plan she went to her room and put on the garments of a dancer, hid her face under a mask and fastened a handsome girdle around her waist, from which hung a dagger. Then she said to Abdalla, "Fetch your tabor, that we may divert our master and his guest."

Ali Baba bade her dance, and she commenced to move gracefully about, while Abdalla played on his tabor. Cogia Houssain watched, but feared that he would have no opportunity of executing his fell purpose.

After Morgiana had danced for some time, she seized the dagger in her right hand and danced wildly, pretending to stab herself the while. As she swept round, she buried the dagger deep in Cogia Houssain's breast and killed him.

Ali Baba and his son, shocked at this action, cried out aloud, "Unhappy wretch! what have you done to ruin me and my family?"

"It was to preserve, not to ruin you," answered Morgiana. "For see here," continued she, opening the pretended Cogia Houssain's garment, and showing the dagger, "what an enemy you had entertained! Look well at him, and you will find him to be both the fictitious oil merchant and the captain of a gang of forty robbers. Remember, too, that he would eat no salt with you. And what would you have more to persuade you of his wicked design?"

Ali Baba, who immediately felt the new obligation he had to Morgiana for saving his life a second time, embraced her. "Morgiana," said he, "I gave you your liberty, and then promised you that my gratitude should not stop there, but that I would soon give you higher proofs of its sincerity, which I now do by making you my daughter-in-law." Then addressing himself to his son, he said, "I believe, son, that you will not refuse Morgiana for your wife. You see that Cogia Houssain sought your friendship with a treacherous design to take away my life. And, if he had succeeded, there is no doubt but he would have sacrificed you also to his revenge. Consider, that by marrying Morgiana you marry the preserver of my family and your own."

The son, far from showing any reluctance, readily consented to the marriage. And a few days afterward, Ali Baba celebrated the nuptials of his son and Morgiana with great solemnity, with a sumptuous feast, and the usual dancing and spectacles.

Ali Baba, fearing that the other two robbers might be alive still, did not visit the cave for a whole year. Finding, however, that they did not seek to disturb him, he then went to the cave, and, having pronounced the words, "Open, Sesame," entered and saw that no one had been there recently. He then knew that he alone in the world knew the secret of the cave; and he rejoiced to think of his good fortune. When he returned to the city he took as much gold as his horse could carry from his inexhaustible storehouse.

Afterward Ali Baba took his son to the cave, taught him the secret, which they handed down to their posterity, who, using their good fortune with moderation, lived in great honor and splendor.

Treasure Island

The greatest of all pirate stories begins when a roaring old sea captain holes up in a little English inn owned by Jim Hawkins' father. Things happen immediately, and before long the old captain is dead, Jim has the treasure map that was hidden in his sea-chest, and with his father's old friends, Doctor Livesey and Squire Trelawney, sails to find the pirate gold. But there is soon trouble aboard ship. Just as they reach the island where the treasure is buried, Jim discovers that Long John Silver—the "honest," amiable old one-legged cook who had helped pick the crew—is actually a pirate, and plans to murder Jim and his friends, dispose of the few honest men aboard, and divide the treasure with the cutthroat crew he has gathered. Now the ship lies rolling off the island while Long John and the mutinous crew bide their time and Jim and his friends plan ways to escape from the trap and save their lives.

HOW MY SHORE ADVENTURE BEGAN

The appearance of the island when I came on deck next morning was altogether changed. Although the breeze had now utterly ceased, we had made a great deal of way during the night, and were now lying becalmed about half a mile to the southeast of the low eastern coast. Grey-colored woods covered a large part of the surface. This even tint was indeed broken up by streaks of yellow sand-break in the lower lands, and by many tall trees of the pine family, out-topping the others—some singly, some in clumps; but the general colouring was uniform and sad. The hills ran up clear above the vegetation in spires of naked rock. All were strangely shaped, and the Spy-glass, which was by three or four hundred feet the tallest on the island, was likewise the strangest in configuration, running up sheer from almost every side, and then suddenly cut off at the top like a pedestal to put a statue on.

The *Hispaniola* was rolling scuppers under in the ocean swell. The booms were tearing at the blocks, the rudder was banging to and fro, and the whole ship creaking, groaning, and jumping like a manufactory. I had to cling tight to the backstay, and the world turned giddily before my eyes; for though I was a good enough sailor when there was way on, this standing still and being rolled about like a bottle was a thing I never learned to stand without a qualm or so, above all in the morning, on an empty stomach.

Perhaps it was this—perhaps it was the look of the island, with its grey, melancholy woods, and wild stone spires, and the surf that we could both see and hear foaming and thundering on the steep beach—at least, although the sun shone bright and hot, and the shore birds were fishing and crying all around us, and you would have thought any one would have been glad to get to land after being so long at sea, my heart sank, as the saying is, into my boots; and from that first look onward, I hated the very thought of Treasure Island.

We had a dreary morning's work before us, for there was no sign of any wind, and the boats had to be got out and manned, and the ship warped three or four miles round the corner of the island, and up the narrow passage to the haven behind Skeleton Island. I volunteered for one of the boats, where I had, of course, no business. The heat was sweltering, and the men grumbled fiercely over their work. Anderson was in command of my boat, and instead of keeping the crew in order, he grumbled as loud as the worst.

"Well," he said, with an oath, "it's not for ever."

I thought this was a very bad sign; for, up to that day, the men had gone briskly and willingly about their business; but the very sight of the island had relaxed the cords of discipline.

All the way in, Long John stood by the steersman and conned the ship. He knew the passage like the palm of his hand; and though the man in the chains got everywhere more water than was down in the chart, John never hesitated once.

"There's a strong scour with the ebb," he said, "and this here passage has been dug out, in a manner of speaking with a spade."

We brought up just where the anchor was in the chart about a third of a mile from each shore, the mainland on one side, and Skeleton Island on the other. The bottom was clean sand. The plunge of our anchor sent up clouds of birds wheeling and crying over the woods; but in less than a minute they were down again, and all was once more silent.

The place was entirely land-locked, buried in woods, the trees coming right down to high-water mark, the shores mostly flat, and the hilltops standing round at a distance in a sort of amphitheatre, one here, one there. Two little rivers, or, rather, two swamps, emptied out into this pond as you might call it; and the foliage round that part of the shore had a kind of poisonous brightness. From the ship, we could see nothing of the house or stockade, for they were quite buried among trees; and if it had not been for the chart on the companion, we might have been the first that had ever anchored there since the island arose out of the seas.

There was not a breath of air moving, nor a sound but that of the surf booming half a mile away along the beaches and against the rocks outside. A peculiar stagnant smell hung over the anchorage—a smell of sodden leaves and rotting tree trunks. I observed the doctor sniffing and sniffing like some one tasting a bad egg.

"I don't know about treasure," he said, "but I'll stake my wig there's fever here."

If the conduct of the men had been alarming in the boat, it became truly threatening when they had come aboard. They lay about the deck growling together in talk. The slightest order was received with a black look, and grudgingly and carelessly obeyed. Even the honest hands must have caught the infection, for there was not one man aboard to mend another. Mutiny, it was plain, hung over us like a thunder-cloud.

And it was not only we of the cabin party who perceived the danger. Long John was hard at work going from group to group, spending himself in good advice, and as for example no man could have shown a better. He fairly outstripped himself in willingness and civility; he was all smiles to every one. If an order were given, John would be on his crutch in an instant, with the cheeriest "Ay, ay, sir!" in the world; and when there was nothing else to do, he kept up one song after another, as if to conceal the discontent of the rest.

Of all the gloomy features of that gloomy afternoon, this obvious anxiety on the part of Long John appeared the worst.

We held a council in the cabin.

"Sir," said the captain, "if I risk another order, the whole ship'll come about our ears by the run. You see, sir, here it is. I get a rough answer, do I not? Well, if I speak back, pikes will be going in two shakes; if I don't, Silver will see there's something under that, and the game's up. Now, we've only one man to rely on."

"And who is that?" asked the squire.

"Silver, sir," returned the captain: "he's as anxious as you and I to smother things up. This is a tiff; he'd soon talk 'em out of it if he had the chance, and what I propose to do is give him the chance. Let's allow the men an afternoon ashore. If they all go, why, we'll fight the ship. If they none of them go, well, then, we hold the cabin, and God defend the right. If some go, you mark my words, sir, Silver'll bring 'em aboard again as mild as lambs."

It was so decided, loaded pistols were served out to all the sure men; Hunter, Joyce, and Redruth were taken into our confidence, and received the news with less surprise and a better spirit than we had looked for, and then the captain went on deck and addressed the crew.

"My lads," said he, "we've had a hot day, and are all tired and out of sorts. A turn ashore'll hurt nobody—the boats are still in the water; you can take the gigs, and as many as please may go ashore for the afternoon. I'll fire a gun half an hour before sundown."

I believe the silly fellows must have thought they would break their shins over treasure as soon as they were landed; for they all came out of their sulks in a moment, and gave a cheer that started the echo in a far-away hill, and sent the birds once more flying and squalling round the anchorage.

The captain was too bright to be in the way. He whipped out of sight in a moment, leaving Silver to arrange the party; and I fancy it was as well he did so. Had he been on deck, he could no longer so much as have pretended not to understand the situation. It was as plain as day. Silver was the captain, and a mighty rebellious crew he had of it. The honest hands—and I was soon to see it proved that there were such on board—must have been very stupid fellows. Or, rather, I suppose the truth was this, that all hands were disaffected by the example of the ringleaders—only some more, some less, and a few, being good fellows in the main, could neither be led nor driven any further. It is one thing to be idle and skulk, and quite another to take a ship and murder a number of innocent men.

At last, however, the party was made up. Six fellows were to stay on board, and the remaining thirteen, including Silver, began to embark.

Then it was that there came into my head the first of the mad notions that contributed so much to save our lives. If six men were left by Silver, it was plain our party could not take and fight the ship; and since only six were left, it was equally plain that the cabin party had no present need of my assistance. It occurred to me at once to go ashore. In a jiffy I had slipped over the side, and curled up in the fore-sheets of the nearest boat, and almost at the same moment she shoved off.

No one took notice of me, only the bow oar saying, "Is that you, Jim? Keep your head down." But Silver, from the other boat, looked sharply over and called out to know if that were me; and from that moment I began to regret what I had done.

The crews raced for the beach; but the boat I was in, having some start, and being at once the lighter and the better manned, shot far ahead of her consort, and the bow had struck among the shore-side trees, and I had caught a branch and swung myself out, and plunged into the nearest thicket, while Silver and the rest were still a hundred yards behind.

"Jim, Jim!" I heard him shouting.

But you may suppose I paid no heed; jumping, ducking, and breaking through, I ran straight before my nose, till I could run no longer.

THE FIRST BLOW

I was so pleased at having given the slip to Long John that I began to enjoy myself and look around me with some interest on the strange land that I was in.

I had crossed a marshy tract full of willows, bulrushes, and odd, outlandish, swampy trees; and had now come out upon the skirts of an open piece of undulating, sandy country, about a mile long, dotted with a few pines, and a great number of contorted trees, not unlike the oak in growth, but pale in the foliage, like willows. On the far side of the open stood one of the hills, with two quaint, craggy peaks, shining vividly in the sun.

I now felt for the first time the joy of exploration. The isle was uninhabited; my shipmates I had left behind, and nothing lived in front of me but dumb brutes and fowls. I turned hither and thither among the trees. Here and there were flowering plants, unknown to me; here and there I saw snakes, and one raised his head from a ledge of rock and hissed at me with a noise not unlike the spinning of a top. Little did I suppose that he was a deadly enemy, and that the noise was the famous rattle.

Then I came to a long thicket of these oak-like trees— live, or evergreen, oaks, I heard afterwards they should be called—which grew low along the sand like brambles, the boughs curiously twisted, the foliage compact, like thatch. The thicket stretched down from the top of one of the sandy knolls, spreading and growing taller as it went, until it reached the margin of the broad, reedy fen, through which the nearest of the little rivers soaked its way into the anchorage. The marsh was steaming in the strong sun, and the outline of the Spy-glass trembled through the haze.

All at once there began to go a sort of bustle among the bulrushes; a wild duck flew up with a quack, another followed, and soon over the whole surface of the marsh a great cloud of birds hung screaming and circling in the air. I judged at once that some of my shipmates must be drawing near along the borders of the fen. Nor was I deceived; for soon I heard the very distant and low tones of a human voice, which, as I continued to give ear, grew steadily louder and nearer.

This put me in a great fear, and I crawled under cover of the nearest live-oak, and squatted there, hearkening, as silent as a mouse.

Another voice answered; and then the first voice, which I now recognised to be Silver's, once more took up the story, and ran on for a long while in a stream, only now and again interrupted by the other. By the sound they must have been talking earnestly, and almost fiercely; but no distinct word came to my hearing.

At last the speakers seemed to have paused, and perhaps to have sat down; for not only did they cease to draw any nearer, but the birds themselves began to grow more quiet, and to settle again to their places in the swamp.

And now I began to feel that I was neglecting my business; that since I had been so foolhardy as to come ashore with these desperadoes, the least I could do was to overhear them at their councils; and that my plain and obvious duty was to draw as close as I could manage, under the favourable ambush of the crouching trees.

I could tell the direction of the speakers pretty exactly, not only by the sound of their voices, but by the behaviour of the few birds that still hung in alarm above the heads of the intruders.

Crawling on all fours, I made steadily but slowly towards them; till at last, raising my head to an aperture among the leaves, I could see clear down into a little green dell beside the marsh, and closely set about with trees, where Long John Silver and another of the crew stood face to face in conversation.

The sun beat full upon them. Silver had thrown his hat beside him on the ground, and his great, smooth, blond face, all shining with heat, was lifted to the other man's in a kind of appeal.

"Mate," he was saying, "it's because I thinks gold dust of you—gold dust, and you may lay to that! If I hadn't took to you like pitch, do you think I'd have been here a-warning of you? All's up—you can't make nor mend; it's to save your neck that I'm a-speaking, and if one of the wild 'uns knew it, where 'ud I be, Tom—now, tell me, where 'ud I be?"

"Silver," said the other man—and I observed he was not only red in the face, but spoke as hoarse as a crow, and his voice shook, too, like a taut rope—"Silver," says he, "you're old, and you're honest, or has the name for it; and you've money, too, which lots of poor sailors hasn't; and you're brave, or I'm mistook. And will you tell me you'll let yourself be led away with that kind of a mess of swabs? Not you! As sure as God sees me, I'd sooner lose my hand. If I turn again my dooty——"

And then all of a sudden he was interrupted by a noise. I had found one of the honest hands—well, here, at that same moment, came news of another. Far away out in the marsh there arose, all of a sudden, a sound like the cry of anger, then another on the back of it; and then one horrid, long-drawn scream. The rocks of the Spy-glass re-echoed it a score of times; the whole troop of marsh-birds rose again, darkening heaven, with a simultaneous whirr; and long after that death yell was still ringing in my brain, silence had re-established its empire, and only the rustle of the redescending birds and the bloom of the distant surges disturbed the languor of the afternoon.

Tom had leaped at the sound, like a horse at the spur; but Silver had not winked an eye. He stood where he was, resting lightly on his crutch, watching his companion like a snake about to spring.

"John!" said the sailor, stretching out his hand.

"Hands off!" cried Silver, leaping back a yard, as it seemed to me, with the speed and security of a trained gymnast.

"Hands off, if you like, John Silver," said the other. "It's a black conscience that can make you feared of me. But, in heaven's name, tell me what was that?"

"That?" returned Silver, smiling away, but warier than ever, his eye a mere pin-point in his big face, but gleaming like a crumb of glass. "That? Oh, I reckon that'll be Alan."

And at this poor Tom flashed out like a hero.

"Alan!" he cried. "Then rest his soul for a true seaman! And as for you, John Silver, long you've been a mate of mine, but you're mate of mine no more. If I die like a dog, I'll die in my dooty. You've killed Alan, have you? Kill me, too, if you can. But I defies you."

And with that, this brave fellow turned his back directly on the cook, and set off walking for the beach. But he was not destined to go far. With a cry, John seized the branch of a tree, whipped the crutch out of his armpit, and sent that uncouth missile hurtling through the air. It struck poor Tom, point foremost, and with stunning violence, right between the shoulders in the middle of his back. His hands flew up, he gave a sort of gasp, and fell.

Whether he were injured much or little, none could ever tell. Like enough, to judge from the sound, his back was broken on the spot. But he had no time given him to recover. Silver, agile as a monkey, even without leg or crutch, was on the top of him next moment, and had twice buried his knife up to the hilt, in that defenceless body. From my place of ambush, I could hear him pant aloud as he struck the blows.

I do not know what it rightly is to faint, but I do know

that for the next little while the whole world swam away from before me in a whirling mist; Silver and the birds, and the tall Spy-glass hilltop, going round and round and topsy-turvy before my eyes, and all manner of bells ringing and distant voices shouting in my ear.

When I came again to myself, the monster had pulled himself together, his crutch under his arm, his hat upon his head. Just before him Tom lay motionless upon the sward; but the murderer minded him not a whit, cleansing his blood-stained knife the while upon a wisp of grass. Everything else was unchanged, the sun still shining mercilessly on the streaming marsh and the tall pinnacle of the mountain, and I could scarce persuade myself that murder had been actually done, and a human life cruelly cut short a moment since, before my eyes.

But now John put his hand into his pocket, brought out a whistle, and blew upon it several modulated blasts, that rang far across the heated air. I could not tell, of course, the meaning of the signal; but it instantly awoke my fears. More men would be coming. I might be discovered. They had already slain two of the honest people; after Tom and Alan, might not I come next?

Instantly I began to extricate myself and crawl back again, with what speed and silence I could manage, to the more open portion of the wood. As I did so, I could hear hails coming and going between the old buccaneer and his comrades, and this sound of danger lent me wings. As soon as I was clear of the thicket, I ran as I never ran before, scarce minding the direction of my flight, so long as it led me from the murderers; and as I ran, fear grew and grew upon me, until it turned into a kind of frenzy.

Indeed, could any one be more entirely lost than I? When the gun fired, how should I dare to go down to the boats among those fiends, still smoking from their crime? Would not the first of them who saw me wring my neck like a snipe's? Would not my absence itself be an evidence to them of my alarm, and therefore of my fatal knowledge? It was all over, I thought. Good-bye to the *Hispaniola*; good-bye to the squire, the doctor, and the captain! There was nothing left for me but death by starvation, or death by the hands of the mutineers.

All this while, as I say, I was still running, and, without taking any notice, I had drawn near to the foot of the little

hill with the two peaks, and had got into a part of the island where the live-oaks grew more widely apart, and seemed more like forest trees in their bearing and dimensions. Mingled with these were a few scattered pines, some fifty, some nearer seventy, feet high. The air, too, smelt more freshly than down beside the marsh.

And here a fresh alarm brought me to a standstill with a thumping heart.

THE MAN OF THE ISLAND

From the side of the hill, which was here steep and stony, a spout of gravel was dislodged, and fell rattling and bounding through the trees. My eyes turned instinc-

tively in that direction, and I saw a figure leap with great rapidity behind the trunk of a pine. What it was, whether bear or man or monkey, I could in no wise tell. It seemed dark and shaggy; more I knew not. But the terror of this new apparition brought me to a stand.

I was now, it seemed, cut off upon both sides; behind me the murderers, before me this lurking nondescript. And immediately I began to prefer the dangers that I knew to those I knew not. Silver himself appeared less terrible in contrast with this creature of the woods, and I turned on my heel, and, looking sharply behind me over my shoulder, began to retrace my steps in the direction of the boats.

Instantly the figure reappeared, and, making a wide circuit, began to head me off. I was tired, at any rate; but had I been as fresh as when I rose, I could see it was in vain for me to contend in speed with such an adversary. From trunk to trunk the creature flitted like a deer, running manlike on two legs, but unlike any man that I had ever seen, stooping almost double as it ran. Yet a man it was, I could no longer be in doubt about that.

I began to recall what I had heard of cannibals. I was within an ace of calling for help. But the mere fact that he was a man, however wild, had somewhat reassured me, and my fear of Silver began to revive in proportion. I stood still, therefore, and cast about for some method of escape; and as I was so thinking, the recollection of my pistol flashed into my mind. As soon as I remembered I was not defenceless, courage glowed again in my heart;

and I set my face resolutely for this man of the island, and walked briskly towards him.

He was concealed, by this time, behind another tree trunk; but he must have been watching me closely, for as soon as I began to move in his direction he reappeared and took a step to meet me. Then he hesitated, drew back, came forward again, and at last, to my wonder and confusion, threw himself on his knees and held out his clasped hands in supplication.

At that I once more stopped.

"Who are you?" I asked.

"Ben Gunn," he answered, and his voice sounded hoarse and awkward, like a rusty lock. "I'm poor Ben Gunn, I am; and I haven't spoke with a Christian these three years."

I could now see that he was a white man like myself, and that his features were even pleasing. His skin, wherever it was exposed, was burnt by the sun; even his lips were black; and his fair eyes looked quite startling in so dark a face. Of all the beggar-men that I had seen or fancied, he was the chief for raggedness. He was clothed with tatters of old ships' canvas and old sea cloth; and this extraordinary patchwork was all held together by a system of the most various and incongruous fastenings, brass buttons, bits of stick, and loops of tarry gaskin. About his waist he wore an old brass-buckled leather belt, which was the one thing solid in his whole accoutrement.

"Three years!" I cried. "Were you shipwrecked?"

"Nay, mate," said he—"marooned."

I had heard the word, and I knew it stood for a horrible kind of punishment common enough among the buccaneers, in which the offender is put ashore with a little powder and shot, and left behind on some desolate and distant island.

"Marooned three years agone," he continued, "and lived on goats since then, and berries, and oysters. Wherever a man is, says I, a man can do for himself. But, mate, my heart is sore for Christian diet. You mightn't happen to have a piece of cheese about you, now? No? Well, many's the long night I've dreamed of cheese—toasted, mostly—and woke up again, and here I were."

"If ever I can get aboard again," said I, "you shall have cheese by the stone."

All this time he had been feeling the stuff of my jacket, smoothing my hands, looking at my boots, and generally, in the intervals of his speech, showing a childish pleasure in the presence of a fellow-creature. But at my last words he perked up into a kind of startled slyness.

"If ever you can get aboard again, says you?" he repeated. "Why, now, who's to hinder you?"

"Not you, I know," was my reply.

"And right you was," he cried. "Now you—what do you call yourself, mate?"

"Jim," I told him.

"Jim, Jim," says he, quite pleased apparently. "Well, now, Jim, I've lived that rough as you'd be ashamed to hear of. Now, for instance, you wouldn't think I had had a pious mother—to look at me?" he asked.

"Why, no, not in particular," I answered.

"Ah, well," said he, "but I had—remarkable pious. And I was a civil, pious boy, and could rattle off my catechism that fast, as you couldn't tell one word from another. And here's what it come to, Jim, and it begun with chuck-farthen on the blessed grave-stones! That's what it begun with, but it went further'n that; and so my mother told me, and predicked the whole, she did, the pious woman! But it were Providence that put me here. I've thought it all out in this here lonely island, and I'm back on piety. You don't catch me tasting rum so much; but just a thimbleful for luck, of course, the first chance I have. I'm bound I'll be good, and I see the way to. And, Jim"—looking all round him, and lowering his voice to a whisper—"I'm rich."

I now felt sure that the poor fellow had gone crazy in his solitude, and I suppose I must have shown the feeling in my face, for he repeated the statement hotly:

"Rich! Rich! I says. And I'll tell you what: I'll make a man of you, Jim. Ah, Jim, you'll bless your stars, you will, you was the first that found me!"

And at this there came suddenly a lowering shadow over his face, and he tightened his grasp upon my hand, and raised a forefinger threateningly before my eyes.

"Now, Jim, you tell me true: that ain't Flint's ship?" he asked.

At this I had a happy inspiration. I began to believe that I had found an ally, and I answered him at once.

"It's not Flint's ship, and Flint is dead; but I'll tell you true, as you ask me—there are some of Flint's hands aboard; worse luck for the rest of us."

"Not a man—with one—leg?" he gasped.

"Silver?" I asked.

"Ah, Silver!" says he; "that were his name."

"He's the cook; and the ringleader, too."

He was still holding me by the wrist, and at that he gave it quite a wring.

"If you was sent by Long John," he said, "I'm as good as pork, and I know it. But where was you, do you suppose?"

I had made my mind up in a moment, and by way of answer told him the whole story of our voyage, and the predicament in which we found ourselves. He heard me with the keenest interest, and when I had done he patted me on the head.

"You're a good lad, Jim," he said; "and you're all in a clove hitch, ain't you? Well, you just put your trust in Ben Gunn—Ben Gunn's the man to do it. Would you think it likely now, that your squire would prove a liberal-minded one in case of help—him being in a clove hitch, as you remark?"

I told him the squire was the most liberal of men.

"Ay, but you see," returned Ben Gunn, "I didn't mean giving me a gate to keep, and a shuit of livery clothes, and such, that's not my mark, Jim. What I mean is, would he be likely to come down to the toon of, say one thousand pounds out of money that's as good as a man's own already?"

"I am sure he would," said I. "As it was, all hands were to share."

"And a passage home?" he added, with a look of great shrewdness.

"Why," I cried, "the squire's a gentleman. And, besides, if we got rid of the others, we should want you to help work the vessel home."

"Ah," said he, "so you would." And he seemed very much relieved.

"Now I'll tell you what," he went on. "So much I'll tell you, and no more. I were in Flint's ship when he buried the treasure; he and six along-six strong seamen. They was ashore nigh on a week, and us standing off and on in the old *Walrus*. One fine day up went the signal, and here comes Flint by himself in a little boat, and his head done up in a blue scarf. The sun was getting up, and mortal white he looked about the cutwater. But, there he was, you mind, and the six all dead—dead and buried. How he done it, not a man aboard us could make out. It was battle, murder, and sudden death, leastways—him against six. Billy Bones was the mate; Long John, he was quartermaster; and they asked him where the treasure was. 'Ah,' says he, 'you can go ashore, if you like, and stay,' he says; 'but as for the ship, she'll beat up for more, by thunder!' That's what he said.

"Well, I was in another ship three years back, and we sighted this island. 'Boys,' said I, 'here's Flint's treasure; let's land and find it.' The cap'n was displeased at that; but my messmates were all of a mind, and landed. Twelve days they looked for it, and every day they had the worse word for me, until one fine morning all hands went aboard. 'As for you, Benjamin Gunn,' says they, 'here's a musket,' they says, 'and a spade and pickaxe. You can stay here and find Flint's money for yourself,' they says.

"Well, Jim, three years have I been here, and not a bite of Christian diet from that day to this. But now, you look here; look at me. Do I look like a man before the mast? No, says you. Nor I weren't, neither, I says."

And with that he winked and pinched me hard.

"Just you mention them words to your squire, Jim," he went on: "Nor he weren't neither—that's the words. Three years he were the man of this island light and dark, fair and rain; and sometimes he would, maybe, think upon a prayer (says you), and sometimes he would, maybe, think of his old mother, so be as she's alive (you'll say); but the most part of Gunn's time (this is what you'll say) —the most part of his time was took up with another matter. And then you'll give him a nip, like I do."

And he pinched me again in the most confidential manner.

"Then," he continued—"then you'll up, and you'll say this: Gunn is a good man (you'll say), and he puts a precious sight more confidence—a precious sight, mind that —in a gen'leman born than in these gen'lemen of fortune, having been one hisself."

"Well," I said, "I don't understand one word that you've been saying. But that's neither here nor there; for how am I to get on board?"

"Ah," said he, "that's the hitch, for sure. Well, there's my boat, that I made with my two hands. I keep her under the white rock. If the worst come to the worst, we might try that after dark. Hi!" he broke out, "what's that?"

For just then, although the sun had still an hour or two to run, all the echoes of the island awoke and bellowed to the thunder of a cannon.

"They have begun to fight!" I cried. "Follow me."

And I began to run towards the anchorage, my terrors all forgotten; while, close at my side, the marooned man in his goatskins trotted easily and lightly.

"Left, left," says he; "keep to your left hand, mate Jim! Under the trees with you! There's where I killed my first goat. They don't come down here now; they're all mast-headed on them mountings for the fear of Benjamin Gunn. Ah! And there's the cetemery"—cemetery, he must have meant. "You see the mounds? I come here and prayed, nows and thens, when I thought maybe a Sunday would be about doo. It weren't quite a chapel, but it seemed more solemn like; and then, says you, Ben Gunn was short-handed—no chapling, nor so much as a Bible and a flag, you says."

So he kept talking as I ran, neither expecting nor receiving any answer.

The cannon-shot was followed, after a considerable interval, by a volley of small arms.

Another pause, and then, not a quarter of a mile in front of me, I beheld the Union Jack flutter in the air above a wood.

WILL JAMES

A Narrow Escape

I was riding along one day whistling a tune, my horse was behaving fine and all was hunkydory and peaceful. Ahead a ways I'd noticed a narrow washout and I kept on a riding. I'd rode over many a one of them, and nothing was there to warn me that I should go around this perticular one.

My horse cleared the opening and I was still a whistling, then, of a sudden my whistling stopped short as I felt the earth go out from under my horse's feet, . . . the next thing I know I was in the bottom of a ten-foot washout and underneath twelve hundred pounds of horseflesh.

I was pinned there to stay, and lucky I thought afterward that my whole body wasn't underneath that horse. It could of just as well been that way, only past experiences with horses had saved me and natural instinct had made me try to stay on top of the horse whether he was upside down or right side up. As it was, I was kind of on the side of him, my head was along his neck and only my left hip and leg felt the pinch of the weight.

The washout was only about three feet wide, at the bottom, just enough room for me and that horse to get wedged in nice. The old pony was fighting and bellering and kicking big hunks of dirt down on top of us. I was kinda worried that he might undermine the bank of the washout and have it cave in on us and bury us alive so I grabbed his head and hugged it toward me thinking that would quiet him down and keep him from tearing things up so much. I figgered that if there'd be any squeezing done it would be on the other side, for as it was I sure had no room to spare.

Well, he fought on for quite a spell, then he laid still for a while. If that horse had been good and gentle I could of maybe got him to lay still long enough so I could try and dig myself out with my hands, but just as soon as I'd move to try anything like that he'd let out a snort that sounded mighty loud in that perticular place and go to fighting again.

His hoofs would start flying and tearing things up and what little dirt I'd scraped away with my fingers would be replaced with a few hundred pounds of the side of the washout. I was having a mighty hard time keeping my head clear and out in the air and the dirt kept accumulating and piling up on top of us till there was nothing but part of the horse's legs, still a going, and our heads sticking out.

Then it comes to me that if that horse keeps on a kicking and bringing down more dirt he'd soon be in a fix where his legs would be all buried and he'd have to be still, but I was sure worried about a big hunk of overhang-

ing dirt he might loosen up while doing that. It looked
like it weighed at least five tons and I didn't want to think
of it dropping down on us.

There was one way where I could win out, and that
was to dig for my six-shooter which it was lucky was on
my right hip and possible to get at. With that six-gun I
could shoot the horse, there'd be no more dirt coming
down and I could easy enough dig myself out with the
same gun, and I could take my time about it too.

That was one way and the best one, but I sure didn't
want to shoot that horse and decided I wouldn't till I just
had to to save him from suffering. Shooting a horse wasn't
appealing to me even in the fix I was in. It would of saved
my carcass for sure but I was finding more pleasure in
looking for other ways out than just that one.

I kept my eye on the hunk of dirt above my head, and
while the pony by me would have another fit once in a
while and small piles of dirt would keep a coming down
I was finding my breathing capacity getting smaller and
smaller. My body was beginning to feel numb from my
chest on down and I felt that the only part of me that was
living was from my chest on up.

I thought of the boys I started out from camp with that
morning and wondered *when* they'd miss me and start
looking for me, and then once again I thought of my six-
gun. If I could get it out and fire a shot once in a while
some of 'em would maybe hear.

I'd been digging pretty steady and with just the idea of
keeping my right arm and head clear. I knowed that I

couldn't get away even if all the dirt was off—the horse was on me and holding me down, but from then on I wanted my gun and I sure went to work for it.

It took me a good hour's time to get it out and my gloves was wore to a frazzle, but I finally managed it, and soon as I shook the dirt out of the barrel I held it straight up and fired. The shot echoed along the washout and sounded like it could be heard for many miles. I waited and listened for an answer and then I noticed where the sun was. It was slanting in where me and my pony was getting buried alive and it was making things all the hotter down there.

By it I figgered it was along about noon, all the boys excepting me would be back to camp from the first "circle" and wouldn't be starting out again for a while. I was about ten miles from camp and when they would start out again I knowed they'd go another direction as all the cattle in the country I was at was run in that morning. The shot I fired had been for nothing.

Riders was often late getting in with cattle and I knowed they hadn't thought anything had happened to me as yet. I also knowed they wouldn't think anything was wrong till that evening when they gathered in to eat, and till then I thought was an ungodly long time to wait.

And what was more, how was they going to find me if they did start looking? I was sure well hid and they'd have to pretty near know the exact spot where I was located, I could make a noise with my gun of course. . . . All them thoughts was mighty cheerful thoughts not to have, but I couldn't dodge 'em. If only that big ton of dirt above my head hadn't been so threatening things would of been easier, but there it was as big as death and I couldn't take my eyes from it.

Finally the sun left us. It was going on west to its setting point and left me still doing some tall thinking. The big horse alongside of me was quiet for good—the dirt had piled up on top of him till his toes disappeared and he *had* to be still. But his breathing wasn't very good to listen to so close to my head, and I didn't find it at all inspiring as to ways and means of getting out of there.

Clods of dirt would still keep a falling off and on but there was signs of 'em quitting since the horse had got quiet. It was too late for me to try to dig out though, but I was still at it and at the same time watching that I didn't tickle or jar the side of the bank that held the all-powerful heavy piece of earth.

As I worked and clawed at the dirt and wished for badger claws instead of bleeding fingers I found that my resting spells was coming oftener and stayed longer. It was just as the sun was going down and when I'd took an *unusual* long rest that I realized I was holding something in my hand that I'd grabbed a hold of when I was ready to quit. It was a clump of rabbit brush that'd fell in from the top with the dirt that'd got loosened—more of it was a hanging up there.

My hand was on my chest as I studied where that piece of brush had come from. I felt a chill run up and down my backbone as I realized that it'd come from no other place

than the big hunk of overhanging dirt. *It was loosening up.*

The thought of that near had me moving, my hand closed in on my shirt just for something to grab a hold of, and as I did that I felt something breaking in my shirt pocket. It was matches.

I held my hand there for a while and done some thinking. I noticed the clump of rabbit brush my hand was still holding and then I looked up ten feet above to where there was lots of the same brush hanging over the edge.

I couldn't think so very fast along about then and I only realized it was dark when I lit a match and it throwed a light, but the rest of the programme didn't need no thinking—everything was in front of me to follow and that's what I did.

I held the match under the piece of rabbit brush I had and it took holt and flamed like that kind of brush does. When I thought the flame was strong enough to stand a little breeze I heaved it as best I could up toward the other brush ten feet above me.

The first attempt wasn't much good, the little piece of brush came back on me, singed me a little and then died. I

tried it again and finally landed it up amongst the brush along the top of the bank. Then I held my breath.

A little flame shot up and throwed a light on the opposite side of the washout. I watched that and seen where the flame seemed to gradually die down. "If that fire don't start," I says out loud, "I'm just as good as done for," which was the truth.

But it did start, slow and aggravating but sure, and pretty soon it gets lit up above, and I can see the sparks fly and some of 'em are falling down on me and the horse but it was sure good to see that light and hear that brush a roaring in flame. I knowed what rabbit brush would do once it got started to burning. I knowed it'd spread and

throw a mighty good light for as long as any of that kind of brush was around. And if I remembered right, that kind of brush was plenty thick along that wash for a good mile or so.

From then on instead of digging I put my efforts to waiting and that was getting to be some painful too, but my hopes had went up a lot since I got such a good signal fire started. I felt sure somebody would ride up and look for me soon, and sure enough, after a while I hear somebody holler, my six-shooter barks out an answer and then I thinks, . . . what if somebody should ride upon that piece of country that's hanging over me and just waiting for some little weight to start it down?

The thought of that sure got my lungs to working. . . . "Stay back," I hollered, "stay back."

"Where are you, Bill?" somebody asks.

"In the bottom of the washout," I answers, "but don't come near the edge of where I'm at or it'll cave in—get in from some other place."

I didn't have to tell them to hurry, they was doing that a plenty and pretty soon half a dozen riders was digging me out with running irons, six-shooters, and everything they could get hold of that'd scatter the dirt. The horse was lifted off of me and I was pulled out to where I could work my legs and get the blood to circulating in 'em.

It took four saddle horses to pull my horse out and straighten him up to stand, and by the time I got through telling the boys what happened, how it happened and all I felt half-ways strong enough to stand up again. With the help of one of the boys I walked over to investigate the hunk of earth that'd been hanging over me and threatening all that long day. There was a crack in the ground and back of it which showed how ready it was to fall. I stuck my boot heel in that crack and shoved a little, and about that time I was pulled away.

The earth seemed to go out from under us as that hunk left, a big cloud of dust went up, and when we looked again the washout was near filled to the top.

CHARLES J. FINGER

A Brace of Cowards

Two lads were aboard the *Gulf of Akaba* when we
left Buenos Aires bound for the Cape Verde Islands, and
both of them were sons of owners, "Preferred Cargo" as
the bos'n put it, "to be carried there and back with special care." That is to say, they were non-paying passengers
with the liberty of the ship, on a three-masted schooner
fitted for freight. The boy from Ohio was blue-eyed, quick-
moving, tall, supple, light on his feet as a greyhound, one
of those who make friends on sight, and from fo'c'sle to
galley his indiscretions were forgiven him. Stuart Feather
easily outshone Juan Moreira, the lad of the pampas.

We were barely out of sight of Cape Santa Maria when
Feather did a trick that tickled even the old mahogany-
faced bos'n. As we bowled along with a steady wind on
our quarter, young Feather climbed out along the bowsprit, went hand over hand up the forestay to the top of
the foremast, then, after a little separated spell, along to
the main top, thence to the mizzen, and so down the backstay to the deck. That, as any seaman knows, is no light

job, being hard on the hands and muscles and taking a level head to boot.

Juan, heavy and thick-set, dared nothing like that. Off the deck he was lost, and when not reading, passed his time staring out to sea, whistling softly between his teeth.

Once he tried to mount the ratlines, intending to join Feather, who sat at ease astride the mainsail yard, but he grew dizzy, I suppose, a dozen feet from the deck, and so came down and tried no more. He had no head for high places. So, naturally, aboard ship, Feather had rather the best of things. For instance, when Miles Seastream fell overboard while painting the davits, Feather was permitted to slip into the dinghy with the rescue party and so have the rare experience of aiding a drowning man, while Juan stood looking on from the deck.

For all that, Juan was interesting and had good things to tell of life in Patagonia: of condors caught; of guanacos killed, and of venturesome men who sought buried treasure in the Andes. But what he told of things that could be done with the boledores was the most amazing. As they hung at his bunk's head, the boledores were more like a toy than a weapon, making a Y-shaped affair when spread out, a thing made of twisted bull hide with balls about the size of an egg at the end of each three-foot thong. Yet, when we went ashore at Cape Verde, he did some odd things. Thrown at a post some twenty yards away, whirling like a triple chain shot, the boledores caught the post in a way that would have seriously entangled any living creature at which it was aimed. The throw was pretty, and there was a swift alacrity about the thrower that was deceptive and led us to think that far less skill and strength was required than was actually the case. When I tried to work the boledores as we walked shoreward after our mountain climb, I became entangled, and received a blow on the head that dazed me.

I tried it just before we came to the tall white church at the edge of town, the church you notice the first thing as you sail in the harbor and the last thing as you leave, for the white spire with the ball which supports a cross stands out against the brown mountain very plainly. On the little green hill behind the church we who were on shore leave sat awhile, talking and eating bananas. We were resting mainly because of that dazing blow on the head I had received.

Someone said something about a fellow he called the Human Fly who climbed the outside of tall buildings. I forget how the subject started, but I know that Feather got into a most amazing labyrinth of explanation about how it was done, telling all about how to keep one's head clear at great heights.

Perhaps he boasted a trifle. Anyway, Billy Walling, who had been everywhere in the world, said that at Benares there was a flag on a high tower which a sailor of his acquaintance had planted there, and so stiff was the climb that no one had been found to remove it. One yarn led to another, to tales of steeplejack work and mountain climbing, and things worked around so that Feather declared that for two cents he would tie anything, the red sash that Juan wore, for instance, to the golden cross on the church.

"Ten minutes is all I want," he said. The idea must have jumped into his head in a moment, for there was no challenging, no silly daring, but when he said it there was a gap of silence.

Juan looked almost scared at the suggestion and drew back a step.

"Scared o' losing that pretty sash?" said Walling, and at that Juan unwound it and handed Feather the two-yard strip without a word.

For a moment Feather's face had a serious and steadfast expression, and, for a space, he stood irresolute. I believe that had one of us said a single discouraging word, what passed afterward would never have been, but we were all silent, each perhaps afraid of being thought scared. An expression of something almost like fear came into Feather's eyes, but he was game, drew himself together smartly, gave his coat to Walling to hold and made for the church door. I clutched his arm and made a perfunctory effort to stop him, but he turned on me sharply.

"Let go," he said as he wrenched loose. "It's no trick at all, I tell you. Nothing near so hard as that climb I did on the ship. Look at the lightning rod. It's easy."

Obviously, the finer edge was gone from his judgment.

In less than two minutes Feather appeared far above and at the little window at the base of the tapering tower. Standing on the sill he waved the scarf; then, forming his hands into a megaphone, he shouted to us.

His words came clear in the still air. "Time me, fellows. I'm off," was what he said.

With him up there to compare by, it became plain that distances were deceiving. As he stretched out his arm, we saw that the lightning rod was all of eight feet from the nearer edge of the little window, though it had seemed within a hand's reach. Again, when Feather did some preliminary testing, we realized that the stone ledge over which he must pass was so narrow that it barely gave toehold. But, full of fertility, he disappeared into the dark of the window, reappeared a moment later with a piece of scantling. That he thrust along in such a way that one end of it was jammed between the rod and the stone and the other rested on a projecting stone ornament above the upper sill of the window. Then, using the scantling as a kind of hand rail, he went with ease, though slowly, along the narrow edge of stone to the copper wire. He vigorously tested a clevis, one of the many which held the rod to the stone; then, jamming his hat down to shade his eyes against the sun glare, he started.

After all, the job was easier than we had imagined, for the clevises were some eight feet apart, and the rod itself far enough away from the sloping stone wall to permit the placing of a foot on the clevis, almost as if in a stirrup. So he seemed to be doing his job with skill and judgment. Once a clevis caught him, entangling his shirt sleeve as he raised his arm, but he easily released himself, and went on and up, swiftly, smoothly, unfalteringly.

Indeed, it seemed to be no trick at all until he reached the base of the stone ball that supported the cross, and the ball, we saw then, was a greater thing than we had supposed, bulging out far beyond the climber. It was plain to see that at the best, he would be able to reach the clevis at the outer circumference only by stretching while his feet were at the angle of ball and spire—a ticklish position.

We heard Feather's voice, though not his words, and Bill Waller certainly spoke for us all when he roared, with long spaces between the words: "All right. You win. Come on down and we'll call it off. Time to be getting aboard." But that the lad did not seem to hear.

It was all very still, almost as if the world watched breathless. Out in the harbor we could see the ship and the dots that were shipmates. It wasn't too far away for them to make out what was going on with the glasses, once their attention was attracted. Close to us a little knot of townspeople had gathered: a barber who had run out in such haste that he bore his brass shaving bowl with him; a porter with his *alpargatas* on his feet; a padre with broad-brimmed hat and little book in his hand, his fingers thrust between the leaves; a panaderia astride of his basket-laden ass; three or four water boys with their great, wicker-covered demijohns, and a barefooted soldier with a rifle, who called upon the climber at regular intervals to come down, but now and then applauded lustily at difficulties overcome. In the town, some were looking from the windows, others watching from roofs or standing in the middle of the street to gaze. As Feather rested before attempting to round the ball, a little fat man, apparently with no very clear notion of what might be done, came running, bearing a coil of light rope which he offered to us, talking the while volubly in Spanish.

Like an ant about to climb a marble, Feather seemed deliberating up there. First the noise of a whistle and then of the ship's bell broke the languor of the day. His motions were perceptibly slower, and for a moment my hopes brightened as I thought that he would descend. He seemed to be crouching, stooping, busy at something; we could not make out what. Then, first one shoe, then the other dropped, struck the spire far below, bounded off, and fell to earth. Another motion of his arm, and his hat floated far out, spinning as it slowly sank. Foolishly enough, I watched the hat and not the lad, and, when I looked again, he was gliding swiftly under the ball, leaning far out, the red sash in his belt flapping bravely. There

were quick movements, and he gained the clevis at the
outer circumference of the ball. It seemed to be no easy
job, and as I looked, I was as sick and dizzy as though I
were up there. For very terror I had to look at those near
me, and the gaze of their beseeching eyes struck a new
anxiety into my soul.

After resting for a moment, the lad reached up and
over; his hand and then his head went out of sight. There
was a kicking, a wriggling, and a very evident straining,
and the upper part of his body was lost to view. He must
have been within an ace of gaining when we heard from
up there a wild scream, and his legs shot into view kicking
furiously; next, the lower half of his body sliding backward and outward. We had a sense of extraordinary activity, of a spasmodic straining. Then came another scream!
At my side, Juan Moreira gave a low moan, broke out
with a cry to God and threw himself on the ground, weeping with fear and horror. Try as I would, I could not look
at the tower then, and my eyes fell on the padre with his
dust-covered soutane. His lips were moving as those of one
who talks without words.

When I dared to look again, somehow Feather had once
more gained the clevis and was sliding up and out of sight
over the upper surface of the ball. But things were different, and the rod that had showed far above the top of the
cross was there no longer; and at the ball the rod bulged
far out, like an inverted handle. It was plain that something had given way; that the rod had slipped and pulled
through somehow, to jam, doubtless, at the angle of cross

and ball. The understanding came upon us at once, and a moment later there was a rushing of men to the little green hill, where, by straining and craning, we could see a huddled figure at the foot of the cross. A great stillness was on the island, a softness that hushed us to whispers. All things seemed at a standstill except for a great swooping eagle that watched from far above.

But those of us whose heads were not craned became aware of Juan running across the bare patch toward the tower door, and he was carrying the coil of rope which the little fat man had brought.

When Juan appeared at the little window we saw that he had been contriving things, for there was a looping arrangement of lines about him. One short length of line held his boledores to a kind of rope belt, another, and longer one, passed from the rope belt to the dark of the little window. Carefully, he hauled the second line out until it hung in a long loop far below, swinging free; then he stuck his boledores into the improvised belt so that the balls hung loose. He was very cool and businesslike, testing this, that, and the other: the ropes, the belt, the boledores, and the scantling that formed the handrail, but especially the boledores. Satisfied at last, he made the trip between window and lightning rod with vast caution, both hands on the scantling, his body close plastered to the wall.

To us he made no signal or sign, but after he had gained the rod, there was another careful testing of everything, a hard pulling at the rod, and a careful dusting of his hands. Then up he went, not gripping with hands and knees, but as a Singhalese climbs a coconut tree, his bare feet walking up the tower, elbows and hands almost touching, hands a little in advance of his feet.

All went well until three fourths of the climb to the stone ball was done, when, by some luckless chance, there came a light, warm, faintly scented breeze that died as soon as it began. Gentle though it was, short as it lived, it was enough to catch the length of looped rope that hung far below. Twice the loop flapped lazily, slowly it slid across the surface of the tower, so slowly indeed that it seemed as if the pressure of a child's little finger could have stayed it. And the line caught somehow in the end of the scantling, and Juan was halted.

He must have guessed correctly what had happened, for he did not look down. There was a faint perking of the rope—once, twice. It seemed pitifully feeble, the strain that he could bring to bear, yet the trick was done. The scantling shifted slightly and the rope hung free again and swung back plumb. The improvised hand rail fell at the window end, struck the tower sill, hung for a brief instant, and slid slantwise. We saw it oddly in the air, slowly turning; saw it strike the ground, stand for a moment on end, then splinter and fall to earth.

But Juan had lost no time and was in the shadow of the globe, somehow braced in the copper rod that was an inverted handle, feet firm against the spire at the base of the ball, body pressing the rod into a V shape. He seemed to be lying far out on something as flimsy as a spider web,

his body almost horizontal, his left hand stiffly stretched
to grasp the wire that passed from his shoulder to the
cross. The slightest slipping of the rod or any careless move
on the part of Feather——

That great quiet which comes on before dusk was upon
the world and the blood-red sun was sinking into a purple
bank of cloud. Far up, our ears caught the sound of voices.
We saw Juan, a black, active mark against a sea-green sky,
and the boledores were hanging loose, were swinging, were
circling. When it seemed as though he would cast them,
his arm was stayed and, for the space of a few heart-beats,
we wondered as we saw the balls hang idle again. A moment later the head and shoulders of Feather showed as
he rose to his knees, clasping fast the cross; then down he
went again out of sight. Again Juan was active and the
boledores swung. They shot upward, opening out into
three flying, circling balls and flew straight to the mark,
whipping and entangling about the arms of the cross. We
heard the sharp crack as they struck the metal. We saw
Feather on his feet, binding fast the twisted hide thongs
and we saw the thrower swarm up the thin line, rest for a
second at the ball's circumference, then pass out of sight,
to reappear standing by the side of Feather.

We found relief then, and the stillness was split with
our yell, and men fell to shaking one another by the hand.
From the street came a fainter yell and the excited soldier
fired his rifle. But our burst of joy was altogether too much
like bragging, and a deep hush followed.

Juan had planned and wrought well. The line he car-

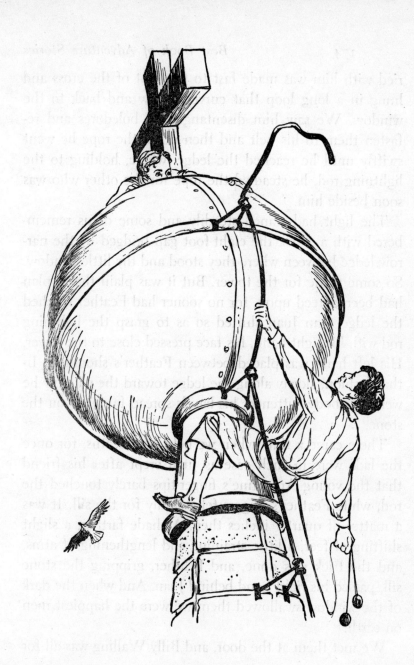

ried with him was made fast to the foot of the cross and hung in a long loop that curved below and back to the window. We saw him disentangle his boledores and refasten them to his belt and then down the rope he went swiftly until he reached the ledge, where, holding to the lightning rod, he steadied the rope for the other who was soon beside him.

The light had waned steadily and some of us remembered with a shock the eight-foot gap bridged by the narrow ledge between where they stood and the little window. So some made for the tower. But it was plain that a plan had been agreed upon, for no sooner had Feather reached the ledge than Juan shifted so as to grasp the lightning rod with his right hand, his face pressed close to the tower. His left hand was placed between Feather's shoulders. In that fashion, slowly along the ledge toward the window he went, his body flattened, his hands spread far apart on the stone.

There came a time when we held our breaths, for once the lads were in such case as Juan crept after his friend that the young Argentine's finger-tips barely touched the rod, while Feather's fingers felt blindly for the sill. It was a matter of quarter inches then. A shade farther, a slight shifting of feet, a little straining and lengthening of arms, and the trick was done, and Feather, gripping the stone sill, passed his right hand behind Juan. And when the dark of the window swallowed them we were the happiest men on earth.

We met them at the door, and Billy Walling was all for

making a fuss, congratulating the lads, and all that kind
of thing. But Feather was strangely quiet, saying almost
nothing, and Juan would accept no thanks or congratula-
tions at all. So we walked down to the beach and pushed
off, a silent and rather gloomy crowd.

In the boat, as we pulled for the ship, the mahogany-
faced bos'n said something to Juan. It was a question
which we did not hear, but Juan said in reply, in his fine,
silky tone:

"No. I was afraid all the time. Really, I have no head
for high places. I did all that because somehow I was afraid
not to."

"I know," said Feather. "I was the same. It was really
cowardice, you know, when you come to look at it. I was
afraid you'd all think me afraid. So it was cowardice."

"It would be that," said the bos'n who was a man of
very few words and vast wisdom.

from MARK TWAIN'S

Life on the Mississippi

Ever since boys were first created, there have been some who dreamed of running away from home and becoming something so grand and famous that even their parents would be impressed. Samuel Clemens was such a boy—and, unlike most, he actually did it. He became a Mississippi River steamboat pilot when that was about the most exciting thing a boy could think of doing. Years later, when he became a writer, he took his pen name from the warning cry of the leadsmen: "Mark twain!" He also wrote a book, one of his best, about his experiences. Here is part of his story about what it was like in those days to have the most exciting job on the biggest river in America.

THE BOY'S AMBITION

When I was a boy, there was but one permanent ambition among my comrades in our village on the west bank of the Mississippi River. That was, to be a steamboatman. We had transient ambitions of other sorts, but they were only transient. When a circus came and went, it left us all burning to become clowns; the first negro minstrel show that ever came to our section left us all suffering to try that kind of life; now and then we had a hope that, if we lived and were good, God would permit us to be pirates. These ambitions faded out, each in its turn; but the ambition to be a steamboatman always remained.

Once a day a cheap, gaudy packet arrived upward from St. Louis, and another downward from Keokuk. Before these events, the day was glorious with expectancy; after them, the day was a dead and empty thing. Not only the boys, but the whole village, felt this. After all these years I can picture that old time to myself now, just as it was then: the white town drowsing in the sunshine of a summer's morning; the streets empty, or pretty nearly so; one or two clerks sitting in front of the Water Street stores, with their splint-bottomed chairs tilted back against the walls, chins on breasts, hats slouched over their faces, asleep—with shingle-shavings enough around to show what broke them down; a sow and a litter of pigs loafing along the sidewalk, doing a good business in watermelon rinds and seeds; two or three lonely little freight piles scattered about the "levee"; a pile of "skids" on the slope of the stone-paved wharf, and the fragrant town drunkard asleep in the shadow of them; two or three wood flats at the head of the wharf, but nobody to listen to the peaceful lapping of the wavelets against them; the great Mississippi, the majestic, the magnificent Mississippi, rolling its mile-wide tide along, shining in the sun; the dense forest away on the other side; the "point" above the town, and the "point" below, bounding the river-glimpse and turning it into a sort of sea, and withal a very still and brilliant and lonely one.

Presently a film of dark smoke appears above one of those remote "points"; instantly a negro drayman, famous for his quick eye and prodigious voice, lifts up the cry, "S-t-e-a-m-boat a-comin'!" and the scene changes! The town drunkard stirs, the clerks wake up, a furious clatter of drays follows, every house and store pours out a human contribution, and all in a twinkling the dead town is alive and moving. Drays, carts, men, boys, all go hurrying from many quarters to a common center, the wharf. Assembled there, the people fasten their eyes upon the coming boat as upon a wonder they are seeing for the first time. And the boat *is* rather a handsome sight, too. She is long and sharp and trim and pretty; she has two tall, fancy-topped chimneys, with a gilded device of some kind swung between them; a fanciful pilot-house, all glass and "gingerbread," perched on top of the "texas" deck behind them; the paddle-boxes are gorgeous with a picture or with gilded rays above the boat's name; the boiler-deck, the hurricane-deck, and the texas deck are fenced and ornamented with clean white railings; there is a flag gallantly flying from the jack-staff; the furnace doors are open and the fires glaring bravely; the upper decks are black with passengers; the captain stands by the big bell, calm, imposing, the envy of all; great volumes of the blackest smoke are rolling and rumbling out of the chimneys—a husbanded grandeur created with a bit of pitch-pine just before arriving at a town; the crew are grouped on the forecastle; the broad stage is run far out over the port bow, and an envied deckhand stands picturesquely on the end of it with a coil of rope in his hand; the pent steam is screaming through the gauge-cocks; the captain lifts his hand, a bell rings, the wheels stop; then they turn back, churning the water to foam, and the steamer is at rest. Then such a scramble as there is to get aboard, and to get ashore, and to take in freight and to discharge freight, all at one and the same time; and such a yelling and cursing as the mates facilitate it all with! Ten minutes later the steamer is under way again, with no flag on the jack-staff and no black smoke issuing from the chimneys. After ten more minutes the town is dead again, and the town drunkard asleep by the skids once more.

My father was a justice of the peace, and I supposed he possessed the power of life and death over all men, and could hang anybody that offended him. This was distinction enough for me as a general thing; but the desire to be a steamboatman kept intruding, nevertheless. I first wanted to be a cabin-boy, so that I could come out with a white apron on and shake a table-cloth over the side, where all my old comrades could see me; later I thought I would rather be the deck-hand who stood on the end of the stage-plank with the coil of rope in his hand, because he was particularly conspicuous. But these were only day-dreams—they were too heavenly to be contemplated as real possibilities.

By and by one of our boys went away. He was not heard of for a long time. At last he turned up as apprentice engineer or "striker" on a steamboat. This thing shook the bottom out of all my Sunday-school teachings. That boy had been notoriously worldly, and I just the reverse; yet he was exalted to this eminence, and I left in obscurity and misery. There was nothing generous about this fellow in his greatness. He would always manage to have a rusty bolt to scrub while his boat tarried at our town, and he would sit on the inside guard and scrub it, where we all could see him and envy him and loathe him. And whenever his boat was laid up he would come home and swell around the town in his blackest and greasiest clothes, so that nobody could help remembering that he was a steamboatman; and he used all sorts of steamboat technicalities in his talk, as if he were so used to them that he forgot common people could not understand them. He would speak of the "labboard" side of a horse in an

easy, natural way that would make one wish he was dead.
And he was always talking about "St. Looy" like an old
citizen; he would refer casually to occasions when he was
"coming down Fourth Street," or when he was "passing
by the Planter's House," or when there was a fire and he
took a turn on the brakes of "the old Big Missouri"; and
then he would go on and lie about how many towns the
size of ours were burned down there that day.

Two or three of the boys had long been persons of consideration among us because they had been to St. Louis
once and had a vague general knowledge of its wonders,
but the day of their glory was over now. They lapsed into
a humble silence, and learned to disappear when the ruth-
less "cub"-engineer approached. This fellow had money,

too, and hair-oil. Also an ignorant silver watch and a showy brass watch-chain. He wore a leather belt and used no suspenders. If ever a youth was cordially admired and hated by his comrades, this one was. No girl could withstand his charms. He "cut out" every boy in the village. When his boat blew up at last, it diffused a tranquil contentment among us such as we had not known for months. But when he came home the next week, alive, renowned, and appeared in church all battered up and bandaged, a shining hero, stared at and wondered over by everybody, it seemed to us that the partiality of Providence for an undeserving reptile had reached a point where it was open to criticism.

This creature's career could produce but one result, and it speedily followed. Boy after boy managed to get on the river. The minister's son became an engineer. The doctor's and the postmaster's sons became "mud clerks"; the wholesale liquor dealer's son became a barkeeper on a boat; four sons of the chief merchant, and two sons of the county judge, became pilots. Pilot was the grandest position of all. The pilot, even in those days of trivial wages, had a princely salary—from a hundred and fifty to two hundred and fifty dollars a month, and no board to pay. Two months of his wages would pay a preacher's salary for a year. Now some of us were left disconsolate. We could not get on the river—at least our parents would not let us.

So, by and by, I ran away. I said I would never come home again till I was a pilot and could come in glory. But somehow I could not manage it. I went meekly aboard a few of the boats that lay packed together like sardines at the long St. Louis wharf, and humbly inquired for the pilots, but got only a cold shoulder and short words from mates and clerks. I had to make the best of this sort of treatment for the time being, but I had comforting day-dreams of a future when I should be a great and honored pilot, with plenty of money, and could kill some of these mates and clerks and pay for them.

A CUB PILOT

But I am wandering from what I was intending to do; that is, make plainer than perhaps appears in the previous chapters some of the peculiar requirements of the science of piloting. First of all, there is one faculty which a pilot must incessantly cultivate until he has brought it to absolute perfection. Nothing short of perfection will do. That faculty is memory. He cannot stop with merely thinking a thing is so and so; he must *know* it; for this is eminently one of the "exact" sciences. With what scorn a pilot was looked upon, in the old times, if he ever ventured to deal in that feeble phrase "I think," instead of the vigorous one, "I know!"

One cannot easily realize what a tremendous thing it is to know every trivial detail of twelve hundred miles of river and know it with absolute exactness. If you will take the longest street in New York, and travel up and down it, conning its features patiently until you know every house and window and lamppost and big and little sign by heart, and know them so accurately that you can instantly name the one you are abreast of when you are set down at random in that street in the middle of an inky black night, you will then have a tolerable notion of the amount and the exactness of a pilot's knowledge who carries the Mississippi River in his head. And then, if you will go on until you know every street-crossing, the character, size, and position of the crossing-stones, and the varying depth of mud in each of these numberless places, you will have some idea of what the pilot must know in order to keep a Mississippi steamer out of trouble. Next, if you will take half of the signs in that long street, and *change their places* once a month, and still manage to know their new positions accurately on dark nights, and keep up with these repeated changes without making any mistakes, you will understand what is required of a pilot's peerless memory by the fickle Mississippi.

I think a pilot's memory is about the most wonderful thing in the world. To know the Old and New Testaments by heart, and be able to recite them glibly, forward or backward, or begin at random anywhere in the book and recite both ways and never trip or make a mistake, is no extravagant mass of knowledge, and no marvelous facility, compared to a pilot's massed knowledge of the Mississippi and his marvelous facility in the handling of it. I make this comparison deliberately, and believe I am not expanding the truth when I do it. Many will think my figure too strong, but pilots will not.

And how easily and comfortably the pilot's memory does its work; how placidly effortless is its way; how *unconsciously* it lays up its vast stores, hour by hour, day by day, and never loses or mislays a single valuable package of them all! Take an instance. Let a leadsman cry, "Half twain! half twain! half twain! half twain! half twain!" until it becomes as monotonous as the ticking of a clock; let conversation be going on all the time, and the pilot be doing his share of the talking, and no longer consciously listening to the leadsman; and in the midst of this endless string of half twains let a single "quarter twain!" be interjected, without emphasis, and then the half-twain cry go on again, just as before: two or three weeks later that pilot can describe with precision the boat's position in the river when that quarter twain was uttered, and give you such a lot of headmarks, stern-marks, and side-marks to guide you, that you ought to be able to take the boat there and put her in that same spot again yourself! The cry of "quarter twain" did not really take his mind from his talk, but his trained faculties instantly photographed the bearings, noted the change of depth, and laid up the important details for future reference without requiring any assistance from *him* in the matter.

If you were walking and talking with a friend, and another friend at your side kept up a monotonous repetition of the vowel sound A, for a couple of blocks, and then in the midst interjected an R, thus, A, A, A, A, A, R, A, A, A, etc., and gave the R no emphasis, you would not be able to state, two or three weeks afterward, that the R had

been put in, nor be able to tell what objects you were passing at the moment it was done. But you could if your memory had been patiently and laboriously trained to do that
sort of thing mechanically.

Give a man a tolerably fair memory to start with, and
piloting will develop it into a very colossus of capability.
But *only in the matters it is daily drilled in.* A time would
come when the man's faculties could not help noticing
land-marks and soundings, and his memory could not help
holding on to them with the grip of a vise; but if you asked
that same man at noon what he had had for breakfast, it
would be ten chances to one that he could not tell you.
Astonishing things can be done with the human memory
if you will devote it faithfully to one particular line of business.

At the time that wages soared so high on the Missouri
River, my chief, Mr. Bixby, went up there and learned
more than a thousand miles of that stream with an ease
and rapidity that were astonishing. When he had seen each
division *once* in the daytime and *once* at night, his educa-
tion was so nearly complete that he took out a "daylight"
license; a few trips later he took out a full license, and
went to piloting day and night—and he ranked A1, too.

Mr. Bixby placed me as steersman for a while under a
pilot whose feats of memory were a constant marvel to me.
However, his memory was born in him, I think, not built.
For instance, somebody would mention a name. Instantly
Mr. Brown would break in:

"Oh, I knew *him.* Sallow-faced, red-headed fellow, with

a little scar on the side of his throat, like a splinter under the flesh. He was only in the Southern trade six months. That was thirteen years ago. I made a trip with him. There was five feet in the upper river then; the *Henry Blake* grounded at the foot of Tower Island drawing four and a half; the *George Elliott* unshipped her rudder on the wreck of the *Sunflower*—"

"Why, the *Sunflower* didn't sink until—"

"*I* know when she sunk; it was three years before that, on the 2d of December; Asa Hardy was captain of her, and his brother John was first clerk; and it was his first trip in her, too; Tom Jones told me these things a week afterward in New Orleans; he was first mate of the *Sunflower*. Captain Hardy stuck a nail in his foot the 6th of July of the next year, and died of the lockjaw on the 15th. His brother John died two years after—3rd of March—erysipelas. I never saw either of the Hardys—they were Alleghany River men—but people who knew them told me all these things. And they said Captain Hardy wore yarn socks winter and summer just the same, and his first wife's name was Jane Shook—she was from New England—and his second one died in a lunatic asylum. It was in the blood. She was from Lexington, Kentucky. Name was Horton before she was married."

And so on, by the hour, the man's tongue would go. He could *not* forget anything. It was simply impossible. The most trivial details remained as distinct and luminous in his head, after they had lain there for years, as the most memorable events. His was not simply a pilot's memory;

its grasp was universal. If he were talking about a trifling letter he had received seven years before, he was pretty sure to deliver you the entire screed from memory. And then, without observing that he was departing from the true line of his talk, he was more than likely to hurl in a long-drawn parenthetical biography of the writer of that letter; and you were lucky indeed if he did not take up that writer's relatives, one by one, and give you their biographies, too.

Such a memory as that is a great misfortune. To it, all occurrences are of the same size. Its possessor cannot distinguish an interesting circumstance from an uninteresting one. As a talker, he is bound to clog his narrative with tiresome details and make himself an insufferable bore. Moreover, he cannot stick to his subject. He picks up every little grain of memory he discerns in his way, and so is led aside. Mr. Brown would start out with the honest intention of telling you a vastly funny anecdote about a dog. He would be "so full of laugh" that he could hardly begin; then his memory would start with the dog's breed and personal appearance; drift into a history of his owner; of his owner's family, with descriptions of weddings and burials that had occurred in it, together with recitals of congratulatory verses and obituary poetry provoked by the same; then this memory would recollect that one of these events occurred during the celebrated "hard winter" of such-and-such a year, and a minute description of that winter would follow, along with the names of people who were frozen to death, and statistics showing the high figures which pork and hay went up to. Pork and hay would suggest corn and fodder; corn and fodder would suggest cows and horses; cows and horses would suggest the circus and certain celebrated bare-back riders; the transition from the circus to the menagerie was easy and natural; from the elephant to equatorial Africa was but a step; then of course the heathen savages would suggest religion; and at the end of three or four hours' tedious jaw, the watch would change, and Brown would go out of the pilot-house muttering extracts from sermons he had heard years before about the efficacy of prayer as a means of grace. And the original first mention would be all you had learned about that dog, after all this waiting and hungering.

A pilot must have a memory; but there are two higher qualities which he must also have. He must have good and quick judgment and decision, and a cool, calm courage that no peril can shake. Give a man the merest trifle of pluck to start with, and by the time he has become a pilot he cannot be unmanned by any danger a steamboat can get into; but one cannot quite say the same for judgment. Judgment is a matter of brains, and a man must *start* with a good stock of that article or he will never succeed as a pilot.

The growth of courage in the pilot-house is steady all the time, but it does not reach a high and satisfactory condition until some time after the young pilot has been "standing his own watch" alone and under the staggering weight of all the responsibilities connected with the position. When the apprentice has become pretty thoroughly acquainted with the river, he goes clattering along so fearlessly with his steamboat, night or day, that he presently begins to imagine that it is *his* courage that animates him; but the first time the pilot steps out and leaves him to his own devices he finds out it was the other man's. He discovers that the article has been left out of his own cargo altogether. The whole river is bristling with exigencies in a moment; he is not prepared for them; he does not know how to meet them; all his knowledge forsakes him; and within fifteen minutes he is as white as a sheet and scared almost to death. Therefore pilots wisely train these cubs by various strategic tricks to look danger in the face a little more calmly. A favorite way of theirs is to play a friendly swindle upon the candidate.

Mr. Bixby served me in this fashion once, and for years afterward I used to blush, even in my sleep, when I thought of it. I had become a good steersman; so good, indeed, that I had all the work to do on our watch, night and day. Mr. Bixby seldom made a suggestion to me; all he ever did was to take the wheel on particularly bad nights or in particularly bad crossings, land the boat when she needed to be landed, play gentleman of leisure nine-tenths of the watch, and collect the wages. The lower river was about bank-full, and if anybody had questioned my ability to run any crossing between Cairo and New Orleans without help or instruction, I should have felt irreparably hurt. The idea of being afraid of any crossing in the lot, in the *daytime*, was a thing too preposterous for con-

templation. Well, one matchless summer's day I was bowl-
ing down the bend above Island 66, brimful of self-conceit
and carrying my nose as high as a giraffe's, when Mr. Bixby
said:

"I am going below awhile. I suppose you know the next
crossing?"

This was almost an affront. It was about the plainest
and simplest crossing in the whole river. One couldn't come
to any harm, whether he ran it right or not; and as for
depth, there never had been any bottom there. I knew all
this, perfectly well.

"Know how to *run* it? Why, I can run it with my eyes
shut."

"How much water is there in it?"

"Well, that is an odd question. I couldn't get bottom
there with a church steeple."

"You think so, do you?"

The very tone of the question shook my confidence.
That was what Mr. Bixby was expecting. He left, without
saying anything more. I began to imagine all sorts of things.
Mr. Bixby, unknown to me, of course, sent somebody
down to the forecastle with some mysterious instructions
to the leadsmen, another messenger was sent to whisper
among the officers, and then Mr. Bixby went into hiding
behind a smoke-stack where he could observe results. Presently the captain stepped out on the hurricane-deck;
next the chief mate appeared; then a clerk. Every moment
or two a straggler was added to my audience; and before I
got to the head of the island I had fifteen or twenty peo-

ple assembled down there under my nose. I began to wonder what the trouble was. As I started across, the captain glanced aloft at me and said, with a sham uneasiness in his voice:

"Where is Mr. Bixby?"

"Gone below, sir."

But that did the business for me. My imagination began to construct dangers out of nothing, and they multiplied faster than I could keep the run of them. All at once I imagined I saw shoal water ahead! The wave of coward agony that surged through me then came near dislocating every joint in me. All my confidence in that crossing vanished. I seized the bell-rope; dropped it, ashamed; seized it again; dropped it once more; clutched it tremblingly once again, and pulled it so feebly that I could hardly hear the stroke myself. Captain and mate sang out instantly, and both together:

"Starboard lead there! and quick about it!"

This was another shock. I began to climb the wheel like a squirrel; but I would hardly get the boat started to port before I would see new dangers on that side, and away I would spin to the other; only to find perils accumulating to starboard, and be crazy to get to port again. Then came the leadsman's sepulchral cry:

"D-e-e-p four!"

Deep four in a bottomless crossing! The terror of it took my breath away.

"M-a-r-k three! M-a-r-k three! Quarter-less-three! Half twain!"

This was frightful! I seized the bell-ropes and stopped the engines.

"Quarter twain! Quarter twain! *Mark* twain!"

I was helpless. I did not know what in the world to do. I was quaking from head to foot, and I could have hung my hat on my eyes, they stuck out so far.

"Quarter-*less*-twain! Nine-and-a-*half!*"

We were *drawing* nine! My hands were in a nerveless flutter. I could not ring a bell intelligibly with them. I flew to the speaking-tube and shouted to the engineer:

"Oh, Ben, if you love me, *back* her! Quick, Ben! Oh, back the immortal *soul* out of her!"

I heard the door close gently. I looked around, and there stood Mr. Bixby, smiling a bland, sweet smile. Then the audience on the hurricane-deck sent up a thundergust of humiliating laughter. I saw it all, now, and I felt meaner than the meanest man in human history. I laid in the lead, set the boat in her marks, came ahead on the engines, and said:

"It was a fine trick to play on an orphan, *wasn't* it? I suppose I'll never hear the last of how I was ass enough to heave the lead at the head of 66."

"Well, no, you won't, maybe. In fact I hope you won't; for I want you to learn something by that experience. Didn't you *know* there was no bottom in that crossing?"

"Yes, sir, I did."

"Very well, then. You shouldn't have allowed me or anybody else to shake your confidence in that knowledge. Try to remember that. And another thing: when you get into a dangerous place, don't turn coward. That isn't going to help matters any."

It was a good enough lesson, but pretty hardly learned. Yet about the hardest part of it was that for months I so often had to hear a phrase which I had conceived a particular distaste for. It was, "Oh, Ben, if you love me, back her!"

from ESTHER FORBES'

Johnny Tremain

Johnny Tremain was 14 and living in Boston in the stirring days just before the Revolutionary War. He had to give up his work as a silversmith apprentice because his hand had been crippled in an accident. But he soon found work as a messenger for "The Sons of Liberty" and was proud to serve such patriots as Sam Adams, John Hancock, and, above all, his hero, Paul Revere. When they were planning the Boston Tea Party, Johnny was afraid that he would not be able to join his friend Rab in this exciting exploit.

SALT-WATER TEA

'First,' Adams said to the boys, 'raise your right hands. Swear by the great name of God Himself never, for as long as you live, to divulge to anyone the secret matters now trusted to you. Do you so swear?'

The boys swore.

Hancock was not looking at them. He sat with his aching head in his hands.

'There's no chance—not one—those ships will be allowed to return. The mass meetings which will be held

almost daily demanding the return of the tea are to arouse
public opinion and to persuade the world we did not turn
to violence until every other course had been blocked to
us. When the twenty days are up, on the night of the sixteenth of December, those ships are going to be boarded.
That tea will be dumped in Boston Harbor. For each ship,
the *Dartmouth*, the *Eleanor*, and the brig, the *Beaver*, we
will need thirty stout, honest, fearless men and boys. Will
you be one, Rab?'

He did not say Rab and Johnny, as the younger boy
noticed. Was this because he thought Johnny too cripple-
handed for chopping open sea chests—or merely because
he knew Rab better and he was older?

'Of course, sir.'

'How many other boys could you find for the night's
work? Strong and trustworthy boys—for if one ounce of
tea is stolen, the whole thing becomes a robbery—not a
protest?'

Rab thought.

'Eight or ten tonight, but give me a little time so I can
feel about a bit and I can furnish fifteen or twenty.'

'Boys who can keep their mouths shut?'

'Yes.'

Paul Revere said, 'I can furnish twenty or more from
about North Square.'

Not one is to be told in advance just what the work will
be, nor who the others are, nor the names of the men who
instigated the tea party—that is, the gentlemen gathered
here tonight. Simply, as they love their country and liberty

and hate tyranny, they are to gather in this shop on the night of December sixteenth, carrying with them such disguises as they can think of, and each armed with an axe or hatchet.'

'It will be as you say.'

The discussion became more general. Each of these three groups must have a leader, men who could keep discipline.

'I'll go, for one,' said Paul Revere.

Doctor Warren warned him. 'Look here, Paul, it has been decided this work must be done by apprentices, strangers—folk little known about Boston. The East India Company may bring suit. If you are recognized . . .'

'I'll risk it.'

Uncle Lorne was motioning to the boys to leave the conspirators. They did not want to leave, but they did.

Both the boys were in their truckle beds. The loft still smelled of tobacco and the spices of the punch.

Johnny moved restlessly on his bed.

'Rab?'

'Uh?'

'Rab . . . those boys you promised. Am I one?'

'Of course.'

'But my hand . . . What will we have to do?'

'Chop open tea chests. Dump tea in the harbor.'

'Rab?'

'Hummmmm?'

'How can I ever . . . chop?'

'You've twenty days to practice in. Logs in back yard need splitting.'

'Rab . . .'

But the older boy was asleep.

Johnny was so wide awake he couldn't close his eyes. Old Meeting struck midnight. He settled himself again. Surely if he tried hard enough he could sleep. He was thinking of those tea ships, the *Dartmouth*, the *Eleanor*, the *Beaver*, great white sails spread softly, sweeping on and on through the night to Boston. Nearer, nearer. He was almost asleep, twitched, and was wide awake. He would not think of the tea ships, but of those logs in the back yard he would practice on. He thought of Doctor Warren. Oh, why had he not let him see his hand? Cilla, waiting and waiting for him at North Square—and then he got there only about when it pleased him. He loved Cilla. She and Rab were the best friends he had ever had. Why was he mean to her? He couldn't think. He would take an axe in his left hand and chop, chop, chop . . . so he fell asleep.

Something large and white was looming up over him— about to run him down. He struggled awake, sat up, and found he was sweating. It was the great sails of the tea ships.

From the bed next to him he heard the soft, slow breathing of the older boy. So much more involved than Johnny in the brewing storm, Rab had been able to drop off immediately. Somehow Johnny must draw into him-

self something of Rab's calm, his nerveless strength. He
began to breathe in unison with the sleeping boy—so
slowly, so softly. He fell into a heavy sleep.

Next morning Johnny was up and out in the back yard
early. At first it seemed impossible to hold an axe in a left
hand, steady it with his bad right. He gritted his teeth and
persevered. Rab said nothing of his struggles. He merely
set type, pulled proofs as usual. But often he was gone
from home, and Johnny knew he was 'feeling about' for
those fifteen to twenty boys he had promised. Would the
others go and Johnny be left behind? He could not bear
the thought, and Rab had promised him that in twenty
days he might learn to chop. Having finished the logs in
Mr. Lorne's back yard, he began chopping (free gratis)
for the Afric Queen.

Almost every day and sometimes all day, the mass meetings at Old South Church went on. Tempers grew higher
and higher. Boston was swept with a passion it had not
known since the Boston Massacre three years before. Riding this wild storm was Sam Adams and his trusty henchmen, directing it, building up the anger until, although
the matter was not publicly mentioned, they would all
see the only thing left for them to do was to destroy the
tea.

Sometimes Rab and Johnny went to these meetings. It
happened they were there when the sheriff arrived and
bade the meeting forthwith to disperse. He said it was

lawless and treasonable. This proclamation from Governor Hutchinson was met with howls and hisses. They voted to disobey the order.

Sometimes the boys slipped over to Griffin's Wharf. By the eighth of December the *Eleanor* had joined the *Dartmouth*. These were strange ships. They had unloaded their cargoes—except the tea. The Town of Boston had ordered them not to unload the tea and the law stated they could not leave until they had unloaded. Nor would the Governor give them a pass to return to England. At Castle Island the British Colonel Leslie had orders to fire upon them if they attempted to sneak out of the harbor. The *Active* and the *Kingfisher*, British men-of-war, stood by ready to blast them out of the water if they obeyed the Town and returned to London with the tea. The ships were held at Griffin's Wharf as though under an enchantment.

Here was none of the usual hustle and bustle. Few of the crew were in sight, but hundreds of spectators gathered every day merely to stare at them. Johnny saw Rotch, the twenty-three-year-old Quaker who owned the *Dartmouth*, running about in despair. The Governor would not let him leave. The Town would not let him unload. Between them he was a ruined man. He feared a mob would burn his ship. There was no mob, and night and day armed citizens guarded the ships. They would see to it that no tea was smuggled ashore and that no harm was done to the ships. Back and forth paced the guard. Many of their faces were familiar to Johnny. One day even John Hancock took his turn with a musket on his shoulder, and the next night he saw Paul Revere.

Then on the fifteenth, the third of the tea ships arrived. This was the brig, the *Beaver*.

The next day, the sixteenth, Johnny woke to hear the rain drumming sadly on the roof, and soon enough once more he heard all the bells of Boston cling-clanging, bidding the inhabitants come once more, and for the last time, to Old South to demand the peaceful return of the ships to England.

By nightfall, when the boys Rab had selected began silently to congregate in the office of the *Observer*, behind locked doors, the rain stopped. Many of them Johnny knew. When they started to assume their disguises, smootch their faces with soot, paint them with red paint, pull on nightcaps, old frocks, torn jackets, blankets with holes cut for their arms, they began giggling and laughing at each other. Rab could silence them with one look, however. No one passing outside the shop must guess that toward twenty boys were at that moment dressing themselves as 'Indians.'

Johnny had taken some pains with his costume. He had sewed for hours on the red blanket Mrs. Lorne had let him cut up and he had a fine mop of feathers standing upright in the old knitted cap he would wear on his head, but when he started to put on his disguise, Rab said no, wait a minute.

Then he divided the boys into three groups. Beside each

ship at the wharf they would find a band of men. 'You,' he said to one group of boys, 'will join the boarding party for the *Dartmouth*. You for the *Eleanor*. You for the *Beaver*.' Each boy was to speak softly to the leader and say, 'Me Know You,' for that was the countersign. They would know the three leaders because each of them would wear a white handkerchief about the neck and a red string about the right wrist. Then he turned to Johnny.

'You can run faster than any of us. Somehow get to Old South Church. Mr. Rotch will be back from begging once more the Governor's permission for the ships to sail within a half-hour. Now, Johnny, you are to listen to what Sam Adams says next. Look you. If Mr. Adams then says, "Now may God help my country," come back here. Then we will take off our disguises and each go home and say nothing. But if he says, "This meeting can do nothing more to save the country," you are to get out of that crowd as fast as you can, and as soon as you get into Corn-hill begin to blow upon this silver whistle. Run as fast as you are able back here to me and keep on blowing. I'll have boys posted in dark corners, close enough to the church, but outside the crowd. Maybe we'll hear you the first time you blow.'

About Old South, standing in the streets, inside the church, waiting for Rotch to return with the very last appeal that could be made to the Governor, was the greatest crowd Boston had ever seen—thousands upon thousands. There was not a chance, not one, Johnny could ever squirm or wriggle his way inside, but he pushed and shoved until he stood close to one of the doors. Farther than this he could not go—unless he walked on people's heads. It was dark already.

Josiah Quincy's voice rang out from within. 'I see the clouds roll and the lightning play, and to that God who rides the whirlwind and directs the storm, I commit my country . . .'

The words thrilled Johnny, but this was not what he was waiting for, and it was not Sam Adams speaking. He was bothered with only one thing. Quincy had a beautiful carrying voice. It was one thing to hear him and another Sam Adams, who did not speak well at all.

The crowd made way for a chaise. 'Rotch is back! Make way for Rotch!' Mr. Rotch passed close to Johnny. He was so young he looked almost ready to cry. This was proof enough that the Governor had still refused. Such a turmoil followed Rotch's entry, Johnny could not hear any one particular voice. What chance had he of hearing Sam Adams's words? He had his whistle in his hand, but he was so jammed into the crowd about the door that he did not believe he would be able to get his hand to his mouth.

'Silence.' That was Quincy again. 'Silence, silence, Mr. Adams will speak.' Johnny twisted and turned and brought the whistle to his lips.

And suddenly there was silence. Johnny guessed there were many in that crowd who, like himself, were hanging on those words. Seemingly Mr. Adams was calmly accepting defeat, dismissing the meeting, for now he was saying, 'This meeting can do nothing more to save the country.'

Johnny gave his first shrill blast on his whistle, and he heard whistles and cries seemingly in all directions, Indian war whoops, and 'Boston Harbor a teapot tonight!' 'Hurrah for Griffin's Wharf!' 'Salt-water tea!' 'Hi, Mohawks, get your axes and pay no taxes!'

Johnny was only afraid all would be over before Rab and his henchmen could get to the wharf. Still shrilling on the whistle, he fought and floundered against the tide of the crowd. It was sweeping toward Griffin's Wharf, he struggling to get back to Salt Lane. Now he was afraid the others would have gone on without him. After all, Rab might have decided that Johnny's legs and ears were better than his hands—and deliberately let him do the work that best suited him. Johnny pushed open the door.

Rab was alone. He had Johnny's blanket coat, his ridiculous befeathered knitted cap in his hands.

'Quick!' he said, and smootched his face with soot, drew a red line across his mouth running from ear to ear. Johnny saw Rab's eyes through the mask of soot. They were glowing with that dark excitement he had seen but twice before. His lips were parted. His teeth looked sharp and white as an animal's. In spite of his calm demeanor, calm voice, he was charged and surcharged with a will to action, a readiness to take and enjoy any desperate chance. Rab had come terrifying alive.

They flung themselves out of the shop.

'Roundabout!' cried Rab. He meant they would get to the wharf by back alleys.

'Come, follow me. *Now we're really going to run.*'

He flew up Salt Lane in the opposite direction from the waterfront. Now they were flinging themselves down back alleys (faster and faster). Once they had a glimpse of a blacksmith shop and other 'Indians' clamoring for soot for their faces. Now slipping over a back-yard fence, now at last on the waterfront, Sea Street, Flounder Alley. They were running so fast it seemed more like a dream of flying than reality.

The day had started with rain and then there had been clouds, but as they reached Griffin's Wharf the moon, full and white, broke free of the clouds. The three ships, the silent hundreds gathering upon the wharf, all were dipped in the pure white light. The crowds were becoming thousands, and there was not one there but guessed what was to be done, and all approved.

Rab was grunting out of the side of his mouth to a thick-set, active-looking man, whom Johnny would have known anywhere, by his walk and the confident lift of his head, was Mr. Revere. 'Me Know You.'

'Me Know You,' Johnny repeated this countersign and took his place behind Mr. Revere. The other boys, held up by the crowd, began arriving, and more men and boys. But Johnny guessed that many who were now quietly joining one of those three groups were acting on the spur of the moment, seeing what was up. They had blacked their faces, seized axes, and come along. They were behaving as quietly and were as obedient to their leaders as those who had been so carefully picked for this work of destruction.

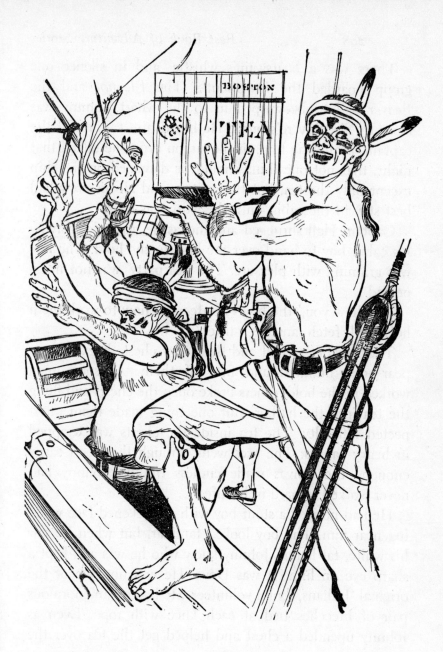

There was a boatswain's whistle, and in silence one group boarded the *Dartmouth*. The *Eleanor* and the *Beaver* had to be warped in to the wharf. Johnny was close to Mr. Revere's heels. He heard him calling for the captain, promising him, in the jargon everyone talked that night, that not one thing should be damaged on the ship except only the tea, but the captain and all his crew had best stay in the cabin until the work was over.

Captain Hall shrugged and did as he was told, leaving his cabin boy to hand over the keys to the hold. The boy was grinning with pleasure. The 'tea party' was not unexpected.

'I'll show you,' the boy volunteered, 'how to work them hoists. I'll fetch lanterns, mister.'

The winches rattled and the heavy chests began to appear—one hundred and fifty of them. As some men worked in the hold, others broke open the chests and flung the tea into the harbor. But one thing made them unexpected difficulty. The tea inside the chests was wrapped in heavy canvas. The axes went through the wood easily enough—the canvas made endless trouble. Johnny had never worked so hard in his life.

He had noticed a stout boy with a blackened face working near him. The boy looked familiar, but when he saw his white, fat hands, Johnny knew who he was and kept a sharp eye on him. It was Dove. He was not one of the original 'Indians,' but a volunteer. He had on an enormous pair of breeches tied at each knee with rope. Even as Johnny upended a chest and helped get the tea over the rail, he kept an eye on Dove. The boy was secretly scooping tea into his breeches. This theft would come to several hundred dollars in value, but more important it would ruin the high moral tone of the party. Johnny whispered to Rab, who put down the axe he had been wielding with such passion and grabbed Dove. It wasn't much of a

scuffle. Soon Dove was whining and admitting that a little of the tea had happened to 'splash' into his breeches. Johnny got them off and kicked them and the many pounds of tea they held into the harbor.

'He swim good,' he grunted at Rab, for everyone was talking 'Indian' that night.

Rab picked up the fat Dove as though he were a rag

baby and flung him into the harbor. The tea was thicker than any seaweed and its fragrance was everywhere.

Not a quarter of a mile away, quite visible in the moonlight, rode the *Active* and the *Kingfisher*. Any moment the tea party might be interrupted by British marines. There was no landing party. Governor Hutchinson had been wise in not sending for their help.

The work on the *Dartmouth* and the *Eleanor* finished about the same time. The *Beaver* took longer, for she had not had time to unload the rest of her cargo, and great care was taken not to injure it. Just as Johnny was about to go over to see if he could help on the *Beaver*, Mr. Revere whispered to him. 'Go get brooms. Cleam um' deck.'

Johnny and a parcel of boys brushed the deck until it was clean as a parlor floor. Then Mr. Revere called the captain to come up and inspect. The tea was utterly gone, but Captain Hall agreed that beyond that there had not been the slightest damage.

It was close upon dawn when the work on all three ships was done. And yet the great, silent audience on the wharf, men, women, and children, had not gone home. As the three groups came off the ships, they formed in fours along the wharf, their axes on their shoulders. Then a hurrah went up and a fife began to play. This was almost the first sound Johnny had heard since the tea party started—except only the crash of axes into sea chests, the squeak of hoists, and a few grunted orders.

Standing quietly in the crowd, he saw Sam Adams, pretending to be a most innocent bystander. It looked to

Johnny as if the dog fox had eaten a couple of fat pullets, and had a third in his mouth.

As they started marching back to the center of town, they passed the Coffin House at the head of Griffin's Wharf. A window opened.

'Well, boys,' said a voice, so cold one hardly knew whether he spoke in anger or not, 'you've had a fine, pleasant evening for your Indian caper, haven't you? But mind . . . you've got to pay the fiddler yet.'

It was the British Admiral Montague.

'Come on down here,' someone yelled, 'and we'll settle that score tonight.'

The Admiral pulled in his head and slapped down the window.

Johnny and Rab knew, and men like the Observers knew, but best of all Sam Adams knew, that the fiddler would have to be paid. England, unable to find the individuals who had destroyed this valuable property, would punish the whole Town of Boston—make every man, woman, and child, Tories and Whigs alike, suffer until this tea was paid for. Nor was she likely to back down on her claim that she might tax the colonists any way she pleased.

Next day, all over Boston, boys and men, some of them with a little paint still showing behind their ears, were so lame they could scarce move their fingers, but none of them—not one—told what it was that had lamed them so. They would stand about and wonder who 'those Mohawks' might have been, or what the British Parliament might do next, but never say what they themselves had been doing, for each was sworn to secrecy.

Only Paul Revere showed no signs of the hard physical strain he had been under all the night before. Not long after dawn he had started on horseback for New York and Philadelphia with an account of the Tea Party. He could chop open tea chests all night, and ride all day.

from HOWARD PYLE'S

The Merry Adventures of Robin Hood

Robin Hood has always been the favorite hero in England—a bold and carefree outlaw, who stole from the rich to give to the poor, the bravest and best archer in all the land, and so delightfully tricky in handling all his enemies. This first adventure with Little John is one of the rare encounters in which Robin Hood does not come out victorious. But he is not at all displeased, for he thus gains a valuable addition to his gallant band. In the grand shooting-match we see him cleverly planning his favorite sport—outwitting the pompous Sheriff of Nottingham.

ROBIN HOOD MEETS LITTLE JOHN

Up rose Robin Hood one merry morn when all the birds were singing blithely among the leaves, and up rose all his merry men, each fellow washing his head and hands in the cold brown brook that leaped laughing from stone to stone. Then said Robin: "For fourteen days have we seen no sport, so now I will go abroad to seek adventures forthwith. But tarry ye, my merry men all, here in the greenwood; only see that ye mind well my call. Three blasts upon the bugle horn I will blow in my hour of need; then come quickly, for I shall want your aid."

So saying, he strode away through the leafy forest glades until he had come to the verge of Sherwood. There he wandered for a long time, through highway and byway, through dingly dell and forest skirts. Now he met a fair buxom lass in a shady lane, and each gave the other a merry word and passed their way; now he saw a fair lady upon an ambling pad, to whom he doffed his cap, and who bowed sedately in return to the fair youth; now he saw a fat monk on a pannier-laden ass; now a gallant knight, with spear and shield and armor that flashed brightly in the sunlight; now a page clad in crimson; and now a stout burgher from good Nottingham Town, pacing along with serious footsteps: all these sights he saw, but adventure found he none.

At last he took a road by the forest skirts; a bypath that dipped toward a broad, pebbly stream spanned by a narrow bridge made of a log of wood. As he drew nigh this bridge he saw a tall stranger coming from the other side. Thereupon Robin quickened his pace, as did the stranger likewise; each thinking to cross first.

"Now stand thou back," quoth Robin, "and let the better man cross first."

"Nay," answered the stranger, "then stand back thine own self, for the better man, I wot, am I."

"That will we presently see," quoth Robin; "and meanwhile stand thou where thou art, or else, by the bright brow of Saint Elfrida, I will show thee right good Nottingham play with a clothyard shaft betwixt thy ribs."

"Now," quoth the stranger, "I will tan thy hide till it be as many colors as a beggar's cloak, if thou darest so much as touch a string of that same bow that thou holdest in thy hands."

"Thou pratest like an ass," said Robin, "for I could send this shaft clean through thy proud heart before a curtal friar could say grace over a roast goose at Michaelmastide."

"And thou pratest like a coward," answered the stranger, "for thou standest there with a good yew bow to shoot at my heart, while I have nought in my hand but a plain blackthorn staff wherewith to meet thee."

"Now," quoth Robin, "by the faith of my heart, never have I had a coward's name in all my life before. I will lay by my trusty bow and eke my arrows, and if thou darest abide my coming, I will go and cut a cudgel to test thy manhood withal."

"Ay, marry, that will I abide thy coming, and joyously, too," quoth the stranger; whereupon he leaned sturdily upon his staff to await Robin.

Then Robin Hood stepped quickly to the coverside and cut a good staff of ground oak, straight, without flaw, and six feet in length, and came back trimming away the tender stems from it, while the stranger waited for him, leaning upon his staff, and whistling as he gazed round about. Robin observed him furtively as he trimmed his

staff, measuring him from top to toe from out the corner of his eye, and thought that he had never seen a lustier or a stouter man. Tall was Robin, but taller was the stranger by a head and a neck, for he was seven feet in height. Broad was Robin across the shoulders, but broader was the stranger by twice the breadth of a palm, while he measured at least an ell around the waist.

"Nevertheless," said Robin to himself, "I will baste thy hide right merrily, my good fellow;" then, aloud, "Lo, here is my good staff, lusty and tough. Now wait my coming, an thou darest, and meet me, an thou fearest not; then we will fight until one or the other of us tumble into the stream by dint of blows."

"Marry, that meeteth my whole heart!" cried the stranger, twirling his staff above his head, betwixt his fingers and thumb, until it whistled again.

Never did the Knights of Arthur's Round Table meet in a stouter fight than did these two. In a moment Robin stepped quickly upon the bridge where the stranger stood; first he made a feint, and then delivered a blow at the stranger's head that, had it met its mark, would have tumbled him speedily into the water; but the stranger turned the blow right deftly, and in return gave one as stout, which Robin also turned as the stranger had done. So they stood, each in his place, neither moving a finger's breadth back, for one good hour, and many blows were given and received by each in that time, till here and there were sore bones and bumps, yet neither thought of crying "Enough," or seemed likely to fall from off the bridge.

Now and then they stopped to rest, and each thought that he never had seen in all his life before such a hand at quarterstaff.

At last Robin gave the stranger a blow upon the ribs that made his jacket smoke like a damp straw thatch in the sun. So shrewd was the stroke that the stranger came within a hair's breadth of falling off the bridge; but he regained himself right quickly, and, by a dexterous blow, gave Robin a crack on the crown that caused the blood to flow. Then Robin grew mad with anger, and smote with all his might at the other; but the stranger warded the blow, and once again thwacked Robin, and this time so fairly that he fell heels over head into the water, as the queen pin falls in a game of bowls.

"And where art thou now, good lad?" shouted the stranger, roaring with laughter.

"Oh, in the flood and floating adown with the tide," cried Robin; nor could he forbear laughing himself at his sorry plight. Then, gaining his feet, he waded to the bank, the little fish speeding hither and thither, all frightened at his splashing.

"Give me thy hand," cried he, when he had reached the bank. "I must needs own thou art a brave and a sturdy soul, and, withal, a good stout stroke with the cudgels. By this and by that, my head hummeth like to a hive of bees on a hot June day."

Then he clapped his horn to his lips, and winded a blast that went echoing sweetly down the forest paths. "Ay, marry," quoth he again, "thou art a tall lad, and eke a brave one, for ne'er, I trow, is there a man betwixt here and Canterbury Town could do the like to me that thou has done."

"And thou," quoth the stranger, laughing, "takest thy cudgelling like a brave heart and a stout yeoman."

But now the distant twigs and branches rustled with the coming of men, and suddenly a score or two of good stout yeomen, all clad in Lincoln green, burst from out the covert, with merry Will Stutely at their head.

"Good master," cried Will, "how is this? Truly thou art all wet from head to foot, and that to the very skin."

"Why, marry," answered jolly Robin, "yon stout fellow hath tumbled me neck and crop into the water, and hath given me a drubbing beside."

"Then shall he not go without a ducking and eke a drubbing himself!" cried Will Stutely. "Have at him, lads!"

Then Will and a score of yeomen leaped upon the stranger, but though they sprang quickly they found him ready and felt him strike right and left with his stout staff, so that, though he went down with press of numbers, some of them rubbed cracked crowns before he was overcome.

"Nay, forbear!" cried Robin, laughing until his sore sides ached again; "he is a right good man and true, and no harm shall befall him. Now hark ye, good youth, wilt thou stay with me and be one of my band? Three suits of Lincoln green shalt thou have each year, beside forty marks in fee, and share with us whatsoever good shall befall us. Thou shalt eat sweet venison and quaff the stoutest ale, and mine own good right-hand man shalt thou be, for never did I see such a cudgel-player in all my life before. Speak! wilt thou be one of my good merry men?"

"That know I not," quoth the stranger, surlily, for he was angry at being so tumbled about. "If ye handle yew bow and apple shaft no better than ye do oaken cudgel, I wot ye are not fit to be called yeomen in my country; but if there be any man here that can shoot a better shaft than I, then will I bethink me of joining with you."

"Now by my faith," said Robin, "thou art a right saucy varlet, sirrah; yet I will stoop to thee as I never stooped to man before. Good Stutely, cut thou a fair white piece of bark four fingers in breadth, and set it forescore yards distant on yonder oak. Now, stranger, hit that fairly with a gray goose shaft and call thyself an archer."

"Ay, marry, that will I," answered he. "Give me a good stout bow and a fair broad arrow, and if I hit it not strip me and beat me blue with bowstrings."

Then he chose the stoutest bow amongst them all, next to Robin's own, and a straight gray goose shaft, well-feathered and smooth, and stepping to the mark—while all the band, sitting or lying upon the greensward, watched to see him shoot—he drew the arrow to his cheek and loosed the shaft right deftly, sending it so straight down the path that it clove the mark in the very centre. "Aha!" cried he, "mend thou that if thou canst;" while even the yeomen clapped their hands at so fair a shot.

"That is a keen shot, indeed," quoth Robin, "mend it

I cannot, but mar it I may, perhaps."

Then taking up his own good stout bow and nocking an arrow with care he shot with his very greatest skill. Straight flew the arrow, and so true that it lit fairly upon the stranger's shaft and split it into splinters. Then all the yeomen leaped to their feet and shouted for joy that their master had shot so well.

"Now by the lusty yew bow of good Saint Withold," cried the stranger, "that is a shot indeed, and never saw I the like in all my life before! Now truly will I be thy man henceforth and for aye. Good Adam Bell was a fair shot, but never shot he so!"

"Then have I gained a right good man this day," quoth jolly Robin. "What name goest thou by, good fellow?"

"Men call me John Little whence I came," answered the stranger.

Then Will Stutely, who loved a good jest, spoke up. "Nay, fair little stranger," said he, "I like not thy name and fain would I have it otherwise. Little art thou indeed, and small of bone and sinew, therefore shalt thou be christened Little John, and I will be thy godfather."

Then Robin Hood and all his band laughed aloud until the stranger began to grow angry.

"An thou make a jest of me," quoth he to Will Stutely, "thou wilt have sore bones and little pay, and that in short season."

"Nay, good friend," said Robin Hood, "bottle thine anger for the name fitteth thee well. Little John shalt thou be called henceforth, and Little John shall it be. So come, my merry men, and we will go and prepare a christening feast for this fair infant."

So turning their backs upon the stream, they plunged into the forest once more, through which they traced their steps till they reached the spot where they dwelt in the depths of the woodland. There had they built huts of bark and branches of trees, and made couches of sweet rushes spread over with skins of fallow deer. Here stood a great oak tree with branches spreading broadly around, beneath which was a seat of green moss where Robin Hood was wont to sit at feast and at merrymaking with his stout men about him. Here they found the rest of the band, some of whom had come in with a brace of fat does. Then they all built great fires and after a time roasted the does and broached a barrel of humming ale. Then when the feast was ready they all sat down, but Robin Hood placed Little John at his right hand, for he was henceforth to be the second in the band.

Then when the feast was done Will Stutely spoke up. "It is now time, I ween, to christen our bonny babe, is it not so, merry boys?" And "Aye! Aye!" cried all, laughing till the woods echoed with their mirth.

"Then seven sponsors shall we have," quoth Will Stutely; and hunting among all the band he chose the seven stoutest men of them all.

"Now by Saint Dunstan," cried Little John, springing to his feet, "more than one of you shall rue it an you lay finger upon me."

But without a word they all ran upon him at once,

seizing him by his legs and arms and holding him tightly in spite of his struggles, and they bore him forth while all stood around to see the sport. Then one came forward who had been chosen to play the priest because he had a bald crown, and in his hand he carried a brimming pot of ale. "Now who bringeth this babe?" asked he right soberly.

"That do I," answered Will Stutely.

"And what name callest thou him?"

"Little John call I him."

"Now Little John," quoth the mock priest, "thou hast not lived heretofore, but only got thee along through the world, but henceforth thou wilt live indeed. When thou livedst not thou wast called John Little, but now that thou dost live indeed, Little John shalt thou be called, so christen I thee." And at these last words he emptied the pot of ale upon Little John's head.

Then all shouted with laughter as they saw the good brown ale stream over Little John's beard and trickle from his nose and chin, while his eyes blinked with the smart of it. At first he was of a mind to be angry, but found he could not because the others were so merry; so he, too, laughed with the rest. Then Robin took this sweet, pretty babe, clothed him all anew from top to toe in Lincoln green, and gave him a good stout bow, and so made him a member of the merry band.

And thus it was that Robin Hood became outlawed; thus a band of merry companions gathered about him, and thus he gained his right-hand man, Little John; And now I will tell how the Sheriff of Nottingham sought to take Robin Hood, and how he failed each time.

THE GRAND SHOOTING-MATCH AT NOTTINGHAM

"Now," thought the Sheriff, "could I but persuade Robin nigh to Nottingham Town so that I could find him, I warrant I would lay hands upon him so stoutly that he would never get away again." Then of a sudden it came to him like a flash that were he to proclaim a great shooting-match and offer some grand prize, Robin Hood might be overpersuaded by his spirit to come to the range. And it was this thought which caused him to cry "Aha!" and smite his palm upon his thigh.

So, as soon as he had returned safely to Nottingham, he sent messengers north and south, and east and west, to proclaim through town, hamlet, and countryside, this grand shooting-match, and every one was bidden that could draw a long bow, and the prize was to be an arrow of pure beaten gold.

When Robin Hood first heard the news of this he was in Lincoln Town, and hastening back to Sherwood Forest he soon called all his merry men about him and spoke to them thus:

"Now hearken, my merry men all, to the news that I have brought from Lincoln Town to-day. Our friend the Sheriff of Nottingham hath proclaimed a shooting-match, and hath sent messengers to tell of it through all the countryside, and the prize is to be a bright golden arrow. Now I fain would have one of us win it, both because of the fairness of the prize and because our sweet friend the Sheriff hath offered it. So we will take our bows and shafts and go there to shoot, for I know right well that merriment will be a-going. What say ye, lads?"

Then young David of Doncaster spoke up and said: "Now listen, I pray thee, good master, unto what I say. I have come straight from our friend Eadom o' the Blue Boar, and there I heard the full news of this same match. But, master, I know from him, and he got it from the Sheriff's man Ralph o' the Scar; that this same knavish Sheriff hath but laid a trap for thee in this shooting-match and wishes nothing so much as to see thee there. So go not, good master, for I know right well he doth seek to entrap thee, but stay within the greenwood lest we all meet dole and woe."

"Now," quoth Robin, "thou art a wise lad and keepest thine ears open and thy mouth shut, as becometh a wise and crafty woodsman. But shall we let it be said that the Sheriff of Nottingham did cow bold Robin Hood and sevenscore as fair archers as are in all merry England? Nay, good David, what thou tellest me maketh me to desire the prize even more than I else should do. But what sayeth our good gossip Swanthold? Is it not 'A hasty man burneth his mouth, and the fool that keepeth his eyes shut falleth into the pit?' Thus he says, truly, therefore we must meet guile with guile. Now some of you clothe yourselves as short-frocked friars, and some as peasants, and some as tinkers, or as beggars, but see that each man taketh a good bow or broadsword, in case need should arise. As for myself, I will shoot for this same golden arrow, and should I win it, we will hang it to the branches of our good greenwood tree for the joy of all the band. How like you the plan, my merry men all?"

Then "Good, good!" cried all the band right heartily.

A fair sight was Nottingham Town on the day of the shooting-match. All along upon the green meadow beneath the town wall stretched a row of benches, one above the other, which were for knight and lady, squire and dame, and rich burghers and their wives; for none but those of rank and quality were to sit there. At the end of the range, near the target, was a raised seat bedecked with ribbons and scarfs and garlands of flowers, for the Sheriff of Nottingham and his dame. The range was twoscore paces broad. At one end stood the target, at the other a tent of striped canvas, from the pole of which fluttered many-colored flags and streamers. In this booth were casks of ale, free to be broached by any of the archers who might wish to quench their thirst.

Across the range from where the seats for the better folk were raised was a railing to keep the poorer people from crowding in front of the target. Already, while it was early, the benches were beginning to fill with people of quality, who kept constantly arriving in little carts, or upon palfreys that curveted gayly to the merry tinkle of silver bells at bridle reins; with these came also the poorer

folk, who sat or lay upon the green grass near the railing
that kept them from off the range. In the great tent the
archers were gathering by twos and threes; some talking
loudly of the fair shots each man had made in his day;
some looking well to their bows, drawing a string betwixt
the fingers to see that there was no fray upon it, or in-
specting arrows, shutting one eye and peering down a
shaft to see that it was not warped, but straight and true,
for neither bow nor shaft should fail at such a time and
for such a prize. And never were such a company of yeomen as were gathered at Nottingham Town that day,
for the very best archers of merry England had come to
this shooting-match. There was Gill o' the Red Cap, the
Sheriff's own head archer, and Diccon Cruikshank of Lincoln Town, and Adam o' the Dell, a man of Tamworth, of
threescore years and more, yet hale and lusty still, who in
his time had shot in the famous match at Woodstock, and
had there beaten that renowned archer, Clym o' the
Clough. And many more famous men of the long bow
were there, whose names have been handed down to us
in goodly ballads of the olden time.

But now all the benches were filled with guests, lord
and lady, burgher and dame, when at last the Sheriff himself came with his lady, he riding with stately mien upon
his milk-white horse and she upon her brown filly.
Upon his head he wore a purple velvet cap, and purple
velvet was his robe, all trimmed about with rich ermine;
his jerkin and hose were of sea-green silk, and his shoes of
black velvet, the pointed toes fastened to his garters with

golden chains. A golden chain hung about his neck, and at his collar was a great carbuncle set in red gold. His lady was dressed in blue velvet, all trimmed with swan's down. So they made a gallant sight as they rode along side by side, and all the people shouted from where they crowded across the space from the gentlefolk.

Then when the Sheriff and his dame had sat down, he bade his herald wind upon his silver horn; who thereupon sounded three blasts that came echoing cheerily back from the gray walls of Nottingham. Then the archers stepped forth to their places, while all the folk shouted with a mighty voice, each man calling upon his favorite yeoman. "Red Cap!" cried some. "Cruikshank!" cried others. "Hey for William o' Leslie!" shouted others yet again; while ladies waved silken scarfs to urge each yeoman to do his best.

Then the herald stood forth and loudly proclaimed the rules of the game as follows:

"Shoot each man from yon mark, which is sevenscore yards and ten from the target. One arrow shooteth each man first, and from all the archers shall the ten that shooteth the fairest shafts be chosen for to shoot again. Two arrows shooteth each man of these ten, then shall the three that shoot the fairest shafts be chosen for to shoot again. Three arrows shooteth each man of those three, and to him that shooteth the fairest shafts shall the prize be given."

Then the Sheriff leaned forward, looking keenly among the press of archers to find whether Robin Hood was amongst them. But no one was there clad in Lincoln green, such as was worn by Robin and his band. "Nevertheless," said the Sheriff to himself, "he may still be there, and I miss him among the crowd of other men. But let me see when but ten men shoot, for I wot he will be among the ten, or I know him not."

And now the archers shot, each man in turn, and the good folk never saw such archery as was done that day. Six arrows were within the clout, four within the black, and only two smote the outer ring; so that when the last arrow sped and struck the target, all the people shouted aloud, for it was noble shooting.

And now but ten men were left of all those that had shot before, and of these ten, six were famous throughout the land, and most of the folk gathered there knew them. These six men were Gilbert o' the Red Cap, Adam o' the Dell, Diccon Cruikshank, William o' Leslie, Hubert o' Cloud, and Swithin o' Hertford. Two others were yeomen of merry Yorkshire, another was a tall stranger in blue, who said he came from London Town, and the last was a tattered stranger in scarlet, who wore a patch over one eye.

"Now," quoth the Sheriff to a man-at-arms who stood near him, "seest thou Robin Hood amongst those ten?"

"Nay, that do I not, your worship," answered the man. "Six of them I know right well. Of those Yorkshire yeomen, one is too tall and the other too short for that bold knave. Robin's beard is as yellow as gold, while yon tattered beggar in scarlet hath a beard of brown, besides be-

ing blind of one eye. As for the stranger in blue, Robin's shoulders, I ween, are three inches broader than his."

"Then," quoth the Sheriff, smiting his thigh angrily, "yon knave is a coward as well as a rogue, and dares not show his face among good men and true."

Then, after they had rested a short time, those ten stout men stepped forth to shoot again. Each man shot two arrows, and as they shot, not a word was spoken, but all the crowd watched with scarce a breath of sound. But when the last had shot his arrow another great shout arose, while many cast their caps aloft for joy of such marvellous shooting.

And now but three men were left of all those that had shot before. One was Gill o' the Red Cap, one the tat-

tered stranger in scarlet, and one Adam o' the Dell of
Tamworth Town. Then all the people called aloud, some
crying, "Ho for Gilbert o' the Red Cap!" and some, "Hey
for stout Adam o' Tamworth!" But not a single man in
the crowd called upon the stranger in scarlet.

"Now, shoot thou well, Gilbert," cried the Sheriff,
"and if thine be the best shaft, fivescore broad silver pen-
nies will I give to thee beside the prize."

"Truly I will do my best," quoth Gilbert, right sturdily.
"A man cannot do aught but his best, but that will I strive
to do this day." So saying, he drew forth a fair smooth arrow with a broad feather and fitted it deftly to the string,
then drawing his bow with care he sped the shaft. Straight
flew the arrow and lit fairly in the clout, a finger breadth

from the centre. "A Gilbert, a Gilbert!" shouted all the crowd; and, "Now, by my faith," cried the Sheriff, smiting his hands together, "that is a shrewd shot."

Then the tattered stranger stepped forth, and all the people laughed as they saw a yellow patch that showed beneath his arm when he raised his elbow to shoot, and also to see him aim with but one eye. He drew the good yew bow quickly, and quickly loosed a shaft; so short was the time that no man could draw a breath betwixt the drawing and the shooting. Yet his arrow lodged nearer the centre than the other by twice the length of a barley-corn.

"Now by all the saints in Paradise!" cried the Sheriff, "that's a lovely shaft in very truth!"

Then Adam o' the Dell shot, carefully and cautiously, and his arrow lodged close beside the stranger's. Then after a short space they all three shot again, and once more each arrow lodged within the clout, but this time Adam o' the Dell's was farthest from the centre, and again the tattered stranger's shot was the best. Then, after another time of rest, they all shot for the third time. This time Gilbert took great heed to his aim, keenly measuring the distance and shooting with shrewdest care. Straight flew the arrow, and all shouted till the very flags that waved in the breeze shook with the sound, and the rooks and daws flew clamoring about the roofs of the old gray tower, for the shaft had lodged close beside the spot that marked the very centre.

"Well done, Gilbert!" cried the Sheriff, right joyously.

"Fain am I to believe the prize is thine, and right fairly won. Now, thou ragged knave, let me see thee shoot a better shaft than that."

Naught spake the stranger but took his place, while all was hushed, and no one spoke or even seemed to breathe, so great was the silence for wonder what he would do. Meanwhile, also, quite still stood the stranger holding his bow in his hand, while one could count five. Then he drew his trusty yew, holding it drawn but a moment, then loosed the string. Straight flew the arrow, and so true that it smote a gray goose feather from off Gilbert's shaft, which fell fluttering through the sunlit air as the stranger's arrow lodged close beside his of the red cap, and in the very centre. No one spoke a word for a while and no one shouted, but each man looked into his neighbor's face amazedly.

"Nay," quoth old Adam o' the Dell presently, drawing a long breath and shaking his head as he spoke; "twoscore years and more have I shot shaft, and maybe not all times bad, but I shoot no more this day, for no man can match with yon stranger, whosoe'er he may be." Then he thrust his shaft into his quiver, rattling, and unstrung his bow without another word.

Then the Sheriff came down from his dais and drew near, in all his silks and velvets, to where the tattered stranger stood leaning upon his stout bow, whilst the good folk crowded around to see the man who shot so wondrously well. "Here, good fellow," quoth the Sheriff, "take thou the prize, and well and fairly hast thou won it, I trow. What may be thy name, and whence comest thou?"

"Men do call me Jock o' Teviotdale, and thence am I come," said the stranger.

"Then, by Our Lady, Jock, thou art the fairest archer that e'er mine eyes beheld, and if thou wilt join my service I will clothe thee with a better coat than that thou hast upon thy back. Thou shalt eat and drink of the best, and at every Christmas-tide fourscore marks shall be thy wage. I trow thou drawest better bow than that same coward knave, Robin Hood, that dared not show his face here this day. Say, good fellow, wilt thou join my service?"

"Nay, that will I not," quoth the stranger, roughly. "I will be mine own, and no man in all merry England shall be my master."

"Then get thee gone, and a murrain seize thee!" cried the Sheriff, and his voice trembled with anger. "And by my faith and troth I have a good part of mind to have thee beaten for thine insolence!" Then he turned upon his heel and strode away.

It was a right motley company that gathered about the noble greenwood tree in Sherwood's depths that same day. A score and more of barefoot friars were there, and some that looked like tinkers, and some that seemed to be sturdy beggars and rustic peasants; and seated upon a mossy couch was one clad in tattered scarlet, with a patch over one eye; and in his hand he held the golden arrow that was the prize of the great shooting-match. Then, amidst a noise of talking and laughter, he took the patch from off his eye and stripped away the scarlet rags from off his body and showed himself all clothed in fair Lincoln green, and quoth he:

"Easy come these things away, but walnut stain cometh not so speedily from yellow hair." Then all laughed louder than before, for it was Robin Hood himself that had won the prize from the Sheriff's very hands.

Then all sat down to the woodland feast and talked amongst themselves of the merry jest that had been played upon the Sheriff and of the adventures that had befallen each member of the band in his disguise. But when the feast was done, Robin Hood took Little John apart and said, "Truly am I vexed in my blood, for I heard the Sheriff say to-day, 'Thou shootest better than that coward knave, Robin Hood, that dared not show his face here this day.' I would fain let him know who it was who won the golden arrow from out his hand, and also that I am no coward such as he takes me to be."

Then Little John said, "Good master, take thou me and Will Stutely and we will send yon fat Sheriff news of all this by a messenger such as he doth not expect."

That day the Sheriff sat at meat in the great hall of his house at Nottingham Town. Long tables stood down the hall, at which sat men-at-arms and household servants and good stout villains [farm-servants], in all fourscore and more. There they talked of the day's shooting as they ate their meat and quaffed their ale. The Sheriff sat at the head of the table upon a raised seat under a canopy, and beside him sat his dame.

"By my troth," said he, "I did reckon full roundly that that knave, Robin Hood, would be at the game to-day. I did not think that he was such a coward. But who could that saucy knave be who answered me to my beard so bravely? I wonder that I did not have him beaten; but there was something about him that spoke of other things than rags and tatters."

Then, even as he finished speaking, something fell rattling among the dishes on the table, while those that sat near started up wondering what it might be. After a while one of the men-at-arms gathered courage enough to pick it up and bring it to the Sheriff. Then every one saw that it was a blunted gray goose shaft, with a fine scroll, about the thickness of a goose quill, tied near to its head. The Sheriff opened the scroll and glanced at it, while the veins upon his forehead swelled and his cheeks grew ruddy with rage as he read, for this was what he saw:

> *Now Heaven bless thy grace this day,*
> *Say all in sweet Sherwood,*
> *For thou didst give the prize away*
> *To merry Robin Hood.*

"Whence came this?" cried the Sheriff in a mighty voice.

"Even through the window, your worship," quoth the man who had handed the shaft to him.

One Alaska Night

A root tripped me and threw me flat in the trail that led through the blueberry thicket. The thick brush closed over me, shutting out the ranks of Alaska hemlock, already somber in the sundown light. Too tired for a moment to stir, I lay, face on my arms, feeling that I'd been foolhardy to start out alone on a ten-mile hike across an unfamiliar peninsula; yet comforting myself with the thought that it could not be much farther to the coast fox ranch, which was my destination.

For some time I had been breasting through this growth of blueberry brush which met thinly above my trail, but as my mind was intent on a story I was planning, I had failed to take this for what it was—a warning of something wrong. Now, nose to the ground, I became aware of a rank, musky odor that brought my head up with a jerk. Something queerly crawling touched my cheek. I slapped my hand over it and, with a chill premonition, looked at what I'd caught—a long tuft of coarse brown hair dangling from a twig above.

One startled glance, and I knew it had been raked from

the side of an Alaskan brown bear—the largest carnivorous animal that walks the world today.

Earlier in the afternoon I had seen an enormous track in a patch of damp clay beside my path and, with a shiver, had placed my own foot inside it. The imprint, from heel to claws, was exactly twice the length of my number two-and-a-half boot.

I would have turned back then, had I not remembered that these beasts commonly avoid trails much traveled by man. Now, with the tuft of hair clutched in my hand and sudden alarm sharpening my perceptions, I scrutinized the path leading forward under the leafy tunnel in which I lay. All along it, evenly spaced in the damp, brown mold, were deep depressions, round and large as dinner plates. The roots across it were plushed with moss and unmarred. Men tread on the roots in their trails; animals step over them. Obviously no human being had passed this way for at least a year.

The truth came with a shock—I had been following a bear trail! It was already getting dark, and I was unarmed.

I had read many articles written by tourist sportsmen setting forth the theory that these fifteen-hundred-pound brutes, literally as big as a horse, will not attack man unless first provoked. But, being an Alaskan, I found this theory of no comfort now. All my life I'd been seeing bear-maimed men brought in from the woods—unarmed men who had been struck down by a single swipe of a brownie's barbed paw. I had seen them with their arms torn from the sockets, their legs raked clean of flesh. Some were dead.

I'm not a hunter. I'm not even a brave woman. And I'd never before been alone in a bear-infested forest with night coming on. In that first chill of apprehension my one absurd desire was to make myself very small, like a wood mouse, and snuggle down under some concealing leaf until the sun came up again. Then I recalled the fact that bears do most of their traveling after dark—and I was lying prone in the middle of one of their thorough-fares.

I leaped to my feet, turned off the trail, and began plowing through the brush, intent only on putting all possible distance between me and that place before dark.

Almost at once the bushes thinned out, and I was able to make good time through stretches of short ferns; but the gray hemlocks linked their boughs above every open space, and the light was fading fast. In the deep gloom there was a curious hush that made me anxious to get out of the timber to the openness of the seacoast. Oddly, it was only now, when I was safely away from the bear trail, that this fact dawned on me—I had no idea which way to go. I was lost.

In that instant of realization, all my strength seemed to ooze out of me into the ground. Then panic came upon me. I had a senseless, almost uncontrollable, impulse to dash madly through the trees, regardless of direction, bears, or anything else. But I got hold of myself, decided on a course, and with forced calmness went forward, watching tensely for that breaking away of the timber which foretells an approach to the sea.

Every step took me deeper into the darkening wilderness. There was no wind. Not a thing moved except myself—not a leaf; not a twig. Even the white hanks of deer moss pendent from the hemlock boughs hung still, like the hair of an old woman, long dead.

The very silence began to frighten me. It was a sly, listening stillness as if, among the trees, some form of life had hushed its action just an instant before my coming, to watch me and fall in behind me after I'd passed. I found myself stepping furtively, trying not to make any noise and straining to hear the slightest sound. I kept glancing back over my shoulder; and every few feet I'd stop suddenly, holding my breath while I studied a moss-grown log, or the long arm of a thorny shrub which I was sure had stirred a second before.

I never could surprise any movement or hear any sound; yet slowly terror was growing in me.

Ferns, moss, bushes—all were losing their green now, and the ground was dim with a swimming vagueness which caused me to miscalculate my steps. I stumbled often. I knew I should stop and build a fire for the night while there was yet light enough to gather a pile of wood. But the desperate hope of reaching the open beach drove me on.

I was groping with my feet, my gaze fixed ahead when, out of the tail of my eye, I saw a blurred stirring in the shadows under the hemlocks. I jerked my head around to look.

Nothing moved.

I went on, tiptoeing now, and presently began to be fearsomely aware of the hemlocks. Hemlocks—somber witch-trees of the North, holding night under their long dark arms. . . . I could have sworn they were moving, slyly closing in around me . . . watching . . . waiting for something unhuman to happen. The mystery and cruelty of the woods seeped into that primeval level of my mind where eerie personalities of childhood tales lie buried. Lesiy, half-human Thing of the forest, with ears like a horse's, and moss-covered legs like a goat's, came alive in the ferny obscurity under the trees. Lesiy, master of bears, who tricks the wayfarer into losing his trail; and then, at dusk, turns him into a laughing maniac by peeping out from behind tree trunks, smiling horribly and beckoning with fingers a foot long. . . . Once I forced myself to go close and touch a yellowish-green fungus fanning out from a hemlock bole—to make sure it was a fungus, and not the face of Lesiy.

I wondered if the "woods-madness" that seizes lost persons was coming upon me so soon.

And then, I paused to stare at a murky clump which I hoped was only bushes looming against the vague knoll ahead. The clump, big as a truck horse, started toward me. It kept coming, slowly, ponderously, swinging a great, low head. Brush rattled under its shambling tread. I smelled the rank, musky odor of bear.

The next instant I had turned from the monster and was running madly through the semidarkness of the forest.

I was nearly exhausted when I burst through the timber and saw the log cabin crouching in the middle of a small, wild meadow of bearweed. Not another thing grew in the clearing except a single towering hemlock tree about fifty feet from the cabin door. I was running toward this refuge with all the speed left in me when, despite the terror I felt to be behind, something in the aspect of the place caused me to slow up. I came to a stop at the hemlock tree and peered apprehensively through the dusk.

There was something distinctly sinister in the very quality of the silence that hung over the cabin. This wasn't due to the boarded windows, the smokeless stovepipe, and the air of desolation that marks every abandoned dwelling in the wilderness. There was something else—a feeling as if death brooded there. The boarded windows on each side of the closed door stared back at me like eye sockets in a brown and weathered skull.

My recoil from the place was so strong that I turned to go back; but after one glance into the black forest where a live monster lurked, I changed my mind. Slipping my belt ax from its sheath, I grasped it firmly and moved forward through the round, rustling leaves of the bearweed. My senses were nervously alert, but my feet were clogged by a nameless dread.

At the edge of the dooryard I came upon a stump and again hesitated. My fingers, absently exploring the stump's broad top, felt a crosshatch of ax marks. A block for chopping firewood, I thought, glancing at the nearby stack of dead hemlock boughs.

For some reason, this evidence of human workaday activity heartened me. I moved on through the whispering bearweed that grew untrampled to the very walls of the cabin and paused before the closed door. It was a home-made door of heavy, unplaned planks, silvered by the beating of many storms. In place of a knob, it had a rawhide latch thong hanging outside. The thong had curled up into a hard, dry knot.

Obviously, no one had drawn this latchstring for many months; yet, when I gave it a pull, I leaped back, expecting —I don't know what.

The creaking door swung in of its own weight, revealing an interior so dark I could distinguish no detail. I listened. All was silent. I sniffed. The place gave off the faint rancid odor that clings to a cabin in which raw furs have been dried.

Suddenly impatient at my senseless hesitancy, I plunged inside and bumped against a crude table in the middle of the floor. My outflung hand encountered a bottle with dribbles of wax on the side. I struck a match, lighted the candle stub still remaining in the neck, and, after shutting the door, turned to inspect my shelter.

In one corner of the single room was a rusty sheet-iron stove; in another a stout pole frame laced with strips of cured bearskin to make a bunk. There was a chair made of slabs, and on the floor two mink-stretchers and a steel bear trap with a broken jaw. That was all. Clearly, this was the very ordinary abode of some trapper who had abandoned it for other fields. Nothing here to alarm even the most timorous woman. Yet—I continued to feel uneasy.

The sensible thing to do now was build a fire and then eat a sandwich. Luckily I had a couple remaining from the lunch I had brought from the trolling boat.

Early in the morning I had left town with some fishermen to get first-hand material for a novel I was planning. By the time my notes were complete, the boat had reached the vicinity of a fox ranch where Lonnie, a schoolmate of mine, was spending the summer with her father, who owned the place. I had never been there, and this part of Alaska was strange to me; but the trollers pointed out a trail cutting in from the beach and crossing the peninsula to the ranch. I persuaded them to put me ashore so that I might walk over and make a short visit, while they fished. They were to call for me late in the evening on their way back to town, fifty miles distant. No doubt they were at the ranch at this moment, and everyone was wondering where I was.

I wondered about that myself. A trail, of course, must lead out from here; and I knew I could find it when the sun came up. As I raked the ashes from the stove, I began searching my memory for all I had heard of this region in which I had lost myself.

The first thing that popped into my mind was the story of five prospectors who, a few years before, had vanished on this peninsula without leaving a trace. Rumor had it that they had met foul play at the hands of a crazy trapper—"Cub Bear" Butler. I didn't know whether or not

the mystery had ever been solved. But—a crazy trapper.
. . . I glanced back over my shoulder, wishing I hadn't
thought about that.

A moment later, ax in hand, I reluctantly went out-of-
doors to the chopping block to cut some wood for the
stove.

A large, round, blood-gold moon, just topping the hemlocks, threw long tree-shadows across the meadow. The
rounded leaves of the bearweed caught the light, making
the clearing look as if it were paved with silver dollars.
Each clumsy blow of my ax rang out unnaturally loud,
then stopped with a thud against the encircling black wall
of timber. My sense of loneliness and isolation deepened.

In nervous haste I chopped an armload of wood, then,
stooping, began piling the sticks on my arm. I was reaching for the last stick which had fallen in the bearweed
when my groping fingers touched something which made
me recoil so violently that all my wood fell to the ground.
Hurriedly I struck a match and, leaning forward, lowered
it until the tiny light fell on the thing which lay half-con-
cealed under the moonlit leaves.

It was a fleshless, skeleton hand, severed at the wrist.

Transfixed with horror I stared at it while tales of
wilderness-crazed men raced through my mind. . . . A
hapless wretch, slumped beside this stump, legs bound,
arms outstretched across the top, and a hairy, gleaming-
eyed maniac whirling an ax——

The match burned my fingers. I dropped it. I was back-
ing away when my eyes, now adjusted to the darkness, fell

on another set of bony fingers thrust out from under a round leaf of bearweed. Then, just beyond that, a third skeleton hand took shape in the gloom.

My brain went into a sickening tailspin. I tried to scream, but could make no sound. I tried to run, but my legs seemed turned to water. Then the hope that my eyes had tricked me in the dim light brought back a measure of

calmness. I struck another match and, sweeping aside the weeds with my foot, bent to look.

They were there—all three of them.

I don't know how I nerved myself to make a thorough search of the ground around that ax-marked stump, but I did. And in the dense bearweed I saw twelve skeleton hands, all severed at the wrist. There wasn't a skull or bone of any other kind.

Somehow I got back inside the candle-lit cabin with an armload of wood, and, shoving the door shut, latched it. The fastening was an unusually sturdy bar of wood, one end of which was affixed to the middle of the door by a peg which allowed it to swing up and down. The other end slipped into a stout wooden stirrup on the log wall. The only way to lift and lower the bar from the outside was by means of the latch thong. I pulled this through its small hole, grateful that the door was strong and that no one could enter unless I lifted the bar.

But—I was hollow with dread. My hands trembled so that I could scarcely build the fire. And my mind kept swirling about Cub Bear Butler, the crazy trapper, and the five prospectors who had vanished. The men were last seen on this peninsula when Butler was living in the vicinity running his trap lines. Was it possible that I had stumbled on to Cub Bear's cabin? Could those skeleton hands belong to——

"But there were only *five* prospectors." I was startled to find I had spoken aloud. There were six pairs of fleshless hands out there bleaching under the Northern moon. To whom did the sixth pair belong?

I was so unstrung by these thoughts that, even after the fire was going, I couldn't eat a sandwich. Instead, after making sure that the door was still barred, I snuffed the candle, knowing it must soon burn out anyway. With my wadded jacket for a pillow, I lay down in the bare bunk, my little ax handy by my side.

I didn't intend to go to sleep, but gradually fatigue began to triumph over nerves. I remember thinking, half-coherently, "If Butler chopped the hands from five men and afterward amputated one of his own, how could he sever his other hand?"

Then my grisly speculations trailed off into sleep.

I don't know what awakened me; but suddenly I found myself sitting bolt upright, heart pounding, ears straining, eyes wide open. In the sooty darkness I could see nothing except a streak of moonlight lancing in through a knothole in one of the slats over the window. The stillness was intense. Yet, I knew that some sound, either inside the cabin or out, had penetrated my sleep.

I was about to get up to light the candle when it came again: *Thump!* . . . *Thump-thump-thump!* Someone was knocking to get in!

I chilled to the pit of my stomach, for the summons, heavy, imperative, was curiously muffled as if the visitor were rapping not with firm knuckles, but with—I shoved the horrible thought from me.

"Who—who's there?" I called unsteadily.

Silence.

Ax in hand, I eased out of the bunk, lighted the candle, and turned to inspect the door. It was barred. Everything in the dim room was just as it had been when I had gone to sleep.

"Who is it?" I demanded in a firmer voice.

The stillness tightened around me. My blood thudded in my eardrums. I knew anyone knocking for admittance at this hour of the night would identify himself—unless he were a——

Again I put from me the thought of a dead man, with no hands. I do not believe in ghosts.

I was trying to convince myself that the knocking had been born of my overwrought nerves when—*Thump! . . . Thump-thump-thump! Thump! . . . Thump-thump-thump!* Twice this time, hollow-loud, seeming to fill the room, yet having that sickening softness—like the fleshy stub of an arm hammering on wood.

Leaden with fright, I managed to reach the door and press my ear against it. "Who—what do you want? Answer me!"

I heard a faint rustling, as of a loose garment brushing against the rough log wall outside. After a dozen seconds had elapsed, I had a sudden, desperate impulse to end the suspense. I lifted the bar, flung open the door, and looked out.

Nothing.

The high moon lighted the clearing with a brilliance almost like that of day, but there was neither movement nor sound in the breathless Northern night.

Puzzled as well as frightened, I went back inside.

No sooner had I dropped the bar in place than it came again—*Thump! . . . Thump-thump-thump!* Instantly I jerked open the door.

No one was there. But the slithering sound, plainer than before, seemed to come from the corner to the right, as if someone had knocked, and then run to play a joke on me.

A flash of anger momentarily banished my fear; I darted

out and ran all the way round the cabin.

There was no one.

I stood in front of the door scrutinizing the chopping block, the low pile of limbs beside it, every inch of the meadow, bright with moonlight to the very edge of the dense timber. The nearest cover—the tall hemlock—was fully fifty feet away. Nothing human, no matter how fleet, could possibly have traversed that distance in the second between the last knock and my abrupt opening of the door. No creature larger than a rabbit could have concealed itself from my searching gaze anywhere in the meadow surrounding the cabin. Indubitably, the clearing lay untenanted by any living being, other than myself.

Then gooseflesh broke out all over me. With a rush of supernatural terror came the thought that I was gazing on no ordinary wild meadow. Under the bearweed were skeleton hands—so many of them that this was literally a meadow of the dead. Only one thing knocks and remains invisible to mortal eyes!

For an instant I was so scared I thought I was going to faint. A sharp, unmistakably real blow on my instep brought me out of it. I became aware that my nerveless hand had let go my ax, and the blunt end had dropped on the most sensitive part of my foot, causing pain so acute that it restored a fraction of my faculties.

I was trembling, and though it was not from cold, I wanted the comfort of a fire—a great, flaming fire. Accordingly, I dragged the pile of dead limbs over to the hut, averting my eyes from what I knew lay in the weeds about the chopping block, and kindled a roaring blaze just outside the door. The crackling, the warmth of it put new courage into me. I sat on the threshold, my back against the doorjamb, and watched the clearing.

Nothing further disturbed me. After a while I began to nod.

I woke with a start, thinking I heard laughter and someone calling my name. Late morning sun flooded the clearing. A pair of excited squirrels, shrieking as though disturbed, were racing up and down the trunk of the lone hemlock. Then I saw a slim, blonde young woman in breeches and a windbreaker, running across the meadow toward me. Lonnie, my friend of the fox ranch! Behind her strode her father, a lean sourdough Alaskan who had, as I well knew, no very high opinion of a woman's ability to take care of herself in the woods.

My joy at their appearance was such that I could have rushed upon them and fallen to embrace their knees. But pride kept me from betraying myself to the quizzical eyes of Lonnie's father, whom I always called "Dad." I assumed a nonchalant manner and strolled out from the door to greet them.

"There, Dad!" said Lonnie, laughing. "I told you she'd be cool as a cucumber!" She gave me a hug. "I knew you'd be all right, but Dad had a fit when you failed to show up last night. Sent two of the ranch hands to search the woods to the north and east. As soon as it was daylight, he and I started out in this direction."

"A woman," declared Dad, "should never go into the woods alone. Women have no bump of location. They're always getting lost." He readjusted the heavy holster on his hip. "I was afraid you'd run into a bear—there are a lot of brownies around this summer. You can thank your lucky star you stumbled on to Butler's cabin."

Butler's cabin! But even as a shivering thrill ran through me, Dad's I-told-you-so manner nettled me.

"It's not only women who get lost," I retorted. "How about those five prospectors who disappeared in these woods a few years ago?"

"Oh, those chaps!" He waved their vanishment aside with the confident air of a man who has a practical solution for every problem. "It's likely they were drowned in the tide-rips off the Cape."

"No, they weren't, Dad," I said quietly. "They were killed—murdered—right here at Butler's cabin."

He and Lonnie stared at me as if they thought I had gone insane. Then Dad began to laugh. "Now, Sis, don't try to put over any of your writer's imaginings on an old fellow like me."

"It's not imagination. Come. I'll show you."

I led the way to the chopping block, and, brushing aside the bearweed with my foot, one by one revealed the skeleton hands, stark white in the sunlight.

Dad looked grave. "By George," he muttered. "This looks bad. I mind there was some talk about Cub Bear Butler, but——" He stooped and picked up one of the bony things.

After a moment's inspection he deliberately tossed it back into the weeds, and brushed his hands together. "Just like a woman!" he drawled, grinning at me. "Those are not human hands, Sister. They're the skeleton paws of cub bears."

I must have looked uncommonly foolish, for he patted my shoulder consolingly. "Don't let that take the wind out of your sails, my dear. Nine men out of ten would have made the same mistake. You see, the skeleton of a bear's paw, particularly the small bones of a cub's, is almost identical with that of the human hand."

"But—why are there no other bones here?"

"Cub Bear Butler, like all other trappers, skinned his catch at the traps in the woods—all except the feet, which demand a good deal of care. He brought the pelts back here to his cabin to skin the paws at his leisure. He trapped only cubs, yearlings. That's how he got his nickname."

Feeling very much deflated, I followed him into the cabin.

"Poor old Cub Bear," he said. "They finally got him."

"Who got him?" I asked, remembering that Butler had been called "the crazy trapper."

"Bears. The Indians round here swear it was the Great She-Bear, the Spirit Bear, who took revenge on him for killing so many cubs. At any rate he was found crumpled down right there"—Dad pointed to a spot just outside the threshold of the open door—"killed as a bear kills a man. He'd been dead only a couple of days, and the tracks of a big brownie were still visible in the dooryard, which wasn't overgrown with bearweed then."

"But I don't understand why he didn't shoot the beast if it jumped him in his own yard."

"Couldn't reach his gun. When they found him, his rifle, his ax, and a fresh cub pelt were all here in the cabin, and the door was barred, and the latch thong broken off."

"What a strange thing!"

"Nothing strange about it. What happened was plain enough. Cub Bear must have come in from his trap line with the pelt. He dropped it when he put his rifle on the table, and then went out—for water, likely—shutting the door behind him. Possibly the mother of the cub he'd just killed did follow him home, and—well, an angry she-brownie is just about the most terrifying creature a man can run up against anywhere. When she went for him, he ran for his cabin to get his rifle and, in his haste, jerked the latch thong so hard he broke it off. Then he couldn't open the door. And it is so stout he couldn't break it in. So—the beast got him."

"How terrible—and ironic!" I shuddered as my mind involuntarily supplied details.

"Tough luck, all right. Bert Slocum, one of my ranch hands now, spent a couple of months here afterward, trapping mink. He came out with a fine, large tale about Cub Bear's ghost hanging around here, and——"

"Ghost," I started, and turned to stare at the spot outside the open door where Butler must have stood frantically beating on the heavy plank barrier trying to get in.

"Yes, so Bert claims." Dad chuckled as if vastly amused. "But Bert's a case. Biggest liar in Alaska. He'd be a good one to put in some of those books you write. The way Bert tells it, Cub Bear——"

Thump! . . . Thump-thump-thump! With the door wide open it came, and before I knew it I had leaped to my feet.

"What in heck's the matter with you, Sis?" inquired Dad. "Bouncing up with your eyes sticking out like a crab's?"

I looked from the empty door to the imperturbable faces of my companions. "Didn't you hear it?" I demanded.

"Hear what?"

"That knocking."

"Oh, those pesky flying squirrels," drawled Dad. "The country's getting overrun with 'em. On a moonlight night a man can't get a wink of sleep, the way they play humpty-dumpty on the roof. They——"

"Flying squirrels," I interrupted, doubtingly. "I'd like to see one—playing."

"No trouble. Just stand there inside the door, sort of hid, and keep your eye on that lone hemlock out in front."

I took up the position he indicated.

After a moment, sure enough, a small, furry form soared out from the top of the tree and, with little legs outspread, came gliding down to land with that soft, solid *thump!* on the roof. Then, quickly, *thump-thump-thump!* it bounded down to the eaves, and off, racing back toward the tree.

"What a cunning little creature," I observed, turning round with what must have been a sickly smile.

As I did so, my attention was caught by the door, swung in so that the outside of it was very close to me. Years of Alaska weather—beating rain and wind and snow, alternating with hot summer sun—had worked the rough grain of the unfinished planks into a coarse, light-gray nap. Visible now on the sunstruck surface, and about even with the top of my head, were curious marks—depressions in the weathernap of the wood, such as might have been made by the edge of heavily pounding fists.

"What are you staring at now, Sis?" Dad broke in on my concentration.

"Those marks on the door."

He laughed. "You must have been pretty excited when you got here last night—knocking that hard. But that's just like a woman—never able to tell whether a cabin's deserted or not." He came to his feet and picking my jacket from the bunk, held it for me. "Come, now. Slip into this. It's time we were toddling. I'm hungry enough to eat boiled owl, and it's eight miles to the ranch."

A few minutes later, as we were walking away across the sunny clearing. I fell a step behind the other two and turned to look back at the cabin in which I had spent the most terrifying night of my life.

I was remembering that two days ago there had been a heavy southeast gale which must have beat directly on that closed door. Yesterday's sun drying out the planks would have raised the woodnap, obliterating any depressions that might have been there before I reached the cabin. Yet—marks were there, as if two fists had pounded on the door. Dad thought I had made them.

I looked down at my hands, and though I don't believe in ghosts, I went a bit queer in the pit of my stomach. The marks were there, plainly visible when the sun struck the door just right. But I knew that my two small fists had never made them.

For I had never knocked, or even thought of knocking, on the door of that grim, deserted cabin in the clearing.

The Voyages of Sinbad the Sailor

In the reign of the Caliph Haroun al-Raschid there dwelt, in Bagdad, a poor porter named Hindbad, who often had to carry heavy burdens, which he could scarcely support. One very hot day he was laboring along a strange street, and overcome by fatigue he sat down near a great house to rest. The porter complimented himself upon his good fortune in finding such a pleasant place, for while he sat there reached his ear sweet sounds of music, and his senses were also soothed by sweet smells. Wondering who lived in so fine a house, he inquired of one of the servants.

"What," said the man, "do you not know that Sinbad the Sailor, the famous circumnavigator of the world, lives here?"

"Alas," replied Hindbad, "what a difference there is between Sinbad's lot and mine. Yet what greater merits does he possess that he should prosper and I starve?"

Now Sinbad happened to overhear this remark, and anxious to see a man who expressed such strange views he sent for Hindbad. Accordingly Hindbad was led into the great hall, where there was a sumptuous repast spread, and a goodly company assembled. The poor porter felt very uncomfortable, until Sinbad bade him draw near, and seating him at his right hand, served him himself, and gave him excellent wine, of which there was abundance upon the sideboard.

When the repast was over, Sinbad asked him why he complained of his condition.

"My lord," replied Hindbad, "I confess that my fatigue put me out of humor, and occasioned me to utter some indiscreet words, which I beg you to pardon."

"Do not think I am so unjust," resumed Sinbad, "as to resent such a complaint. But that you may know that my wealth has not been acquired without labor, I will recite the history of my travels for your benefit; and I think that, when you have heard it, you will acknowledge how wonderful have been my adventures." Sinbad then related the story of his first voyage as follows:

THE FIRST VOYAGE

When still a very young man I inherited a large fortune from my father, and at once set about amusing myself. I lived luxuriously, and soon found that money was decreasing, while nothing was added to replace my spending. Quickly seeing the folly of my ways, I invested the remainder of my fortune with some merchants of Bussorah, and joined them in their voyage, which was toward the Indies by way of the Persian Gulf.

In our voyage we touched at several islands, where we sold or exchanged our goods. One day, while under sail, we were becalmed near a small island, but little elevated above the level of the water, and resembling a green meadow. The captain ordered his sails to be furled, and permitted such persons as were so inclined to land; of this number I was one.

But while we were enjoying ourselves in eating and drinking, and recovering ourselves from the fatigue of the sea, the island on a sudden trembled, and shook us terribly.

The trembling of the island was perceived on board the ship, and we were called upon to re-embark speedily, or we should all be lost; for what we took for an island proved to be the back of a sea monster. The nimblest got into the sloop, others betook themselves to swimming; but for myself I was still upon the back of the creature, when he dived into the sea, and I had time only to catch hold of a piece of wood that we had brought out of the ship to make a fire. Meanwhile, the captain, having received those on board who were in the sloop, and taken up some of those that swam, resolved to improve the favorable gale that had just risen, and hoisting his sails pursued his voyage, so that it was impossible for me to recover the ship.

Thus was I exposed to the mercy of the waves. I struggled for my life all the rest of the day and the following night. By this time I found my strength gone, and despaired of saving my life, when happily a wave threw me against an island. I struggled up the steep bank by aid of some roots, and lay down upon the ground half dead, until the sun appeared. Then, though I was very feeble, both from hard labor and want of food, I crept along to find some herbs fit to eat, and had the good luck not only to procure some, but likewise to discover a spring of excellent

water, which contributed much to recover me. As I advanced farther into the island, I was not a little surprised and startled to hear a voice and see a man, who asked me who I was. I related to him my adventure, after which, taking me by the hand, he led me into a cave, where there were several other people, no less amazed to see me than I was to see them.

I partook of some provisions which they offered me. I then asked them what they did in such a desert place, to which they answered that they were grooms belonging to Maharajah, sovereign of the island, and that they were about to lead the King's horses back to the palace. They added that they were to return home on the morrow, and, had I been one day later, I must have perished, because the inhabited part of the island was at a great distance, and it would have been impossible for me to have got thither without a guide.

When the grooms set out I accompanied them, and was duly presented to the Maharajah, who was much interested in my adventure, and bade me stay with him as long as I desired.

Being a merchant, I met with men of my own profession, and particularly inquired for those who were strangers, that perchance I might hear news from Bagdad, or find an opportunity to return. For the Maharajah's capital is situated on the seacoast, and has a fine harbor, where ships arrive daily from the different quarters of the world. I frequented also the society of the learned Indians, and took delight to hear them converse; but withal, I took care to make my court regularly to the Maharajah, and conversed with the governors and petty kings, his tributaries, that were about him. They put a thousand questions respecting my country; and I, being willing to inform myself as to their laws and customs, asked them concerning everything which I thought worth knowing.

There belongs to this King an island named Cassel.

They assured me that every night a noise of drums was heard there, whence the mariners fancied that it was the residence of Degial. I determined to visit this wonderful place, and in my way thither saw fishes of one hundred and two hundred cubits long, that occasion more fear than hurt; for they are so timorous that they will fly upon the rattling of two sticks or boards. I saw likewise other fish, which had heads like owls.

As I was one day at the port after my return, the ship in which I had set sail arrived, and the crew began to unload the goods. I saw my own bales with my name upon them, and going up to the captain said, "I am that Sinbad whom you thought to be dead, and those bales are mine."

When the captain heard me speak thus, he exclaimed, "Heavens! whom can we trust in these times? There is no faith left among men. I saw Sinbad perish with my own eyes, as did also the passengers on board, and yet you tell me you are that Sinbad. What impudence is this? To look on you, one would take you to be a man of probity, and yet you tell a horrible falsehood, in order to possess yourself of what does not belong to you."

After much discussion, the captain was convinced of the truth of my words, and, having seen me identified by members of the crew, he handed me over my goods, congratulating me upon my escape.

I took out what was most valuable in my bales, and presented them to the Maharajah, who, knowing my misfortune, asked me how I came by such rarities. I acquainted him with the circumstance of their recovery. He was pleased at my good luck, accepted my present, and in return gave me one much more considerable. Thereupon, I took leave of him, and went aboard the same ship, after I had exchanged my goods for the commodities of that country. We passed by several islands, and at last arrived at Bussorah, from whence I came to this city, with the value of one hundred thousand sequins.

Sinbad stopped here, and ordered the musicians to proceed with their concert, which the story had interrupted. The company continued enjoying themselves till the evening, and it was time to retire, when Sinbad sent for a purse of one hundred sequins, and giving it to the porter said, "Take this, Hindbad, return to your home, and come back tomorrow to hear more of my adventures." The porter went away, astonished at the honor done and the present made him, and arrayed in his best apparel returned to Sinbad's house next day. After he had graciously received and feasted his guest, Sinbad continued his narrative:

THE SECOND VOYAGE

I designed, after my first voyage, to spend the rest of my days at Bagdad; but it was not long ere I grew weary of an indolent life, and, therefore, I set out a second time upon a voyage. We embarked on board a good ship, and, after recommending ourselves to God, set sail. We traded from island to island, and exchanged commodities with great profit. One day we landed at an island covered with several sorts of fruit trees, but we could see neither man nor animal. We went to take a little fresh air in the meadows, along the streams that watered them. While some diverted themselves with gathering flowers, and others fruits, I took my wine and provisions, and sat down near a stream betwixt two high trees, which formed a thick shade. I made a good meal, and afterward fell asleep. I cannot tell how long I slept, but when I awoke the ship was gone.

I was much alarmed at finding the ship gone. I got up and looked around me, but could not see one of the merchants who landed with me. I perceived the ship under sail, but at such a distance that I lost sight of her in a short time. I upbraided myself a hundred times for not being content with the produce of my first voyage, that might have sufficed me all my life. But all this was in vain, and my repentance too late. Not knowing what to do, I climbed up to the top of a lofty tree, whence I looked about on all sides, to see if I could discover anything that could give me hopes. When I gazed over the land I beheld something white; and coming down, I took what provision I had left, and went toward it, the distance being so great that I could not distinguish what it was.

As I approached, I thought it to be a white dome, of a prodigious height and extent; and when I came up to it, I touched it, and found it to be very smooth. I went round to see if it was open on any side, but saw it was not, and that there was no climbing up to the top, as it was so smooth. It was at least fifty paces round.

By this time the sun was about to set, and all of a sudden the sky became as dark as if it had been covered with a thick cloud. I was much astonished at this sudden darkness, but much more when I found it occasioned by a bird of monstrous size, that came flying toward me. I remembered that I had often heard mariners speak of a miraculous bird called a roc, and conceived that the great dome which I so much admired must be its egg. In a short time, the bird alighted, and sat over the egg. As I perceived her coming, I crept close to the egg, so that I had before me one of the legs of the bird, which was as big as the trunk of a tree. I tied myself strongly to it with my turban, in hopes that the roc next morning would carry me with her out of this desert island. After having passed the night in this condition, the bird flew away as soon as it was daylight, and carried me so high that I could not discern the earth; she afterward descended with so much rapidity that I lost my senses. But when I found myself on the ground, I speedily untied the knot, and had scarcely done so, when the roc, having taken up a serpent of a great length in her bill, flew away.

The spot where it left me was encompassed on all sides by mountains, which seemed to reach above the clouds, and so steep that there was no possibility of getting out of the valley. This was a new perplexity; so that when I compared this place with the desert island from which the roc had brought me, I found that I had gained nothing by the change.

As I walked through this valley, I perceived it was strewn with diamonds, some of which were of a surprising size. I took pleasure in looking upon them. But shortly I saw at a distance some objects that greatly diminished my satisfaction, and which I could not view without terror, namely, a great number of serpents, so monstrous that the least of them was capable of swallowing an elephant. They retired in the daytime to their dens, where they hid themselves from the roc, their enemy, and came out only in the night.

I spent the day in walking about in the valley, resting myself at times in such places as I thought most convenient. When night came on, I went into a cave, where I thought I might repose in safety. I secured the entrance, which was low and narrow, with a great stone to preserve me from the serpents; but not so far as to exclude the light. I supped on part of my provisions, but the serpents, which began hissing round me, put me into such extreme fear that you may easily imagine I did not sleep. When day appeared, the serpents retired, and I came out of the cave trembling. I can justly say that I walked upon diamonds without feeling any inclination to touch them. At last I sat down, and notwithstanding my apprehensions, not having closed my eyes during the night, fell asleep, after having eaten a little more of my provision. But I had scarcely shut my eyes when something that fell by me with a great noise awaked me. This was a large piece of raw meat; and at the same time I saw several others fall down from the rocks in different places.

I had always regarded as fabulous what I had heard sailors and others relate of the valley of diamonds, and of the stratagems employed by merchants to obtain jewels from thence; but now I found that they had stated nothing but the truth. For as a fact, the merchants come to the neighborhood of this valley, when the eagles have young ones, and throwing great joints of meat into the valley, the diamonds, upon whose points they fall, stick to them. The eagles, which are stronger in this country than anywhere else, pounce with great force upon those pieces of meat, and carry them to their nests on the precipices of the rocks to feed their young. The merchants at this time run to their nests, disturb and drive off the eagles by their shouts, and take away the diamonds that stick to the meat.

The happy idea struck me that here was a means of escape from my living tomb; so I collected a number of the largest diamonds, with which I filled my wallet, which I tied to my girdle. Then I fastened one of the joints of meat to the middle of my back by means of my turban cloth, and lay down with my face to the ground.

I had scarcely placed myself in this posture when the eagles came. Each of them seized a piece of meat, and one of the strongest having taken me up, with the piece of meat to which I was fastened, carried me to his nest on the top of the mountain. The merchants began their shouting to frighten the eagles; and when they had obliged them to quit their prey, one of them came to the nest where I was. He was much alarmed when he saw me. But recovering himself, instead of inquiring how I came

thither, began to quarrel with me, and asked why I stole
his goods.

"You will treat me," replied I, "with more civility,
when you know me better. Do not be uneasy; I have diamonds enough for you and myself, more than all the other
merchants together. Whatever they have they owe to
chance, but I selected for myself in the bottom of the valley those which you see in this bag."

I had scarcely done speaking, when the other merchants
came crowding about us, much astonished to see me. But
they were much more surprised when I told them my
story. Yet they did not so much admire my stratagem to
effect my deliverance as my courage in putting it into
execution.

They conducted me to their encampment, and there,
having opened my bag, they were surprised at the large-
ness of my diamonds, and confessed that in all the courts
which they had visited they had never seen any of such
size and perfection. I prayed the merchant, who owned
the nest to which I had been carried (for every merchant
had his own), to take as many for his share as he pleased.
He contented himself with one, and that too the least of
them; and when I pressed him to take more, without fear
of doing me injury, he said, "No, I am very well satisfied
with this which is valuable enough to save me the trouble
of making any more voyages, and will raise as great a fortune as I desire."

I spent the night with the merchants, to whom I related my story a second time, for the satisfaction of those

who had not heard it. I could not moderate my joy when I found myself delivered from the danger I have mentioned. I thought myself in a dream, and could scarcely believe myself out of danger. When at length I reached home I gave large presents to the poor, and lived luxuriously upon my hard-earned wealth.

Then Sinbad ended the account of his second voyage, and, having given Hindbad another hundred sequins, asked him to come on the next day to hear his further adventures.

THE FIFTH VOYAGE

The pleasures I enjoyed had again charms enough to make me forget all the troubles and calamities I had undergone, but could not cure me of my inclination to make new voyages. I therefore bought goods and departed with them for the best seaport. There, that I might not be obliged to depend upon a captain, but have a ship at my own command, I remained till one was built at my own charge. When the ship was ready, I went on board with my goods; but not having enough to load her, I agreed to take with me several merchants of different nations with their merchandise.

We sailed with the first fair wind, and after a long voyage, the first place we touched at was a desert island, where we found an egg of a roc, equal in size to the one I previously mentioned. There was a young roc in it just ready to be hatched, and its bill had begun to appear.

The merchants who landed with me broke the egg with hatchets, and pulled out the young roc piecemeal, and roasted it. I had earnestly entreated them not to meddle with the egg, but they would not listen to me.

Scarcely had they finished their repast when there appeared in the air at a considerable distance from us two great clouds. The captain whom I had hired to navigate my ship, knowing by experience what they meant, said they were the male and female roc that belonged to the young one, and pressed us to re-embark with all speed, to prevent the misfortune which he saw would otherwise befall us. We hastened on board, and set sail with all possible expedition.

In the meantime, the two rocs approached the island with a frightful noise, which they redoubled when they saw the egg broken and their young one gone. They flew back in the direction they had come, and disappeared for some time, while we made all the sail we could to endeavor to prevent that which unhappily befell us.

They soon returned, however, and we observed that each of them carried between its talons stones of a monstrous size. When they came directly over my ship, they hovered, and one of them let fall a stone, but by the dexterity of the steersman it missed us, and falling into the sea, divided the water so that we could almost see the bottom. The other roc, to our misfortune, threw his massive burden so exactly upon the middle of the ship as to split it into a thousand pieces. The mariners and passengers were all crushed to death, or drowned. I myself would have been among the latter, but as I came to the surface, I fortunately caught hold of a piece of the wreck, and swimming sometimes with one hand, and sometimes with the other, but always holding fast to my board, the wind and the tide favoring me, I came to an island, whose shore was very steep. I overcame that difficulty, however, and got ashore.

I sat down upon the grass, to recover myself from my fatigue, after which I went into the island to explore it. It seemed to be a delightful garden. I found trees everywhere, some of them bearing green, and others ripe fruits, and streams of fresh pure water running in pleasant meanders. I ate of the fruits, which I found excellent, and drank of the water, which was very sweet and good.

When night closed in, I lay down upon the grass in a convenient spot, but could not sleep more than an hour at a time, my mind being apprehensive of danger. I spent the best part of the night in alarm, and reproached myself for my imprudence in not remaining at home, rather than undertaking this last voyage. These reflections carried me so far that I began to form a design against my life; but daylight dispersed these melancholy thoughts. I got up, and walked among the trees, but not without some fears.

As I advanced into the island, I came upon an old man who appeared very weak and infirm. He was sitting on the bank of a stream, and at first I took him to be one who had been shipwrecked like myself. I went toward him and saluted him, but he only slightly bowed his head. I asked him why he sat so still, but instead of answering me, he made a sign for me to take him upon my back, and carry him over the brook, signifying that it was to gather fruit.

I believed him really to be in need of my assistance. So I took him upon my back, and having carried him over, bade him get down, and for that end stooped, that he might get off with ease. But instead of doing so the old man, who to me appeared quite decrepit, clasped his legs nimbly about my neck, so tightly that I swooned.

Notwithstanding my fainting, the ill-natured old fellow kept fast about my neck, but opened his legs a little to give me time to recover my breath. When I had done so, he thrust one of his feet against my stomach, and struck me so rudely on the side with the other, that he forced me to rise up against my will. Having arisen, he made me walk under the trees, and forced me now and then to stop, to gather and eat fruit such as we found. He never left me all day, and when I lay down to rest at night, laid himself down with me, holding always fast about my neck. Every morning he pushed me to make me awake, and afterward obliged me to get up and walk, and pressed me with his feet. You may judge, then, what trouble I was in, to be loaded with such a burden of which I could not rid myself.

One day I found in my way several dry calabashes that had fallen from a tree. I took a large one, and after cleaning it, pressed into it some juice of grapes, which abounded in the island. Having filled the calabash, I put it by in a convenient place, and going thither again some days after, I tasted it, and found the wine so good that it soon made me forget my sorrow, gave me new vigor, and so exhilarated my spirits that I began to sing and dance as I walked along.

The old man, perceiving the effect which this liquor had upon me, and that I carried him with more ease than before, made me a sign to give him some of it. I handed him the calabash, and the liquor pleasing his palate, he drank it all off, and was soon so intoxicated that his grip released. Seizing this opportunity, I threw him upon the ground, where he lay without motion. I then took up a great stone, and crushed his head to pieces.

I was extremely glad to be thus freed forever from this troublesome fellow. I now walked toward the beach, where I met the crew of a ship that had cast anchor to take in water. They were surprised to see me, but more so at hearing the particulars of my adventures. "You fell," said they, "into the hands of the Old Man of the Sea, and are the first who ever escaped strangling by his malicious tricks. He never quitted those he had once made himself master of, till he had destroyed them, and he has made this island notorious by the number of men he has slain; so that the merchants and mariners who landed upon it, durst not advance into the island but in numbers at a time." After saying this, they carried me with them to the ship. The captain received me with great kindness when they told him what had befallen me. He put out to sea, and after some days' sail, we arrived at the harbor of a great city, the houses of which were built of hewn stone.

One of the merchants who had taken me into his friendship invited me to go along with him. He gave me a large bag, and having recommended me to some people of the town, who used to gather coconuts, desired them to take me with them. "Go," said he, "follow them, and act as you see them do, but do not separate from them, otherwise you may endanger your life." Having thus spoken, he gave me provisions for the journey, and I went with them.

We came to a thick forest of coco palms, very lofty, with trunks so smooth that it was not possible to climb to the branches that bore the fruit. When we entered the forest we saw a great number of apes of various sizes, who fled as soon as they perceived us, and climbed up to the top of the trees with surprising swiftness.

The merchants in whose company I was gathered stones and threw them at the apes on the trees. I did the same, and the apes out of revenge threw coconuts at us so fast, and with such gestures, as sufficiently showed their anger and resentment. We gathered up the coconuts, and from time to time threw stones to provoke the apes. By this stratagem we filled our bags with coconuts. I soon sold mine, and returned several times to the forest for more. By this means I made a considerable sum.

The vessel in which I had come sailed with some merchants, who loaded her with coconuts. I expected the arrival of another, which anchored soon after for the like loading. I embarked in her all the coconuts I had, and when she was ready to sail, took leave of the merchant who had been so kind to me. But he could not embark with me, because he had not finished his business at the port. We sailed toward the islands where pepper grows in great plenty. From thence we went to the Isle of Comari, where the best species of wood of aloes grows, and whose inhabitants have made it an inviolable law to themselves to drink no wine. I exchanged my coconuts in those islands for pepper and wood of aloes, and went with other merchants pearl-fishing. I hired divers, who brought me up some that were very large and pure. Later I embarked in a vessel that happily arrived at Bussorah. From thence I returned to Bagdad, where I made vast sums from my pepper, wood of aloes, and pearls. I gave the tenth of my gains in alms, as I had done upon my return from my other voyages, and rested from my journeys.

from ALEXANDRE DUMAS

The Count of Monte Cristo

Edmond Dantès had been imprisoned, unjustly ac-
cused of plotting to restore Napoleon to the French
throne. Shut up in the Château d'If, a strong fortress
standing on an island of solid rock, his only friend had
been the Abbé Faria. And now he was dead. But while
Dantès sits mourning over the body of his dead com-
panion, he suddenly sees a possibility of attempting a
daring break for freedom.

DANTÈS' ESCAPE FROM THE CHÂTEAU D'IF

In the bed, at full length, faintly lighted by a dim
ray that entered through the window, Dantès saw a sack
of coarse cloth, under the ample folds of which he could
distinctly discern a long, stiff form: it was Faria's shroud.
All was over then. Dantès was separated from his old
friend. Faria, the helpful, kind companion, to whom he
had become so attached, to whom he owed so much, existed now but in his memory. He sat on the edge of the
bed and became a prey to deep and bitter melancholy.

Alone! He was quite alone once more! Alone! No longer to see, to hear the voice of, the only human being that attached him to life! Would it not be better to seek his Maker, as Faria had done, to learn the mystery of life even at the risk of passing through the dismal gates of suffering?

The idea of suicide, which had been dispelled by his friend and which he himself had forgotten in his presence, rose again before him like a phantom beside Faria's corpse.

"If I could only die," he said, "I should go where he has gone. But how am I to die? It is quite simple," said he with a smile. "I will stay here, throw myself on the first one who enters, strangle him, and then I shall be guillotined."

Dantès, however, recoiled from such an infamous death, and swiftly passed from despair to an ardent desire for life and liberty. "Die? Oh, no!" he cried out, "it would hardly have been worth-while to live, to suffer so much, and then to die now. No, I desire to live, to fight to the end. I wish to reconquer the happiness that has been taken from me. Before I die, I have my executioners to punish, and possibly also some friends to recompense. Yet they will forget me here, and I shall only leave this dungeon in the same way that Faria has done."

As he uttered these words, Edmond stood stock-still, with eyes fixed like a man struck by a sudden and terrifying idea.

"Oh, who has given me this thought?" he murmured.

"My God, comes this from Thee? Since it is only the dead who go free from here, I must take the place of the dead!"

Without giving himself time to reconsider his decision, and as though he would not give reflection time to destroy his desperate resolution, he leaned over the hideous sack, slit it open with the knife Faria had made, took the dead body out, carried it to his own cell, and placed it on his bed, put round the head the piece of rag he always wore, covered it with the bedclothes, kissed for the last time the ice-cold forehead, endeavored to shut the rebellious eyes, which were still open, and stared so horribly, and turned the head to the wall so that, when the jailer brought his evening meal, he would think he had gone to bed as he often did. Then he returned to the other cell, took the needle and thread from the cupboard, flung off his rags that the men might feel naked flesh under the sacking, slipped into the sack, placed himself in the same position as the corpse, and sewed the sack up again from the inside. If the jailers had entered then, they would have heard the beating of his heart.

Now this is what Dantès intended doing. If the gravediggers discovered that they were carrying a live body instead of a dead one, he would give them no time for thought. He would slit the sack open with his knife from top to bottom, jump out, and, taking advantage of their terror, escape; if they tried to stop him, he would use his knife. If they took him to the cemetery and placed him in a grave, he would allow himself to be covered with earth; then, as it was night, as soon as the gravediggers had

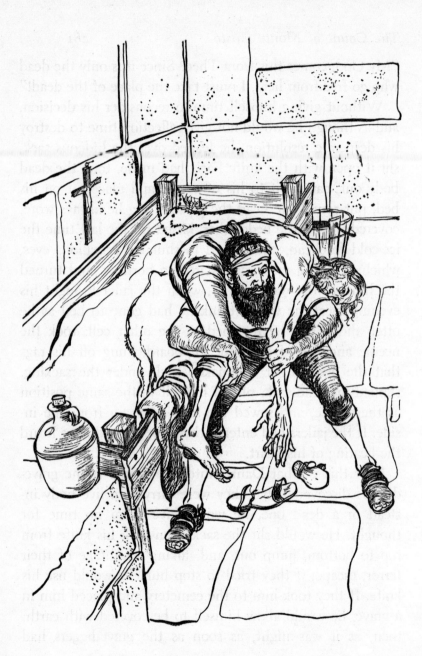

turned their backs, he would cut his way through the soft
earth and escape; he hoped the weight would not be too
heavy for him to raise.

He had eaten nothing since the previous evening, but
he had not thought of his hunger in the morning, neither
did he think of it now. His position was much too pre-
carious to allow him time for any thought but that of
flight.

At last, toward the time appointed by the governor, he
heard footsteps on the staircase. He realized that the moment had come, he summoned all his courage and held
his breath.

The door was opened, a subdued light reached his eyes.
Through the sacking that covered him he saw two shadows approach the bed. There was a third one at the door
holding a lantern in his hand. Each of the two men who
had approached the bed took the sack by one of its two
extremities.

"He is very heavy for such a thin old man," said one of
them as he raised the head.

"They say that each year adds half a pound to the
weight of one's bones," said the other, taking the feet.

They carried away the sham corpse on the bier. Edmond made himself rigid. The procession, lighted by the
man with the lantern, descended the stairs. All at once
Dantès felt the cold fresh night air and the sharp north-
west wind, and the sensation filled him at once with joy
and with anguish.

The men went about twenty yards, then stopped and

dropped the bier onto the ground. One of them went away, and Dantès heard his footsteps on the stones.

"Where am I?" he asked himself.

"He is by no means a light load, you know," said the man who remained behind, seating himself on the edge of the bier.

Dantès' impulse was to make his escape, but, fortunately, he did not attempt it. He heard one of the men draw near and drop a heavy object on the ground; at the same moment a cord was tied round his feet, cutting into his flesh.

"Well, have you made the knot?" one of the men asked.

"Yes, and it is well made. I can answer for that."

"Let's on, then."

The bier was lifted once more, and the procession proceeded. The noise of the waves breaking against the rocks on which the Château is built sounded more distinctly to Dantès with each step they took.

"Wretched weather!" said one of the men, "the sea will not be very inviting tonight."

"Yes, the abbé runs a great risk of getting wet," said the other, and they burst out laughing.

Dantès could not understand the jest, nevertheless his hair began to stand on end.

"Here we are at last!"

"No, farther on, farther on! You know the last one was dashed on the rocks, and the next day the governor called us a couple of lazy rascals."

They went another five yards, and then Dantès felt

them take him by the head and feet and swing him to and fro.

"One! Two! Three!"

With the last word, Dantès felt himself flung into space. He passed through the air like a wounded bird falling, falling, ever falling with a rapidity which turned his heart to ice. At last—though it seemed to him like an eternity of time—there came a terrific splash; and as he dropped like an arrow into the icy cold water he uttered a scream which was immediately choked by his immersion.

Dantès had been flung into the sea, into whose depths he was being dragged down by a cannon ball tied to his feet.

The sea is the cemetery of the Château d'If.

Though stunned and almost suffocated, Dantès had yet the presence of mind to hold his breath and, as he grasped the open knife in his right hand ready for any emergency, he rapidly ripped open the sack, extricated his arm and then his head; but in spite of his efforts to raise the cannon ball, he still felt himself being dragged down and down. He bent his back into an arch in his en-deavor to reach the cord that bound his legs, and, after a desperate struggle, he severed it at the very moment when he felt that suffocation was getting the upper hand of him. He kicked out vigorously and rose unhampered to the surface, while the cannon ball dragged to the un-known depths the sacking which had so nearly become his shroud.

Dantès merely paused to take a deep breath and then

he dived again to avoid being seen. When he rose the second time, he was already fifty yards from the spot where he had been thrown into the sea. He saw above him a black and tempestuous sky; before him was the vast expanse of dark, surging waters; while behind him, more gloomy than the sea and more somber than the sky, rose the granite giant like some menacing phantom, whose dark summit appeared to Dantès like an arm stretched out to seize its prey. He had always been reckoned the best swimmer in Marseilles, and he was now anxious to rise to the surface to try his strength against the waves. To his joy he found that his enforced inaction had not in any way impaired his strength and agility, and he felt he could still master the element in which he had so often sported when a boy.

An hour passed. Exalted by the feeling of liberty, Dantès continued to cleave the waves in what he reckoned should be a direct line for the Isle of Tiboulen. Suddenly it seemed to him that the sky, which was already black, was becoming blacker than ever, and that a thick, heavy cloud was rolling down on him. At the same time he felt a violent pain in his knee. With the incalculable rapidity of imagination, he thought it was a shot that had struck him, and he expected every moment to hear the report. But there was no sound. He stretched out his hand and encountered an obstacle; he drew his leg up and felt land; he then saw what it was he had mistaken for a cloud. Twenty yards from him rose a mass of strangely formed rocks looking like an immense fire petrified at the moment of its most violent combustion: it was the Isle of Tiboulen.

Dantès rose, advanced a few steps, and, with a prayer of gratitude on his lips, stretched himself out on the jagged rocks which seemed to him more restful and comfortable than the softest bed he had ever slept on. Then, in spite of the wind and storm, in spite of the rain that began to fall, worn out with fatigue as he was, he fell into the delicious sleep of a man whose body becomes torpid but whose mind remains alert in the consciousness of unexpected happiness.

For an hour he slept thus, and was awakened by the roar of a tremendous clap of thunder. A flash of lightning that seemed to open the heavens to the very throne of God, illuminated all around, and by its light he saw about a quarter of a mile away, between the Isle of Lemaire and Cap Croisille, a small fishing boat borne along by the wind, and riding like a phantom on the top of a wave only to disappear in the abyss below. A second later it appeared on the crest of another wave advancing with terrifying rapidity. By the light of another flash, he saw four men clinging to the masts and rigging; a fifth was clinging to the broken rudder. Then he heard a terrific crash followed by agonizing cries. As he clung to his rock like a limpet, another flash revealed to him the little boat smashed to pieces, and, amongst the wreckage, heads with despairing faces, and arms stretched heavenward. Then all was dark again. There was nothing left but tempest.

By degrees the wind abated; the huge gray clouds rolled toward the west. Shortly afterward a long, reddish streak

was seen along the horizon; the waves leaped and frol-
icked, and a sudden light played on their foamy crests,
turning them into golden plumes. Daylight had come.

It must have been five o'clock in the morning; the sea
continued to grow calm. "In two or three hours," Dantès
said to himself, "the turnkeys will enter my cell, find the
dead body of my poor friend, recognize him, seek me in
vain, and give the alarm. Then they will find the aperture
and the passage; they will question the men who flung me
into the sea and who must have heard the cry I uttered.
Boats filled with armed soldiers will immediately give
chase to the wretched fugitive who, they know, cannot
be far off. The cannon will warn the whole coast that no
one shall give shelter to a naked, famished wanderer. The
spies and police of Marseilles will be notified, and they
will beat the coast while the Governor of the Château d'If
beats the sea. And what will become of me pursued by
land and by sea? I am hungry and cold and have even
lost my knife. I am at the mercy of the first peasant who
cares to hand me over to the police for the reward of
twenty francs. Oh God! my God! Thou knowest I have
suffered to excess; help me now that I cannot help myself!"

As Dantès finished this fervent prayer that was torn
from his exhausted and anguished heart, he saw appearing
on the horizon what he recognized as a Genoses *tartan*
coming from Marseilles.

"To think that I could join this vessel in half an hour
if it were not for the fear of being questioned, recognized
as a fugitive, and taken back to Marseilles," said Dantès, to

himself. "What am I to do? What can I say? What story can I invent which might sound credible? I might pass as one of the sailors wrecked last night." So saying he turned his gaze toward the wreck and gave a sudden start. There, caught on a point of rock, he perceived the cap of one of the shipwrecked sailors, and close by still floated some of the planks of the unfortunate vessel.

Dantès soon thought out a plan and as quickly put it into action. He dived into the sea, swam to the cap, placed it on his head, seized one of the timbers, and turning back, struck out in a direction which would cut the course the vessel must take.

The boat changed her course, steering toward him, and Dantès saw that they made ready to lower a boat. He summoned all his strength to swim toward it, but his arms began to stiffen, his legs lost their flexibility, and his movements became heavy and difficult. Breath was failing him. A wave that he had not the strength to surmount passed over his head, covering him with foam. Then he saw and heard nothing more.

When he opened his eyes again, Dantès found himself on the deck of the *tartan;* a sailor was rubbing his limbs with a woolen cloth, another was holding a gourd to his mouth, and a third, who was the master of the vessel, was looking at him with that feeling of pity which is uppermost in the hearts of most people when face to face with a misfortune which they escaped yesterday, and of which they may be the victim tomorrow.

"Who are you?" the skipper asked in bad French.

"I am a Maltese sailor," replied Dantès in equally bad
Italian. "We were coming from Syracuse laden with
wine and grain. We were caught in a storm last night off
Cape Morgion, and we were wrecked on the rocks you see
yonder."

"Where have you come from?"

"From those rocks over there. Fortunately for me I was
able to cling to them, but our poor captain and my three
companions were drowned. I believe I am the sole survivor. I saw your ship, and I risked swimming towards
you. Thank you," he continued, "you have saved my
life. I was lost when one of your sailors caught hold of my
hair."

"It was I," said a sailor with a frank and open face, en-

circled by long black whiskers. "It was time, too, for you were sinking."

"Yes," said Dantès, holding out his hand to him. "I know, and I thank you once more."

"Lord! but you nearly frightened me," the sailor replied. "You looked more like a brigand than an honest man with your beard six inches long and your hair a foot in length."

Dantès suddenly recollected that neither his hair nor his beard had been cut all the time that he had been at the Château d'If.

"Once when I was in danger," he cried, "I made a vow to the Madonna of Piedigrotta not to cut my hair or beard for ten years. The time is up this very day, and I nearly celebrated the event by being drowned."

"Now, what are we going to do with you?" asked the skipper.

"Alas! do with me what you will," replied Dantès. "The bark I sailed in is lost, my captain is dead, and I nearly shared the same fate. Fortunately I am a good sailor. Leave me at the first port you touch at, and I shall be sure to find employment in some merchantman."

"Take the helm and let us see how you frame."

The young man did as he was bid. Ascertaining by a slight pressure that the vessel answered to the rudder, he saw that, without being a first-rate sailor, she was yet tolerably obedient.

"Man the lee-braces," he cried.

The four seamen, who composed the crew, obeyed, whilst the skipper looked on.

"Haul away!"

They obeyed.

"Belay!"

This order was also executed, and, instead of tacking about, the vessel made straight for the Isle of Rion, leaving it about twenty fathoms to starboard.

"Bravo!" said the captain.

"Bravo!" repeated the sailors.

And they all regarded with astonishment this man whose eye had recovered an intelligence and his body a vigor they were far from suspecting him to possess.

"You see," said Dantès, handing over the tiller to the helmsman, "I shall be of some use to you, at any rate during the voyage. If you do not want me at Leghorn, you can leave me there, and with the first wages I earn, I will pay you for my food and for the clothes you lend me."

"Very well," said the captain. "We can fix things up if you are not too exacting."

"Give me what you give the others," returned Dantès.

"Hallo! What's the matter at the Château d'If?" exclaimed the captain.

A small white cloud crowned the summit of the bastion of the Château d'If. At the same moment, the faint report of a gun was heard. The sailors all looked at one another.

"A prisoner has escaped from the Château d'If, and they are firing the alarm gun," said Dantès calmly.

"What is the day of the month?" he presently asked of Jacopo, the sailor who had saved him and who now sat beside him.

"The twenty-eighth of February."

"What year?"

"Have you forgotten that you ask such a question?"

"I was so frightened last night," replied Dantès, with a smile, "that I have almost lost my memory. What year is it?"

"The year eighteen-twenty-nine," returned Jacopo.

It was fourteen years to the very day since Dantès' arrest. He was nineteen when he entered the Château d'If; he was thirty-three when he escaped.

from DANIEL DEFOE'S

Robinson Crusoe

The idea of a person shipwrecked on a desert island and thrown completely on his own resources has always been enormously appealing to both children and adults. Robinson Crusoe was one of the earliest of the desert island stories—it has since had hundreds of imitations—and it is still the best. Nobody has ever surpassed Defoe in his account of the thousands of fascinating details in the struggle for existence of this most famous of all castaways. When we meet Robinson Crusoe here his ship has just been wrecked during a violent hurricane and he finds himself the sole survivor on a barren island in the Pacific.

EXPLORING THE ISLAND

When I waked it was broad day, the weather clear, and the storm abated, so that the sea did not rage and swell as before; but that which surprised me most was, that the ship was lifted off in the night from the sand where she lay by the swelling of the tide, and was driven up almost as far as the rock which I first mentioned, where I had been so bruised by the dashing against it. This being within about a mile from the shore where I was, and the ship seeming to stand upright still, I wished myself on board, that, at least, I might save some necessary things for my use.

When I came down from my apartment in the tree, I looked about me again, and the first thing I found was the boat, which lay as the wind and the sea had tossed her, up upon the land, about two miles on my right hand. I walked as far as I could upon the shore to have got to her, but found a neck or inlet of water between me and the boat, which was about half a mile broad; so I came back for the present, being more intent upon getting at the ship, where I hoped to find something for my present subsistence.

A little after noon I found the sea very calm, and the tide ebbed so far out that I could come within a quarter of a mile of the ship, and here I found a fresh renewing of my grief; for I saw evidently, that if we had kept on board, we had been all safe, that is to say, we had all got safe on shore, and I had not been so miserable as to be left entirely destitute of all comfort and company, as I now was. This forced tears from my eyes again, but as there was little relief in that, I resolved, if possible, to get to the ship, so I pulled off my clothes, for the weather was hot to extremity, and took the water. But when I came to the ship, my difficulty was still greater to know how to get on board, for as she lay a-ground, and high out of the water, there was nothing within my reach to lay hold of. I swam round her twice, and the second time I spied a small piece of rope, which I wondered I did not see at first, hang down by the fore-chains so low as that with great difficulty I got hold of it, and by the help of that rope got up into the forecastle of the ship.

Here I found that the ship was bulged, and had a great deal of water in her hold, but that she lay so on the side

of a bank of hard sand, or rather earth, that her stern lay lifted up upon the bank, and her head low almost to the water. By this means all her quarter was free, and all that was in that part was dry; for you may be sure my first work was to search and to see what was spoiled and what was free; and first I found that all the ship's provisions were dry and untouched by the water; and being very well disposed to eat, I went to the bread-room and filled my pockets with biscuit, and ate it as I went about other things, for I had no time to lose. I also found some rum in the great cabin, of which I took a large dram, and which I had indeed need enough of to spirit me for what was before me. Now I wanted nothing but a boat to furnish myself with many things which I foresaw would be very necessary to me.

It was in vain to sit still and wish for what was not to be had, and this extremity roused my application. We had several spare yards, and two or three large spars of wood, and a spare top-mast or two in the ship. I resolved to fall to work with these, and flung as many of them overboard as I could manage for their weight, tying every one with a rope that they might not drive away. When this was done I went down the ship's side, and pulling them to me, I tied four of them fast together at both ends, as well as I could, in the form of a raft, and laying two or three short pieces of plank upon them cross-ways, I found I could walk upon it very well, but that it was not able to bear any great weight, the pieces being too light. So I went to work, and with the carpenter's saw I cut a spare top-mast into three lengths, and added them to my raft, with a great deal of labour and pains: but hope of furnishing myself with necessaries encouraged me to go beyond what I should have been able to have done upon another occasion.

My raft was now strong enough to bear any reasonable weight; my next care was what to load it with, and how to preserve what I laid upon it from the surf of the sea;

but I was not long considering this. I first laid all the planks or boards upon it that I could get, and having considered well what I most wanted, I first got three of the seamen's chests, which I had broken open and emptied, and lowered them down upon my raft. The first of these I filled with provisions, namely, bread, rice, three Dutch cheeses, five pieces of dried goat's flesh, which we lived much upon, and a little remainder of European corn which had been laid by for some fowls which we brought to sea with us, but the fowls were killed. There had been some barley and wheat together; but, to my great disappointment, I found afterwards that the rats had eaten or spoiled it all. As for liquors, I found several cases of bottles belonging to our skipper, in which were some cordial waters, and in all about five or six gallons of arrack; these I stowed by themselves, there being no need to put them into the chest, nor no room for them.

While I was doing this, I found the tide began to flow, though very calm; and I had the mortification to see my coat, shirt, and waistcoat, which I had left on shore upon the sand, swim away; as for my breeches, which were only linen and open-kneed, I swam on board in them and my stockings. However, this put me upon rummaging for clothes, of which I found enough, but took no more than I wanted for present use; for I had other things which my eye was more upon—as, first, tools to work with on shore; and it was after long searching that I found out the carpenter's chest, which was indeed a very useful prize to me, and much more valuable than a ship-loading of gold would

have been at that time. I got it down to my raft, even whole as it was, without losing time to look into it, for I knew in general what it contained.

My next care was for some ammunition and arms. There were two very good fowling-pieces in the great cabin, and two pistols; these I secured first, with some powder-horns, and a small bag of shot, and two old rusty swords. I knew there were three barrels of powder in the ship, but knew not where our gunner had stowed them; but with much search I found them, two of them dry and good, the third had taken water. Those two I got to my raft, with the arms; and now I thought myself pretty well freighted, and began to think how I should get to shore with them, having neither sail, oar, nor rudder, and the least cap-full of wind would have overset all my navigation.

I had three encouragements: a smooth, calm sea, the tide rising and setting into the shore, and what little wind there was blew me towards the land. And thus, having found two or three broken oars belonging to the boat, and besides the tools which were in the chest, I found two saws, an axe and a hammer, and with this cargo I put to sea. For a mile, or thereabouts, my raft went very well, only that I found it drive a little distant from the place where I had landed before, by which I perceived that there was some indraft of the water, and consequently I hoped to find some creek or river there, which I might make use of as a port to get to land with my cargo.

As I imagined, so it was. There appeared before me a little opening of the land, and I found a strong current

of the tide set into it, so I guided my raft as well as I could
to keep in the middle of the stream. But here I had like
to have suffered a second shipwreck, which, if I had, I
think verily would have broke my heart. For knowing
nothing of the coast, my raft run a-ground at one end of
it upon a shoal, and not being a-ground at the other end,
it wanted but a little that all my cargo had slipped off
towards that end that was afloat, and so fallen into the
water. I did my utmost, by setting my back against the
chests, to keep them in their places, but could not thrust
off the raft with all my strength, neither durst I stir from
the posture I was in; but holding up the chests with all
my might, stood in that manner near half an hour, in
which time the rising of the water brought me a little
more upon a level. And a little after, the water still rising,
my raft floated again, and I thrust her off with the oar I
had into the channel; and then driving up higher, I at
length found myself in the mouth of a little river, with
land on both sides, and a strong current or tide running
up. I looked on both sides for a proper place to get to
shore, for I was not willing to be driven too high up the
river, hoping in time to see some ship at sea, and therefore resolved to place myself as near the coast as I could.

At length I spied a little cove on the right shore of the
creek, to which, with great pain and difficulty, I guided
my raft, and at last got so near, as that, reaching ground
with my oar, I could thrust her directly in. But here I had
liked to have dipped all my cargo in the sea again; for that
shore lying pretty steep, that is to say sloping, there was

no place to land, but where one end of the float, if it run on shore, would lie so high, and the other sink lower as before, that it would endanger my cargo again. All that I could do, was to wait till the tide was at the highest, keeping the raft with my oar like an anchor to hold the side of it fast to the shore, near a flat piece of ground, which I expected the water would flow over; and so it did. As soon as I found water enough (for my raft drew about a foot of water), I thrust her on upon that flat piece of ground, and there fastened or moored her by sticking my two broken oars into the ground; one on one side near one end, and one on the other side near the other end. And thus I lay till the water ebbed away, and left my raft and all my cargo safe on shore.

My next work was to view the country, and seek a proper place for my habitation, and where to stow my goods to secure them from whatever might happen. Where I was I yet knew not; whether on the continent or on an island, whether inhabited or not inhabited, whether in danger of wild beasts or not. There was a hill not above a mile from me, which rose up very steep and high, and which seemed to over-top some other hills which lay as in a ridge from it northward. I took out one of the fowling-pieces, and one of the pistols and an horn of powder, and thus armed, I travelled for discovery up to the top of that hill; where, after I had with great labour and difficulty got to the top, I saw my fate to my great affliction, namely, that I was in an island environed every way with the sea, no land to be seen, except some rocks which lay a great way off, and two small islands less than this, which lay about three leagues to the west.

I found also that the island I was in was barren, and, as I saw good reason to believe, uninhabited, except by wild beasts, of whom however I saw none; yet I saw abundance of fowls, but knew not their kinds, neither when I killed them could I tell what was fit for food, and what not. At my coming back, I shot at a great bird, which I saw sitting upon a tree on the side of a great wood—I believe it was the first gun that had been fired there since the creation of the world. I had no sooner fired, but from all parts of the wood there arose an innumerable number of fowls of many sorts, making a confused screaming, and crying every one according to his usual note; but not one of them of any kind that I knew. As for the creature I killed, I took it to be a kind of hawk, its colour and beak resembling it, but had no talons or claws more than common; its flesh was carrion and fit for nothing.

Contented with this discovery, I came back to my raft, and fell to work to bring my cargo on shore, which took me up the rest of that day. And what to do with myself at night I knew not, nor indeed where to rest; for I was afraid to lie down on the ground, not knowing but some wild beast might devour me, though, as I afterwards found, there was really no need for those fears.

However, as well as I could, I barricaded myself round with the chests and boards that I had brought on shore, and made a kind of a hut for that night's lodging. As for food, I yet saw not which way to supply myself, except that I had seen two or three creatures, like hares, run out of the wood where I shot the bird.

I now began to consider that I might yet get a great many things out of the ship which would be useful to me, and particularly some of the rigging and sails, and such other things as might come to land, and I resolved to make another voyage to board the vessel, if possible. And as I knew that the first storm that blew must necessarily break her all in pieces, I resolved to set all other things apart till I got everything out of the ship that I could get. Then I called a council, that is to say, in my thoughts, whether I should take back the raft. But this appeared impracticable, so I resolved to go as before, when the tide was down, and I did so, only that I stripped before I went from my hut, having nothing on but a chequered shirt, and a pair of linen trousers, and a pair of pumps on my feet.

I got on board the ship, as before, and prepared a second raft, and having had experience of the first, I neither made this so unwieldy, nor loaded it so hard. Yet I brought away several things very useful to me; as first, in the carpenter's stores, I found two or three bags full of nails and spikes, a great screw jack, a dozen or two of hatchets, and above all, that most useful thing called a grindstone. All these I secured, together with several things belonging to the gunner, particularly two or three iron crows, and two barrels of musket-bullets, seven muskets, and another fowling-piece, with some small quantity of powder more, a large bag full of small shot, and a great roll of sheet lead. But this last was so heavy I could not hoist it up to get it over the ship's side.

Besides these things, I took all the men's clothes that I could find, and a spare fore-top-sail, hammock, and some bedding; and with this I loaded my second raft, and brought them all safe on shore, to my very great comfort.

I was under some apprehensions during my absence from the land, that at least my provisions might be devoured on shore; but when I came back, I found no sign of any visitor, only there sat a creature like a wild cat upon one of the chests, which, when I came towards it, ran away a little distance, and then stood still. She sat very composed and unconcerned, and looked full in my face, as if she had a mind to be acquainted with me. I presented my gun at her, but as she did not understand it, she was perfectly unconcerned at it, nor did she offer to stir away. Upon which I tossed her a bit of biscuit, though by the way I was not very free of it, for my store was not great. However, I spared her a bit, I say, and she went to it, smelled it, ate it, and looked, as pleased, for more; but I thanked her, and could spare no more, so she marched off.

Having got my second cargo on shore, though I was fain to open the barrels of powder, and bring them by parcels (for they were too heavy, being large casks), I went to work to make me a little tent with the sail and some poles which I cut for that purpose; and into this tent I brought everything that I knew would spoil, either with rain or sun, and I piled all the empty chests and casks up in a circle round the tent, to fortify it from any sudden attempt, either from man or beast.

When I had done this, I blocked up the door of the tent with some boards within, and an empty chest set up on-end without; and spreading one of the beds on the ground, laying my two pistols just at my head, and my gun at length by me, I went to bed for the first time, and slept very quietly all night, for I was very weary and heavy. For the night before I had slept little, and had laboured very hard all day, as well to fetch all those things from the ship as to get them on shore.

I had the biggest magazine of all kinds now that ever were laid up, I believe, for one man, but I was not satisfied still; for while the ship sat upright in that posture, I thought I ought to get everything out of her that I could. So every day at low water I went on board, and brought away something or other; but particularly the third time I went, I brought away as much of the rigging as I could, as also all the small ropes and rope-twine I could get, with a piece of spare canvas, which was to mend the sails upon occasion, and the barrel of wet gunpowder. In a word, I brought away all the sails first and last, only that I was fain to cut them in pieces, and bring as much at a time as I could; for they were no more useful to be sails, but as mere canvas only.

But that which comforted me more still, was that, last of all, after I had made five or six such voyages as these, and thought I had nothing more to expect from the ship that was worth my meddling with; I say, after all this, I found a great hogshead of bread, and three large runlets of rum or spirits, and a box of sugar, and a barrel of fine flour. This was surprising to me, because I had given over expecting any more provisions, except what was spoiled by the water. I soon emptied the hogshead of that bread, and wrapped it up, parcel by parcel, in pieces of the sails, which I cut out; and, in a word, I got all this safe on shore also.

The next day I made another voyage; and now, having plundered the ship of what was portable and fit to hand out, I began with the cables; and cutting the great cable into pieces, such as I could move, I got two cables and a hawser on shore, with all the iron-work I could get; and having cut down the spritsail-yard, and the mizen-yard, and everything I could to make a large raft, I loaded it with all those heavy goods and came away. But my good luck began now to leave me. For this raft was so unwieldy and so overladen, that after I had entered the little cove, where I had landed the rest of my goods, not being able to guide it so handily as I did the other, it overset, and threw me and all my cargo into the water. As for myself it was no great harm, for I was near the shore; but as to my cargo, it was great part of it lost, especially the iron, which I expected would have been of great use to me. However, when the tide was out, I got most of the pieces of cable ashore, and some of the iron, though with infinite labour; for I was fain to dip for it into the water—a work which fatigued me very much. After this, I went every day on board and brought away what I could get.

I had been now thirteen days on shore, and had been

eleven times on board the ship, in which time I had
brought away all that one pair of hands could be well supposed capable to bring; though I believe verily, had the
calm weather held, I should have brought away the whole
ship, piece by piece. But preparing the twelfth time to go
on board, I found the wind begin to rise; however, at low
water I went on board, and though I thought I had rum-
maged the cabin so effectually, as that nothing more could
be found, yet I discovered a locker with drawers in it, in
one of which I found two or three razors, and one pair
of large scissors, with some ten or a dozen of good knives
and forks. In another I found about thirty-six pounds
value in money, some European coin, some Brasil, some
pieces of eight, some gold, some silver.

I smiled to myself at the sight of this money. "O Drug!"
said I, aloud, "what art thou good for? thou art not worth
to me, no, not the taking off the ground. One of these
knives is worth all this heap. I have no manner of use for
thee, even remain where thou art and go to the bottom,
as a creature whose life is not worth saving." However,
upon second thoughts, I took it away, and wrapping all
this in a piece of canvas, I began to think of making another raft. But while I was preparing this, I found the sky
overcast, and the wind began to rise, and in a quarter of
an hour it blew a fresh gale from the shore. It presently
occurred to me, that it was in vain to pretend to make a
raft with the wind off shore, and that it was my business
to be gone before the tide of flood began, otherwise I
might not be able to reach the shore at all. Accordingly

I let myself down into the water, and swam across the channel, which lay between the ship and the sands, and even that with difficulty enough, partly with the weight of things I had about me, and partly the roughness of the water; for the wind rose very hastily, and before it was quite high water it blew a storm.

But I was gotten home to my little tent, where I lay with all my wealth about me very secure. It blew very hard all that night; and in the morning when I looked out, behold no more ship was to be seen. I was a little surprised, but recovered myself with this satisfactory reflection; namely, that I had lost no time, nor abated any diligence, to get everything out of her that could be useful to me; and that indeed there was little left in her that I was able to bring away, if I had had more time.

I now gave over any more thoughts of the ship, or of any thing out of her, except what might drive on shore from her wreck, as indeed divers pieces of her afterwards did; but those things were of small use to me.

My thoughts were now wholly employed about securing myself against either savages (if any should appear) or wild beasts, if any were in the island; and I had many thoughts of the method how to do this, and what kind of dwelling to make; whether I should make me a cave in the earth, or a tent upon the earth; and, in short, I resolved upon both, of the manner, and description of which it may not be improper to give an account.

I soon found the place I was in was not for my settlement, particularly because it was upon a low moorish

ground near the sea, and I believed would not be whole-
some, and more particularly because there was no fresh
water near it, so I resolved to find a more healthy and
more convenient spot of ground.

I consulted several things in my situation which I found
would be proper for me. Health, and fresh water, I just
now mentioned; shelter from the heat of the sun; security
from ravenous creatures, whether man or beast; a view to
the sea, that if God sent any ship in sight, I might not lose
any advantage for my deliverance, of which I was not willing to banish all my expectation yet.

In search of a place proper for this, I found a little
plain on the side of a rising hill, whose front towards this
little plain was steep as a house-side, so that nothing could
come down upon me from the top. On the side of this
rock there was a hollow place, worn a little way in, like
the entrance or door of a cave: but there was not really
any cave or way into the rock at all.

On the flat of the green, just before this hollow place,
I resolved to pitch my tent. This plain was not above an
hundred yards broad, and about twice as long, and lay like
a green before my door, and at the end it descended irreg-
ularly every way down into the low grounds by the sea-side.
It was on the N.N.W. side of the hill, so that I was sheltered from the heat every day, till it came to a W. and by
S. sun, or thereabouts, which in those countries is near
the setting.

Before I set up my tent, I drew a half circle before the
hollow place, which took in about ten yards in its semi-

diameter, from the rock, and twenty yards in its diameter, from its beginning and ending. In this half circle I pitched two rows of strong stakes, driving them into the ground till they stood very firm, like piles, the biggest end being out of the ground about five foot and a half, and sharpened on the top; the two rows did not stand above six inches from one another.

Then I took the pieces of cable which I had cut in the ship, and laid them in rows one upon another, within the circle between these two rows of stakes, up to the top, placing other stakes in the inside, leaning against them, about two foot and a half high, like a spur to a post. And this fence was so strong, that neither man nor beast could get into it or over it. This cost me a great deal of time and labour, especially to cut the piles in the woods, bring them to the place, and drive them into the earth.

The entrance into this place I made to be not by a door, but by a short ladder to go over the top; which ladder, when I was in, I lifted over after me. And so I was completely fenced in and fortified, as I thought, from all the world, and consequently slept secure in the night, which otherwise I could not have done; though, as it appeared afterward, there was no need of all this caution from the enemies that I apprehended danger from.

ROBERT HYATT

The Terrible Stranger

Winter it was, and the night drawn down cold and dark above the white ground. The chariot tracks were deep as a man's arm. The raw wind swept across the Plain of Macha, howling spitefully around the Royal House; it beat upon doors and windows, screaming away into the night.

All was light and warmth inside. The glow of blazing logs reddened the walls and glimmered in the silver and bronze of the ornaments that adorned them. The smell of burning wood was in the air, and the voices of poets and of harps drifted from the king's chamber. The huge Warriors' Hall was a happy place this night, where a group of Knights of the Red Branch of Ulster had drawn their chairs of carved yew wood close to the fire.

Wonderful peace and contentment there was over them all—or, at any rate, contentment—for it had been a good year, this year of '64 that was closing. They talked of their victories, of the vastness of the herds and the richness of the crops of Ulster. And they didn't fail to mention how all the power and the glory of the kingdom was a credit to themselves.

Suddenly the noise of their voices ceased. And it wasn't the music that stopped them, either; nor yet that the door burst open with a great slam; nor even the big swirl of snow that blew in at them and kept whirling around the room. No, it was the terrible figure they saw standing there that put the silence on them—a tall man, big and awkward and ugly, with stooped shoulders and ravenous yellow eyes and a scraggly beard the color of peat. He had an old cowhide wrapped about him, and in his hand he held an enormous ax that he swung clumsily as he lumbered into the room.

Legair, a big man with reddish yellow hair, faced him. "What do you want?" he demanded.

The stranger glowered at him. "I am looking for a man," he rumbled, and his voice seemed to come from far down in the cowhide.

Fergus gave a twist to his red beard. "A man shouldn't be hard to find," he said. And he looked down at himself proudly. "Who are you?"

"Hoth," answered the stranger.

"H'm! Well, what sort of man is it you want?"

Hoth plucked a hair from his beard and dropped it on the gleaming edge of his ax, where it fell in two pieces.

"The man I want," he said, "is the kind that is hard to find. He is hard to find in good times, and he is hard to find in bad times. But I don't know that there is a better when he *is* found. And that is the kind who will keep an agreement."

Shane spoke up at that, a brown, gloomy man with a

fearsome voice. "You would have to go out of the kingdom to find one that wouldn't," he growled.

"An Ulsterman keeps his word," said Scel. "I remember well the time—"

"It is expected of him," Mac Roi interrupted.

Hoth looked around and his eyes seemed to see into
all the corners, even up into the black beams overhead.

"That is all I want," he said; "just the keeping of an
agreement."

"What a pity Cuchulain is not here," said Fergus. "He
is a great lad for keeping his word. There are not many
like Cuchulain and me. What sort of agreement is it you
want kept?"

"This," replied Hoth. "I am looking for a man who
will keep this agreement with me; he is to cut off my
head tonight; I to cut off his head tomorrow night."

Fergus made a neat little curl on the end of his beard.
"You give him all the advantage," he remarked.

"Advantage or no advantage," Hoth growled, "that
is the agreement: he to cut off my head tonight; I to cut
off his head tomorrow night."

"Cuchulain would like that," said Shane; "anything
that had cutting off heads in it. He would keep his agreement, too, Cuchulain would, if he were here. Not but
it is a queer enough one."

"It is the one I want," Hoth mumbled. "Where is this
Cuchulain?"

Legair got up. "Cuchulain is away now, but he is not
the only man that keeps his word," said he, and he flung

off his purple cloak. "Neither Cuchulain nor any man is the equal of myself. I am the Winner of Battles. Is there a single warrior in all Ireland that ever got the better of me? Is there one that can compare with me? Are there any ten men that are half as good as I am? Are there? You say you want me to cut off your head?"

"Mine, tonight," Hoth said solemnly; "yours, tomorrow night. That is the agreement, if you are ready to make it."

"Where is my sword?" Legair shouted. "Someone fetch me my sword!"

"You may have the ax," said Hoth.

"But what will you defend yourself with?"

"There is to be no defending ourselves. That is the agreement."

Legair thought for a moment. "You are sure that I understand you aright?" he asked. "I am to cut off your head now. Then tomorrow night you are to cut off my head?"

"That is it."

"There'll be no sending someone else and having him say he is to do it for you?"

"There will not."

Legair took the ax. "I wanted to be sure," he said. "I don't mind telling you that you are spoiling a good deal of my pleasure, in refusing to defend yourself. Would you want me to cut it off for you as you stand, or would you prefer—"

"You can please yourself," said Hoth.

"You're very accommodating," Legair said politely. He felt the blade of the ax. "That is a grand edge. If it is all the same with you, then let someone get a block of wood. You might as well be comfortable."

So a block of wood was brought, and Hoth knelt down and stretched his neck across it.

"And I to cut off your head tomorrow night," he rumbled in his thunderous voice.

"Aye," said Legair, and he winked at Scel, who had drawn his chair close and was watching very earnestly. Then Legair swung the ax high in the air, gave it a couple of twirls, and brought it down on Hoth's neck with a mighty stroke that sent the head bounding off into a corner. There it lay with its eyes catching the light of the fire and flickering little yellow flames. A log fell over in the fire, so that a sudden flare shone full on Hoth's body.

"It will be no easy matter for *him* to cut off your head tomorrow," remarked Scel, peering down at it. "I well remember the time—"

"When *I* cut off heads," Legair snorted, "they're off." And he glared defiantly about him.

"You may give me the ax now," said a voice. It was a tired-sounding voice, and not so strong as the voices of most of the Ulstermen; but there was something very familiar about it. Legair looked around quickly, but there wasn't a sound out of any of the warriors.

"My ax!" repeated the voice. Legair spun around, and there was the body of Hoth getting up from its knees. It stood for a moment in a half-puzzled sort of way; then it seemed to make up its mind, and off it walked to where the head was lying. It picked up the head and tucked it under an arm. That seemed to make Hoth feel better for, now that he had collected himself again, he came over to Legair briskly, took his ax, and started for the door.

"Tomorrow night, yours," said Hoth's head from under his arm. Then he pulled the old cowhide around him and lumbered out into the darkness.

Legair, the Battle-Winner, sat down with a thud on the block of wood that Hoth only a moment before had finished with.

"Never in all my life," said Scel, "have I seen anyone do a thing like that. I remember well the time—"

"I wonder where he comes from," interrupted Mac Roi.

"What Legair is wondering," said Shane, "is whether or not Hoth will come back."

Then Legair looked down and saw what he was sitting on; he bounded to his feet with a shout. "I've been cheated."

"Cheated?" asked Shane. "How is that?"

"What business had he picking up his head again?" Legair yelled, striding rapidly up and down the room. "Cheated!" he roared. "That's what I've been. A man has no right to pick up his head, once it has been chopped off." He felt the back of his own neck, and all the anger went out of him, leaving only sorrow.

"I never could do a thing like that," Legair continued. "I never could." He shook his head dejectedly. "Not but what it is a fine thing to be able to do. And now what a fine fix I'm in!" He gave a great sigh. "Ah, well," said he, "I'm a man who keeps his agreements." And with that he went out.

But when the next night came, there wasn't a sign of Legair, the Battle-Winner. There was the fire blazing in the huge fireplace, and there was Fergus sitting in front of it; and there was Scel and Shane; and ever so many others of the fighting men of Ulster. But not a sign of Legair.

A great deal of talk there was, too, about his not appearing. And right in the middle of it all who should arrive but Conal, the Victorious, a big stout man with fair hair that was like a bushel basket on top of his head.

Fergus nodded to him. "Ah, Conal, it's you, is it?"

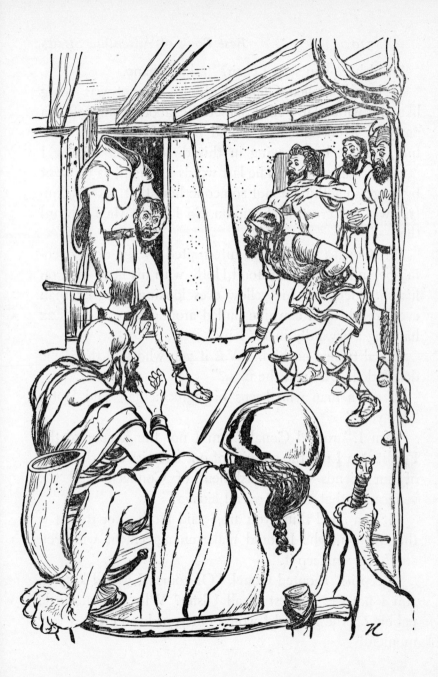

"And have you seen Legair?" asked Shane.

"I have," replied Conal; "and his chariot was going like the wind. He yelled something about going after a party of Munstermen. I would have offered to go with him, but he kept waving in this direction, so I knew I must be wanted here. The last words I caught, as he went by, were something about someone here that said Cuchulain was our greatest champion. So I knew when I heard that—"

But Conal's words were interrupted by the door opening behind him. There stood Hoth, with his head back on his shoulders and his yellow eyes looking hungrier than ever, and his old cowhide pulled around him, and his ax hanging awkwardly in his hand.

Conal turned on him. "Was it you who said that?" he demanded. "Are you the man?"

"I am a man who keeps his agreements," said Hoth. "Are you?"

"Am I?" roared Conal. "Am I not the Keeper of the Fords? Am I not the scourge of our enemies and the hope of our friends—the punishment of Connacht and the vengeance that sweeps over Leinster?"

"It is a good thing you are," said Hoth, "for if that is the truth, maybe I could make an agreement with you and have you keep it."

"Keep it!" shouted Conal. "Of course I would keep it. Am I not the greatest in all Ulster? Why, for one little pebble off the ground I would cut your head off this very moment!"

"That is the agreement I would make with you," said Hoth.

"What agreement?"

"You to cut off my head tonight; I to cut off yours tomorrow night. Would you keep that agreement?"

Conal drew his sword with a grand flourish.

"Would I?"

"I am to cut off your head tomorrow night," Hoth warned him.

"So you are!" Conal laughed as he whirled his great sword in the air and brought it across Hoth's neck like a flash of light.

"Hah!" sneered Conal. "He'll be no trouble to anyone now." And he turned his back and started to walk off. But he hadn't gone far before he noticed the queer hush that was upon everyone. He turned and saw Hoth's body getting up on its knees.

"You could have used my ax," said Hoth's head, "only you were in such a hurry." And Hoth's body picked up the head and put it carefully under its arm and walked out. With a slow sort of dignity he walked, too. It was easy to see that Hoth didn't altogether like the way he had been hurried.

"Tomorrow night, yours," said the gory head.

Conal, the Victorious, one of the greatest of all Knights of the Red Branch, sat down as if his knees had been cut from under him. Every hair in his bushy beard was standing as straight as a young pine tree.

When the next night came, there was no sign either of

Legair, the Battle-Winner, or of Conal, the Victorious. Back came Hoth, the same as before, with his yellow eyes gleaming, his old cowhide wrapped about him, ax in his hand, and his big branch over his head. There was a great host of knights gathered around the fireplace; but, when Hoth glowered around at them, there was nothing but silence.

"Well?" said Hoth in his rumbling voice.

"Aye," said Fergus. "It *is* a cold night, for a fact."

"Never mind the cold," snapped Hoth. "What about the agreement I made?"

"You made no agreement with me," Fergus said huskily, his beard sticking out like the bowsprit of a ship.

"I would, though," Hoth offered, "if I thought you would keep it."

Fergus smiled politely. "I would be glad to accommodate you, but I promised to go to Cruachan tomorrow. And I'm a great man to keep my promises. There has never been a time when anyone could say—"

That was as far as Fergus got. The door burst open with a slam that was three times as great as any slam it ever had made before. And into the room bounded a small, dark man with a gorgeous purple cloak on him.

"Cuchulain himself!" exclaimed Shane.

There stood Cuchulain, eyeing them all, his sword in his hand—his sword with its hilt of gold, its point that would bend back to the hilt, and its blade that would cut a hair on water or a man in half so swiftly that the one half wouldn't know when the other half had gone from it.

"Look here, Cuchulain," said Fergus, "they tell me a party of Connachtmen has been seen over beyond Coolgair. Wouldn't it be a good thing for you to run them out?"

"Conal has gone after them," answered Cuchulain. "Only he said it was Ath and Forair they were."

"Conal?"

"Aye, I met him, and he told me that some stranger was here, saying that I—"

Hoth walked in front of him. "It was I," he said.

"It was, was it?" shouted Cuchulain. "Defend yourself then!" And he whirled his great sword around his head.

Hoth leaned on his ax, and stood there facing Cuchulain. "I have no need for defense," said he, "so long as you'll keep your agreements." At that a red flush came to Cuchulain's face and his cheeks glowed, and his eyes shone with the warrior's flame that would come upon him in moments of anger.

"Never," he shouted, "has an agreement of mine gone unkept. Never have I turned my back on an enemy, nor on a friend, although whole armies avoid me. Forty heads with one stroke of my sword can I—"

"Cuchulain!" cried Fergus. "I wouldn't—"

"What do I care whether you would or not?" Cuchulain whirled on Fergus. "Forty heads with a single stroke—"

"It is an agreement with you that I want," interrupted Hoth, "if you'll keep it."

"Keep it?" roared Cuchulain, who was on fire with

wrath. "Keep it? I'll keep any agreement with anyone anywhere. Take your ax and defend yourself!"

"There's no need for that," replied Hoth softly. "You can cut off my head now, if you'll agree to let me cut off yours tomorrow night. That's all—"

Before anyone could say another word there was a flash like that of lightning. And there was Cuchulain letting the point of his sword come to rest on the ground, and there was Hoth standing in front of him swaying on his feet, as if a strong wind had struck him. He put one hand up to his neck, did Hoth, and he felt it; yet he could feel nothing amiss. But when he tried to turn his head, it rolled off his shoulders and tumbled to the ground.

"O Cuchulain! Cuchulain!" groaned Fergus. "How often have I warned you about your hasty temper!"

Cuchulain looked from one to the other in great puzzlement at the way they were behaving—until he happened to glance down at the body of Hoth, which was busy picking up its head. Cuchulain stood as if suddenly turned to stone.

Hoth took the head and put it under his arm, as he had done twice before, although he seemed to be more tired than ever this time. His feet dragged as he walked toward the door, and his hand shook, and he nearly dropped his ax as he drew the old cowhide around him.

"Tomorrow night, your head," said Hoth's head as he went out.

"O Cuchulain! Cuchulain!" moaned Fergus. "Will you ever—will you look at what you have done."

"Maybe Hoth will not come back," said Scel. "After all, a man can't go on getting his head cut off. There must be an end to it sometime. He'll wear out. I remember well—"

Cuchulain looked at them all in great amazement.

"It is the first time I ever saw a man pick up his own head," he said, "and hundreds of heads have fallen at my feet."

"He has done it twice before."

"Twice before?"

"Aye! Legair and Conal cut off Hoth's head, but neither of them came back for their part of the agreement. So there is no need of your—"

"I shall be here," said Cuchulain, and he drew his purple cloak around him and took a couple of steps toward the door. Then he stopped. "In fact, I'll stay here," he said.

"Now, Cuchulain, listen to me," began Fergus. "You didn't rightly know how this was going to turn out. How could you? What right has a man to put his head back on him again, after your cutting it off so beautifully? And it was *off.* I couldn't have cut it off better myself. Besides—"

Cuchulain waved him away. "It makes no difference," he said. "My agreement must be kept. I shall be here."

And he was, too, the very next night, when Hoth came in with his swirl of snow and the cold wind that caused everyone to move closer to the fire. Right in the center of Warriors' Hall Cuchulain stood, and never a move out of him, until Hoth lumbered up to him with his old cowhide steaming in the warm air and his yellow eyes burning as if there was a fire raging inside of him.

"So you're here!" said Hoth.

"I am." Cuchulain's voice was very quiet, and there was no warrior's flame in him any more.

"Ah," said Fergus, "this is a bad day that is come upon us. Why did it have to be himself that must be taken from us in all the greatness of his glory? Go, tell Conachar the way things are, Scel."

So Scel went to the Royal Chamber and told the great King Conachar of the terrible things that had come to pass, and the king hurried to Warriors' Hall, his full-moon face looking pale. For Scel had left nothing out, even in so hasty a telling of the story.

There they were then, all gathered in the Warriors' Hall, King Conachar and Fergus and a host of the greatest men of Ulster. Cuchulain stood sad and alone by a big block of wood. Hoth stood at his side.

"O Cuchulain," lamented the king, "is there no way out?"

"There is not," answered Cuchulain, "though I wish there were." And he looked all around the great hall, with its glow of ruddy lights and its deep shadows and the shields of silver and bronze hanging on the walls.

"There is no way out," he continued, "for, when a man like me gives his word, that is the end of the matter."

Then he turned to Hoth. "Is there anything keeping you?" he asked.

"There is not," said Hoth, "unless it be the need of

having you kneel down."

So Cuchulain knelt down and put his head across the block of wood, so that his neck was a fair invitation to the ax.

Hoth watched him for a moment, then he walked all around him. "Ah!" said he, thoughtfully. Then he took another walk in the other direction. "H'm!" said he.

Then Hoth took the ax and ran his fingers along the edge of the blade. "It is sharp," he remarked, and his voice was as slow as a chariot being dragged over boulders. "Yet I wonder if it is sharp enough."

"Get on with what you're doing," Cuchulain ordered.

Hoth let the ax drop to the ground with a thud, and stood there resting on the handle of it. "You would not want your head cut off with a blunt ax, would you?" he asked.

"What do I care? Get on with it!"

"But you ought to care," Hoth warned. "It makes a great difference to a man, when getting his head cut off, whether the ax is sharp or not." He plucked a hair out of his head and let it drop across the blade. "It is not dull," he said, as the hair divided itself. "Still, it is not so sharp." Then after considering for awhile he said: "Well, maybe it will do. Still I don't know. . . ."

"Will you get on?" thundered Cuchulain, his face getting redder than flames from his stooping and his thin lips beginning to twitch with anger. "How much longer must I wait?"

"Your sword was sharp, when you used it on my neck,"

said Hoth reproachfully. "But I think maybe the ax will do. Let me see now."

He raised the blade over his head and, as he raised it, he seemed to lengthen the way a shadow lengthens as the sun goes down. He raised it so high that the head of it struck the very beams of the roof; and for a moment he held it there, poised, and the red light of the fire gleamed on its edge. So great was the silence that even the logs in their blazing ceased to crackle. Then Hoth brought the ax down. In a mighty sweep it came, like a bolt falling out of the sky; only he turned the blade so that, instead of striking Cuchulain, it went past him, and the head of the ax struck the floor. It struck with such a force that every man was shaken almost out of his seat.

Cuchulain remained kneeling by the block of wood, with his neck resting upon it and his head bowed at the farther side of it.

"Ah, well," said Hoth, and his voice sounded a little less tired now, "you can get up, Cuchulain. You are the one man that kept his agreement with me; so you had better keep your head where it belongs, for it is too good a head to have rolling about on the ground. Indeed, there are few men who would rather have their necks severed than break their promises."

Hoth looked around him with a slow look. "A kingdom," said he, "cannot last long when the agreements of its people are broken."

When he looked at Conachar, the king was scowling angrily. But Fergus was chuckling softly to himself.

Then Hoth pulled his old cowhide around him. "I'm going back to Dun Curoi now," said he.

By that they knew he was not Hoth at all, but Curoi, a man deeply versed in enchantment, famous throughout Ireland for the magic spells he could cast.

The Mysterious Island

Jules Verne is probably best known for 20,000 Leagues Under the Sea, but The Mysterious Island *is still one of his most exciting books. Three years before this story opens four men and a boy, carried in their balloon by a raging storm, had been wrecked on an uncharted Pacific island. Later, they were joined by another castaway, Ayrton. By hard work and inventiveness the little group carved out a comfortable life on Lincoln Island. They lived in Granite House—a cave high up in a cliff. But with all their comforts they still yearned for home and a ship that would take them there. Finally, one day they sighted a sail. They rejoiced as it came closer and closer . . . until they made out the color of its flag—black. It was a pirate ship!*

THE PIRATE SHIP

There was no longer any doubt as to the pirates' intentions. They had dropped anchor at a short distance from the island, and it was evident that the next day by means of their boats they purposed to land on the beach!

Cyrus Harding and his companions were ready to act,

but, determined though they were, they must not forget to be prudent. Perhaps their presence might still be concealed in the event of the pirates contenting themselves with landing on the shore without examining the interior of the island. It might be, indeed, that their only intention was to obtain fresh water from the Mercy, and it was not impossible that the bridge, thrown across a mile and a half from the mouth and the manufactory at the Chimneys might escape their notice.

But why was that flag hoisted at the brig's peak? What was that shot fired for? Pure bravado doubtless, unless it was a sign of the act of taking possession. Harding knew now that the vessel was well armed. And what had the colonists of Lincoln Island to reply to the pirates' guns? A few muskets only.

"However," observed Cyrus Harding, "here we are in an impregnable position. The enemy cannot discover the mouth of the outlet, now that it is hidden under reeds and grass, and consequently it would be impossible for them to penetrate into Granite House."

"But our plantations, our poultry-yard, our corral, all, everything!" exclaimed Pencroft, stamping his foot. "They may spoil everything, destroy everything in a few hours!"

"Everything, Pencroft," answered Harding, "and we have no means of preventing them."

"Are they numerous? that is the question," said Gideon Spilett. "If they are not more than a dozen, we shall be able to stop them, but forty, fifty, more perhaps!"

"Captain Harding," then said Ayrton, advancing towards the engineer, "will you give me leave?"

"For what, my friend?"

"To go to that vessel to find out the strength of her crew."

"But Ayrton—" answered the engineer, hesitating, "you will risk your life—"

"Why not, sir?"

"That is more than your duty."

"I have more than my duty to do," replied Ayrton.

"Will you go to the ship in the boat?" asked Gideon Spilett.

"No, sir, but I will swim. A boat would be seen where a man may glide between wind and water."

"Do you know that the brig is a mile and a quarter from the shore?" said Herbert.

"I am a good swimmer, Mr. Herbert."

"I tell you it is risking your life," said the engineer.

"That is no matter," answered Ayrton. "Captain Harding, I ask this as a favor. Perhaps it will be a means of raising me in my own eyes!"

"Go, Ayrton," replied the engineer, who felt sure that a refusal would have deeply wounded the former convict, now become an honest man.

"I will accompany you," said Pencroft.

"You mistrust me!" said Ayrton quickly.

Then more humbly,—

"Alas!"

"No! no!" exclaimed Harding with animation, "no, Ayrton, Pencroft does not mistrust you. You interpret his words wrongly."

"Indeed," returned the sailor, "I only propose to accompany Ayrton as far as the islet. It may be, although it is scarcely possible, that one of these villains has landed, and in that case two men will not be too many to hinder him from giving the alarm. I will wait for Ayrton on the islet, and he shall go alone to the vessel, since he has proposed to do so." These things agreed to, Ayrton made preparations for his departure. His plan was bold, but it might succeed, thanks to the darkness of the night. Once arrived at the vessel's side, Ayrton, holding on to the main chains, might reconnoiter the number and perhaps overhear the intentions of the pirates.

Ayrton and Pencroft, followed by their companions, descended to the beach. Ayrton undressed and rubbed himself with grease, so as to suffer less from the temperature of the water, which was still cold. He might, indeed, be obliged to remain in it for several hours.

Pencroft and Neb, during this time, had gone to fetch the boat, moored a few hundred feet higher up, on the bank of the Mercy, and by the time they returned, Ayrton was ready to start. A coat was thrown over his shoulders, and the settlers all came round him to press his hand.

Ayrton then shoved off with Pencroft in the boat.

It was half-past ten in the evening when the two adventurers disappeared in the darkness. Their companions returned to wait at the Chimneys.

The channel was easily traversed, and the boat touched the opposite shore of the islet. This was not done without precaution, for fear lest the pirates might be roaming

about there. But after a careful survey, it was evident that
the islet was deserted. Ayrton then, followed by Pencroft,
crossed it with a rapid step, scaring the birds nestled in
the holes of the rocks; then, without hesitating, he
plunged into the sea, and swam noiselessly in the direction
of the ship, in which a few lights had recently appeared,
showing her exact situation. As to Pencroft, he crouched
down in a cleft of the rock, and awaited the return of his
companion.

In the meanwhile, Ayrton, swimming with a vigorous
stroke, glided through the sheet of water without produc-
ing the slightest ripple. His head just emerged above it
and his eyes were fixed on the dark hull of the brig, from
which the lights were reflected in the water. He thought
only of the duty which he had promised to accomplish,
and nothing of the danger which he ran, not only on board
the ship, but in the sea, often frequented by sharks. The
current bore him along and he rapidly receded from the
shore.

Half an hour afterwards, Ayrton, without having been
either seen or heard, arrived at the ship and caught hold
of the main-chains. He took breath, then, hoisting himself up, he managed to reach the extremity of the cutwater. There were drying several pairs of sailors' trousers.
He put on a pair. Then settling himself firmly, he listened.
They were not sleeping on board the brig. On the contrary, they were talking, singing, laughing. And these were
the sentences, accompanied with oaths, which principally
struck Ayrton:—

"Our brig is a famous acquisition."

"She sails well, and merits her name of the 'Speedy.' "

"She would show all the navy of Norfolk a clean pair of heels."

"Hurrah for her captain!"

"Hurrah for Bob Harvey!"

What Ayrton felt when he overheard this fragment of conversation may be understood when it is known that in this Bob Harvey he recognized one of his old Australian companions, a daring sailor, who had continued his criminal career. Bob Harvey had seized, on the shores of Norfolk Island, this brig, which was loaded with arms, ammunition, utensils, and tools of all sorts, destined for one of the Sandwich Islands. All his gang had gone on board, and pirates after having been convicts, these wretches, more ferocious than the Malays themselves, scoured the Pacific, destroying vessels, and massacring their crews.

The convicts spoke loudly, they recounted their deeds, drinking deeply at the same time, and this is what Ayrton gathered. The actual crew of the "Speedy" was composed solely of English prisoners, escaped from Norfolk Island. It would be difficult to imagine a collection of greater ruffians. Sometimes,—although very rarely,—not withstanding the extreme surveillance of which they were the object, many managed to escape, and seizing vessels which they surprised, they infested the Polynesian Archipelagoes.

Thus had Bob Harvey and his companions done. Thus had Ayrton formerly wished to do. Bob Harvey had seized the brig "Speedy," anchored in sight of Norfolk Island; the crew had been massacred; and for a year this ship had scoured the Pacific, under the command of Harvey, now a pirate, and well known to Ayrton!

The convicts were, for the most part, assembled under the poop; but a few, stretched on the deck, were talking loudly.

The conversation still continued amid shouts and libations. Ayrton learned that chance alone had brought the "Speedy" in sight of Lincoln Island; Bob Harvey had never yet set foot on it; but, as Cyrus Harding had conjectured, finding this unknown land in his course, its position being marked on no chart, he had formed the project of visiting it, and, if he found it suitable, of making it the brig's headquarters.

As to the black flag hoisted at the "Speedy's" peak, and the gun which had been fired, in imitation of men-of-war when they lower their colors, it was pure piratical bravado. It was in no way a signal, and no communication yet existed between the convicts and Lincoln Island.

The settlers' domain was now menaced with terrible danger. Evidently the island, with its water, its harbor, its resources of all kinds so increased in value by the colonists, and the concealment afforded by Granite House, could not but be convenient for the convicts. In their hands it would become an excellent place of refuge, and, being unknown, it would assure them, for a long time perhaps, impunity and security. Evidently, also, the lives of the settlers would not be respected, and Bob Harvey and his accomplices' first care would be to massacre them without mercy. Harding and his companions had, therefore, not even the choice of flying and hiding themselves in the island, since the convicts intended to reside there, and since, in the event of the "Speedy" departing on an expedition, it was probable that some of the crew would remain on shore, so as to settle themselves there. Therefore, it would be necessary to fight, to destroy every one of these scoundrels, unworthy of pity, and against whom any means would be right. So thought Ayrton, and he well knew that Cyrus Harding would be of his way of thinking.

But was resistance and, in the last place, victory possible? That would depend on the equipment of the brig, and the number of men which she carried.

This Ayrton resolved to learn at any cost, and as an hour after his arrival the vociferations had begun to die away, and as a large number of the convicts were already buried in a drunken sleep, Ayrton did not hesitate to venture onto the "Speedy's" deck, which the extinguished lanterns now left in total darkness. He hoisted himself onto the cutwater, and by the bowsprit arrived at the forecastle. Then, gliding among the convicts stretched here and there, he made the round of the ship, and found that the "Speedy" carried four guns, which would throw shot of from eight to ten pounds in weight. He found also, on touching them, that these guns were breech-loaders. They were, therefore, of modern make, easily used, and of terrible effect.

As to the men lying on the deck, they were about ten in number, but it was to be supposed that more were sleeping down below. Besides, by listening to them, Ayrton had understood that there were fifty on board. That was a large number for the six settlers of Lincoln Island to contend with! But now, thanks to Ayrton's devotion, Cyrus Harding would not be surprised, he would know the strength of his adversaries, and would make his arrangements accordingly.

There was nothing more for Ayrton to do but to return, and render to his companions an account of the mission with which he had charged himself, and he prepared to regain the bows of the brig, so that he might let himself down into the water.

But to this man, whose wish was, as he had said, to do more than his duty, there came an heroic thought. This was to sacrifice his own life, but save the island and the colonists. Cyrus Harding evidently could not resist fifty ruffians, all well armed, who, either by penetrating by main force into Granite House, or by starving out the besieged, could obtain from them what they wanted. And then he thought of his preservers—those who had made him again a man, and an honest man, those to whom he owed all—murdered without pity, their works destroyed, their island turned into a pirates' den! He said to himself that he, Ayrton, was the principal cause of so many disasters, since his old companion, Bob Harvey, had but realized his own plans, and a feeling of horror took possession of him. Then he was seized with an irresistible desire to blow up the brig, and with her, all whom she had on board. He would perish in the explosion, but he would have done his duty.

Ayrton did not hesitate. To reach the powder-room, which is always situated in the after-part of a vessel, was easy. There would be no want of powder in a vessel which followed such a trade, and a spark would be enough to destroy it in an instant.

Ayrton stole carefully along the between-decks, strewn with numerous sleepers, overcome more by drunkenness than sleep. A lantern was lighted at the foot of the main-mast, round which was hung a gun-rack, furnished with weapons of all sorts.

Ayrton took a revolver from the rack, and assured himself that it was loaded and primed. Nothing more was needed to accomplish the work of destruction. He then glided towards the stern, so as to arrive under the brig's poop at the powder-magazine.

It was difficult to proceed along the dimly lighted deck without stumbling over some half-sleeping convict, who retorted by oaths and kicks. Ayrton was, therefore, more than once obliged to halt. But at last he arrived at the partition dividing the after-cabin, and found the door opening into the magazine itself.

Ayrton, compelled to force it open, set to work. It was a difficult operation to perform without noise, for he had to break a padlock. But under his vigorous hand, the padlock broke, and the door was open.

At that moment a hand was laid on Ayrton's shoulder.

"What are you doing here?" asked a tall man, in a harsh voice, who, standing in the shadow, quickly threw the light of a lantern on Ayrton's face.

Ayrton drew back. In the rapid flash of the lantern, he had recognized his former accomplice, Bob Harvey, who could not have known him, as he must have thought Ayrton long since dead.

"What are you doing here?" again said Bob Harvey, seizing Ayrton by the waistband.

But Ayrton, without replying, wrenched himself from his grasp and attempted to rush into the magazine. A shot fired into the midst of the powder-casks, and all would be over!

"Help, lads!" shouted Bob Harvey.

At his shout two or three pirates awoke, jumped up, and, rushing on Ayrton, endeavored to throw him down. He soon extricated himself from their grasp. He fired his revolver, and two of the convicts fell, but a glow from a knife which he could not ward off made a gash in his shoulder.

Ayrton perceived that he could no longer hope to carry out his project. Bob Harvey had reclosed the door of the powder-magazine, and a movement on the deck indicated a general awakening of the pirates. Ayrton must reserve himself to fight at the side of Cyrus Harding. There was nothing for him but flight!

But was flight still possible? It was doubtful, yet Ayrton resolved to dare everything in order to rejoin his companions.

Four barrels of the revolver were still undischarged. Two were fired—one, aimed at Bob Harvey, did not wound him, or at any rate only slightly, and Ayrton, profiting by the momentary retreat of his adversaries, rushed towards the companion-ladder to gain the deck. Passing before the lantern, he smashed it with a blow from the butt of his revolver. A profound darkness ensued, which favored his flight. Two or three pirates, awakened by the noise, were descending the ladder at the same moment. A fifth shot from Ayrton laid one low, and the others drew back, not understanding what was going on. Ayrton was on deck in two bounds, and three seconds later, having discharged his last barrel in the face of a pirate who was about to seize him by the throat, he leaped over the bulwarks into the sea.

Ayrton had not made six strokes before shots were splashing around him like hail.

What were Pencroft's feelings, sheltered under a rock on the islet! what were those of Harding, the reporter, Herbert, and Neb, crouched in the Chimneys, when they heard the reports on board the brig! They rushed out on to the beach, and, their guns shouldered, they stood ready to repel any attack.

They had no doubt about it themselves! Ayrton, surprised by the pirates, had been murdered, and, perhaps, the wretches would profit by the night to make a descent on the island!

Half an hour was passed in terrible anxiety. The firing had ceased, and yet neither Ayrton nor Pencroft had reappeared. Was the islet invaded? Ought they not to fly to the help of Ayrton and Pencroft? But how? The tide being high at that time, rendered the channel impassable. The boat was not there! We may imagine the horrible anxiety which took possession of Harding and his companions!

At last, towards half-past twelve, a boat, carrying two men, touched the beach. It was Ayrton, slightly wounded in the shoulder, and Pencroft, safe and sound, whom their friends received with open arms.

All immediately took refuge in the Chimneys. There Ayrton recounted all that had passed, even to his plan for blowing up the brig, which he had attempted to put into execution.

All hands were extended to Ayrton, who did not conceal from them that their situation was serious. The pirates had been alarmed. They knew that Lincoln Island was inhabited. They would land upon it in numbers and well armed. They would respect nothing. Should the settlers fall into their hands, they must expect no mercy!

"Well, we shall know how to die!" said the reporter.

"Let us go in and watch," answered the engineer.

"Have we any chance of escape, captain?" asked the sailor.

"Yes, Pencroft."

"Hum! six against fifty!"

"Yes! six! without counting—"

"Who?" asked Pencroft.

Cyrus did not reply, but pointed upwards.

The night passed without incident. The colonists were on the *qui vive*, and did not leave their post at the Chimneys. The pirates, on their side, did not appear to have made any attempt to land. Since the last shots fired at Ayrton not a report, not even a sound, had betrayed the presence of the brig in the neighborhood of the island. It might have been fancied that she had weighed anchor, thinking that she had to deal with her match, and had left the coast.

But it was no such thing, and when day began to dawn the settlers could see a confused mass through the morning mist. It was the "Speedy."

"These, my friends," said the engineer, "are the arrangements which appear to me best to make before the fog completely clears away. It hides us from the eyes of the pirates, and we can act without attracting their attention. The most important thing is, that the convicts should believe that the inhabitants of the island are numerous, and consequently capable of resisting them. I therefore propose that we divide into three parties, the first of which shall be posted at the Chimneys, the second at the mouth of the Mercy. As to the third, I think it would be best to place it on the islet, so as to prevent, or at all events delay, any attempt at landing. We have the use of two rifles and four muskets. Each of us will be armed, and, as we are amply provided with powder and shot, we need not spare our fire. We have nothing to fear from the muskets nor even from the guns of the brig. What can they do against these rocks? And, as we shall not fire from the windows of

Granite House, the pirates will not think of causing ir-
reparable damage by throwing shell against it. What is to
be feared is, the necessity of meeting hand-to-hand, since
the convicts have numbers on their side. We must therefore, try to prevent them from landing, but without dis-
covering ourselves. Therefore, do not economize the ammunition. Fire often, but with a sure aim. We have each
eight or ten enemies to kill, and they must be killed!"

Cyrus Harding had clearly represented their situation,
although he spoke in the calmest voice, as if it was a question of directing a piece of work, and not ordering a battle.
His companions approved these arrangements without
even uttering a word. There was nothing more to be done
but for each to take his place before the fog should be
completely dissipated. Neb and Pencroft immediately
ascended to Granite House and brought back a sufficient
quantity of ammunition. Gideon Spilett and Ayrton, both
very good marksmen, were armed with the two rifles,
which carried nearly a mile. The four other muskets were
divided among Harding, Neb, Pencroft, and Herbert.

The posts were arranged in the following manner:—

Cyrus Harding and Herbert remained in ambush at
the Chimneys, thus commanding the shore to the foot of
Granite House.

Gideon Spilett and Neb crouched among the rocks at
the mouth of the Mercy, from which the drawbridges
had been raised, so as to prevent any one from crossing
in a boat or landing on the opposite shore.

As to Ayrton and Pencroft, they shoved off in the boat,

and prepared to cross the channel and to take up two separate stations on the islet. In this way, shots being fired from four different points at once, the convicts would be led to believe that the island was both largely peopled and strongly defended.

In the event of a landing being effected without their having been able to prevent it, and also if they saw that they were on the point of being cut off by the brig's boat, Ayrton and Pencroft were to return in their boat to the shore and proceed towards the threatened spot.

Before starting to occupy their posts, the colonists for the last time wrung each other's hands.

Pencroft succeeded in controlling himself sufficiently to suppress his emotion when he embraced Herbert, his boy! and then they separated.

In a few moments Harding and Herbert on one side, Spilett and Neb on the other, had disappeared behind the rocks, and five minutes later Ayrton and Pencroft, having without difficulty crossed the channel, disembarked on the islet and concealed themselves in the clefts of its eastern shore.

None of them could have been seen, for they themselves could scarcely distinguish the brig in the fog.

It was half-past six in the morning.

Soon the fog began to clear away, and the topmasts of the brig issued from the vapor. For some minutes great masses rolled over the surface of the sea, then a breeze sprang up, which rapidly dispelled the mist.

The "Speedy" now appeared in full view, with a spring

on her cable, her head to the north, presenting her larboard side to the island. Just as Harding had calculated, she was not more than a mile and a quarter from the coast.

The sinister black flag floated from the peak.

The engineer, with his telescope, could see that the four guns on board were pointed at the island. They were evidently ready to fire at a moment's notice.

In the meanwhile the "Speedy" remained silent. About thirty pirates could be seen moving on the deck. A few were on the poop; two others posted in the shrouds, and armed with spy-glasses, were attentively surveying the island.

Certainly, Bob Harvey and his crew would not be able easily to give an account of what had happened during the night on board the brig. Had this half-naked man, who had forced the door of the powder-magazine, and with whom they had struggled, who had six times discharged his revolver at them, who had killed one and wounded two others, escaped their shot? Had he been able to swim to shore? Whence did he come? What had been his object? Had his design really been to blow up the brig, as Bob Harvey had thought? All this must be confused enough to the convicts' minds. But what they could no longer doubt was that the unknown island before which the "Speedy" had cast anchor was inhabited, and that there was, perhaps, a numerous colony ready to defend it. And yet no one was to be seen, neither on the shore, nor on the heights. The beach appeared to be absolutely deserted. At any rate, there was no trace of dwellings. Had the inhabitants fled into the interior? Thus probably the pirate captain reasoned, and doubtless, like a prudent man, he wished to reconnoiter the locality before he allowed his men to venture there.

During an hour and a half, no indication of attack or landing could be observed on board the brig. Evidently Bob Harvey was hesitating. Even with his strongest telescopes he could not have perceived one of the settlers crouched among the rocks. It was not even probable that his attention had been awakened by the screen of green branches and creepers hiding the windows of Granite House, and showing rather conspicuously on the bare rock. Indeed, how could he imagine that a dwelling was hollowed out, at that height, in the solid granite. From Claw Cape to the Mandible Capes, in all the extent of Union Bay, there was nothing to lead him to suppose that the island was or could be inhabited.

At eight o'clock, however, the colonists observed a movement on board the "Speedy." A boat was lowered, and seven men jumped into her. They were armed with muskets; one took the yoke-lines, four others the oars, and the two others, kneeling in the bows, ready to fire, reconnoitered the island. Their object was no doubt to make an examination but not to land, for in the latter case they would have come in larger numbers. The pirates from their look-out could have seen that the coast was sheltered by an islet, separated from it by a channel half a mile in width. However, it was soon evident to Cyrus Harding, on observing the direction followed by the boat, that they would not attempt to penetrate into the channel, but would land on the islet.

Pencroft and Ayrton, each hidden in a narrow cleft of the rock, saw them coming directly towards them, and waited till they were within range.

The boat advanced with extreme caution. The oars only dipped into the water at long intervals. It could now be seen that one of the convicts held a lead-line in his hand, and that he wished to fathom the depth of the channel hollowed out by the current of the Mercy. This showed that it was Bob Harvey's intention to bring his brig as near as possible to the coast. About thirty pirates, scattered in the rigging, followed every movement of the boat, and took the bearings of certain landmarks which would allow them to approach without danger. The boat was not more than two cables-lengths off the islet when she stopped. The man at the tiller stood up and looked for the best place at which to land.

At that moment two shots were heard. Smoke curled up from among the rocks of the islet. The man at the helm and the man with the lead-line fell backwards into the boat. Ayrton's and Pencroft's balls had struck them both at the same moment.

Almost immediately a louder report was heard, a cloud of smoke issued from the brig's side, and a ball, striking the summit of the rock which sheltered Ayrton and Pencroft, made it fly in splinters, but the two marksmen remained unhurt.

Horrible imprecations burst from the boat, which im-

mediately continued its way. The man who had been at
the tiller was replaced by one of his comrades, and the oars
were rapidly plunged into the water. However, instead
of returning on board as might have been expected, the
boat coasted along the islet, so as to round its southern
point. The pirates pulled vigorously at their oars that they
might get out of range of the bullets.

They advanced to within five cables-lengths of that
part of the shore terminated by Flotsam Point, and after
having rounded it in a semicircular line, still protected by
the brig's guns, they proceeded towards the mouth of the
Mercy.

Their evident intention was to penetrate into the channel, and cut off the colonists posted on the islet, in such a
way, that whatever their number might be, being placed
between the fire from the boat and the fire from the brig,
they would find themselves in a very disadvantageous position.

A quarter of an hour passed while the boat advanced
in this direction. Absolute silence, perfect calm reigned
in the air and on the water.

Pencroft and Ayrton, although they knew they ran the
risk of being cut off, had not left their post, both that they
did not wish to show themselves as yet to their assailants,
and expose themselves to the "Speedy's" guns, and that
they relied on Neb and Gideon Spilett, watching at the
mouth of the river, and on Cyrus Harding and Herbert,
in ambush among the rocks at the Chimneys.

Twenty minutes after the first shots were fired, the boat

was less than two cables-lengths off the Mercy. As the tide
was beginning to rise with its accustomed violence, caused
by the narrowness of the straits, the pirates were drawn
towards the river, and it was only by dint of hard rowing
that they were able to keep in the middle of the channel.
But, as they were passing within good range of the mouth
of the Mercy, two balls saluted them, and two more of
their number were laid in the bottom of the boat. Neb
and Spilett had not missed their aim.

The brig immediately sent a second ball on the post
betrayed by the smoke, but without any other result than
that of splintering the rock.

The boat now contained only three able men. Carried
on by the current, it shot through the channel with the
rapidity of an arrow, passed before Harding and Herbert,
who, not thinking it within range, withheld their fire,
then, rounding the northern point of the islet with the
two remaining oars, they pulled towards the brig.

Hitherto the settlers had nothing to complain of. Their
adversaries had certainly had the worst of it. The latter already counted four men seriously wounded if not dead;
they, on the contrary, unwounded, had not missed a shot.
If the pirates continued to attack them in this way, if they
renewed their attempt to land by means of a boat, they
could be destroyed one by one.

It was now seen how advantageous the engineer's arrangements had been. The pirates would think that they
had to deal with numerous and well-armed adversaries,
whom they could not easily get the better of.

Half an hour passed before the boat, having to pull against the current, could get alongside the "Speedy." Frightful cries were heard when they returned on board with the wounded, and two or three guns were fired with no result.

But now about a dozen other convicts, maddened with rage, and possibly by the effect of the evening's potations, threw themselves into the boat. A second boat was also lowered, in which eight men took their places, and while the first pulled straight for the islet, to dislodge the colonists from thence the second maneuvered so as to force the entrance of the Mercy.

The situation was evidently becoming very dangerous for Pencroft and Ayrton, and they saw that they must regain the mainland.

However, they waited till the first boat was within range, when two well-directed balls threw its crew into disorder. Then, Pencroft and Ayrton, abandoning their posts, under fire from the dozen muskets, ran across the islet at full speed, jumped into their boat, crossed the channel at the moment the second boat reached the southern end, and ran to hide themselves in the Chimneys.

They had scarcely rejoined Cyrus Harding and Herbert, before the islet was overrun with pirates in every direction. Almost at the same moment, fresh reports resounded from the Mercy station, to which the second boat was rapidly approaching. Two, out of the eight men who manned her, were mortally wounded by Gideon

Spilett and Neb, and the boat herself, carried irresistibly onto the reefs, was stove in at the mouth of the Mercy. But the six survivors, holding their muskets above their heads to preserve them from contact with the water, managed to land on the right bank of the river. Then, finding they were exposed to the fire of the ambush there, they fled in the direction of Flotsam Point, out of range of the balls.

The actual situation was this: on the islet were a dozen convicts, of whom some were no doubt wounded, but who had still a boat at their disposal; on the island were six, but who could not by any possibility reach Granite House, as they could not cross the river, all the bridges being raised.

"Hallo," exclaimed Pencroft as he rushed into the Chimneys, "hallo, captain! What do you think of it, now?"

"I think," answered the engineer, "that the combat will now take a new form, for it cannot be supposed that the convicts will be so foolish as to remain in a position so unfavorable for them!"

"They won't cross the channel," said the sailor. "Ayrton and Mr. Spilett's rifles are there to prevent them. You know that they carry more than a mile!"

"No doubt," replied Herbert; "but what can two rifles do against the brig's guns?"

"Well, the brig isn't in the channel yet, I fancy!" said Pencroft.

"But suppose she does come there?" said Harding.

"That's impossible, for she would risk running aground and being lost!"

"It is possible," said Ayrton. "The convicts might profit by the high tide to enter the channel, with the risk of grounding at low tide, it is true; but then, under the fire from her guns, our posts would be no longer tenable."

"Confound them!" exclaimed Pencroft, "it really seems as if the blackguards were preparing to weigh anchor."

"Perhaps we shall be obliged to take refuge in Granite House!" observed Herbert.

"We must wait!" answered Cyrus Harding.

"But Mr. Spilett and Neb?" said Pencroft.

"They will know when it is best to rejoin us. Be ready, Ayrton. It is yours and Spilett's rifles which must speak now."

It was only too true. The "Speedy" was beginning to weigh her anchor, and her intention was evidently to approach the islet. The tide would be rising for an hour and a half, and the ebb current being already weakened, it would be easy for the brig to advance. But as to entering the channel, Pencroft, contrary to Ayrton's opinion, could not believe that she would dare to attempt it.

In the meanwhile, the pirates who occupied the islet had gradually advanced to the opposite shore, and were now only separated from the mainland by the channel.

Being armed with muskets alone, they could do no harm to the settlers, in ambush at the Chimneys and the mouth of the Mercy; but, not knowing the latter to be supplied with long range rifles, they on their side did not believe themselves to be exposed. Quite uncovered, therefore, they surveyed the islet, and examined the shore.

Their illusion was of short duration. Ayrton's and Gideon Spilett's rifles then spoke, and no doubt imparted some very disagreeable intelligence to two of the convicts, for they fell backwards.

Then there was a general helter-skelter. The ten others, not even stopping to pick up their dead or wounded companions, fled to the other side of the islet, tumbled into the boat which had brought them, and pulled away with all their strength.

"Eight less!" exclaimed Pencroft. "Really, one would have thought that Mr. Spilett and Ayrton had given the word to fire together!"

"Gentlemen," said Ayrton, as he reloaded his gun, "this is becoming more serious. The brig is making sail!"

"The anchor is weighed!" exclaimed Pencroft.

"Yes, and she is already moving."

In fact, they could distinctly hear the creaking of the windlass. The "Speedy" was at first held by her anchor; then, when that had been raised, she began to drift towards the shore. The wind was blowing from the sea; the jib and the fore-topsail were hoisted, and the vessel gradually approached the island.

From the two posts of the Mercy and the Chimneys they watched her without giving a sign of life, but not without some emotion. What could be more terrible for the colonists than to be exposed, at a short distance, to the brig's guns, without being able to reply with any effect? How could they then prevent the pirates from landing?

Cyrus Harding felt this strongly, and he asked himself what it would be possible to do. Before long, he would be called upon for his determination. But what was it to be? To shut themselves up in Granite House, to be besieged there, to remain there for weeks, for months even, since they had an abundance of provisions? So far good! But after that? The pirates would not the less be masters of the island, which they would ravage at their pleasure, and in time, they would end by having their revenge on the prisoners in Granite House.

However, one chance yet remained; it was that Bob Harvey, after all, would not venture his ship into the channel, and that he would keep outside the islet. He would be still separated from the coast by half a mile, and at that distance his shot could not be very destructive.

"Never!" repeated Pencroft, "Bob Harvey will never, if he is a good seaman, enter that channel! He knows well that it would risk the brig, if the sea got up ever so little! And what would become of him without his vessel?"

In the meanwhile the brig approached the islet, and it could be seen that she was endeavoring to make the lower end. The breeze was light, and as the current had then lost much of its force, Bob Harvey had absolute command over his vessel.

The route previously followed by the boats had allowed her to reconnoiter the channel, and she boldly entered it.

The pirate's design was now only too evident; he wished to bring her broadside to bear on the Chimneys and from there to reply with shell and ball to the shot which had till then decimated her crew.

Soon the "Speedy" reached the point of the islet; she rounded it with ease; the mainsail was braced up, and the brig hugging the wind, stood across the mouth of the Mercy.

"The scoundrels! they are coming!" said Pencroft.

At that moment, Cyrus Harding, Ayrton, the sailor, and Herbert, were rejoined by Neb and Gideon Spilett.

The reporter and his companion had judged it best to abandon the post at the Mercy, from which they could do nothing against the ship, and they had acted wisely. It was better that the colonists should be together at the moment when they were about to engage in a decisive action. Gideon Spilett and Neb had arrived by dodging behind the rocks, though not without attracting a shower of bullets, which had not, however, reached them.

"Spilett! Neb!" cried the engineer. "You are not wounded?"

"No," answered the reporter, "a few bruises only from the ricochet! But that cursed brig has entered the channel!"

"Yes," replied Pencroft, "and in ten minutes she will have anchored before Granite House!"

"Have you formed any plan, Cyrus?" asked the reporter.

"We must take refuge in Granite House while there is still time, and the convicts cannot see us."

"That is my opinion, too," replied Gideon Spilett, "but once shut up—"

"We must be guided by circumstances," said the engineer.

"Let us be off, then, and make haste!" said the reporter.

"Would you not wish, captain, that Ayrton and I should remain here?" asked the sailor.

"What would be the use of that, Pencroft?" replied Harding. "No. We will not separate!"

There was not a moment to be lost. The colonists left the Chimneys. A bend of the cliff prevented them from being seen by those in the brig, but two or three reports, and the crash of bullets on the rock, told them that the "Speedy" was at no great distance.

To spring into the lift, hoist themselves up to the door of Granite House, to rush into the large room, was the work of a minute only.

It was quite time, for the settlers, through the branches, could see the "Speedy," surrounded with smoke, gliding up the channel. The firing was incessant, and shot from the four guns struck blindly, both on the Mercy post, although it was not occupied, and on the Chimneys. The rocks were splintered, and cheers accompanied each discharge. However, they were hoping that Granite House would be spared, thanks to Harding's precaution of concealing the windows, when a shot, piercing the door, penetrated into the passage.

"We are discovered!" exclaimed Pencroft.

The colonists had not, perhaps, been seen, but it was certain that Bob Harvey had thought proper to send a ball through the suspected foliage which concealed that part of the cliff. Soon he redoubled his attack, when another ball having torn away the leafy screen, disclosed a gaping aperture in the granite.

The colonists' situation was desperate. Their retreat was discovered. They could not oppose any obstacle to these missiles, nor protect the stone, which flew in splinters around them. There was nothing to be done but to take refuge in the upper passage of Granite House, and leave their dwelling to be devastated, when a deep roar was heard, followed by frightful cries!

Cyrus Harding and his companions rushed to one of the windows—

The brig irresistibly raised on a sort of water-spout, had just split in two, and in less than ten seconds she was swallowed up with all her criminal crew!

from SIR JOHN HUNT'S

The Conquest
of Everest

Mount Everest, the tallest peak on the surface of the earth, has always been a symbol of the unknown and the unobtainable. There have been legends about an enchanted "keep" beyond which no man could pass; and of an "abominable snowman," a kind of prehistoric man-eating creature who lived on its slopes. Between 1922 and 1954 eleven major expeditions attempted to reach its peak. All had failed—several within a thousand feet of the top. In 1954 a British expedition led by Sir John Hunt finally conquered the unconquerable. Two of the younger members of the party, Sir Edmund Hillary and the Sherpa guide Tenzing, were chosen to make the final ascent—and the results were announced to the world on the coronation day of Queen Elizabeth II. This chapter which describes the final successful assault on the summit is written by Sir Edmund Hillary.

THE SUMMIT

Early on the morning of May 27th I awoke from an uneasy sleep feeling very cold and miserable. We were

on the South Col of Everest. My companions in our Pyra-
mid tent, Lowe, Gregory, and Tenzing, were all tossing
and turning in unsuccessful efforts to gain relief from the
bitter cold. The relentless wind was blowing in all its fury
and the constant loud drumming on the tent made deep
sleep impossible. Reluctantly removing my hand from my
sleeping bag, I looked at my watch. It was 4 A.M. In the
flickering light of a match, the thermometer lying against
the tent wall read -25° Centigrade [13 below zero].

We had hoped to establish a camp high on the southeast ridge that day, but the force of the wind obviously
made a start impossible. We must, however, be prepared
to go on if the wind should drop. I nudged the uncom-
plaining Tenzing with my elbow and murmured a few
words about food and drink, then callously snuggled my
way back into my bag again. Soon the purring of the Primus and the general warming of the atmosphere stirred
us into life and while we munched biscuits and drank hot
water flavored with lemon crystals and heaps of sugar,
Lowe, Gregory, and I discussed rather pessimistically our
plans for the day.

At 9 A.M. the wind was still blowing fiercely, and clad
in all my warm clothing I crawled out of the tent and
crossed to the small Meade tent housing John Hunt,
Charles Evans, and Tom Bourdillon. Hunt agreed that
any start under these conditions was impossible. Ang
Temba had become sick and was obviously incapable of
carrying up any farther. So we decided to send him down
with Evans and Bourdillon when they left for Camp VII

about midday. Hunt decided at the last moment to accompany this party, owing to Bourdillon's condition, and Lowe and I assisted a very weary foursome to climb the slopes above the camp and then watched them start off on their slow and exhausting trip down to Camp VII.

All day the wind blew furiously and it was in a somewhat desperate spirit that we organized the loads for the establishment of the ridge camp on the following day. Any delay in our departure from the South Col could only result in increased deterioration and consequent weakness. The violent wind gave us another unpleasant night, but we were all breathing oxygen at one liter per minute and this enabled us to doze uneasily for seven or eight hours.

Early in the morning the wind was still blowing strongly, but about 8 A.M. it ceased considerably and we decided to leave. However, another blow had fallen— Pemba had been violently ill all night and was obviously not capable of going on. Only one Sherpa porter, Ang Nyima, was left to carry for us out of our original band of three. Our only alternative was to carry the camp ourselves, as to abandon the attempt was unthinkable. We repacked the loads, eliminating anything not vitally necessary and having no choice because of our reduced manpower but to cut down vital supplies of oxygen.

At 8.45 A.M. Lowe, Gregory, and Ang Nyima departed, all carrying over forty pounds each and breathing oxygen at four liters a minute. Tenzing and I were to leave later so that we could follow quickly up the steps made by the other party and so conserve energy and oxygen. We loaded all our personal clothing, sleeping bags, and air mattresses, together with some food, onto our oxygen sets and left at 10 A.M., carrying fifty pounds apiece.

We followed slowly up the long slopes to the foot of the great couloir and then climbed the veritable staircase hewn by Lowe in the firm steep snow of the couloir. As we moved slowly up the steps we were bombarded by a constant stream of ice chips falling from well above us where Lowe and Gregory were cutting steps across to the southeast ridge. We reached the ridge at midday and joined the other party. Nearby was the tattered ruin of the Swiss tent of the previous spring, and it added an air of loneliness and desolation to this remarkable viewpoint. From here Lambert and Tenzing had made their gallant attempt to reach the summit after a night spent without sleeping bags.

It was a wonderful spot with tremendous views in every direction and we indulged in an orgy of photography. We were all feeling extremely well and felt confident of placing our camp high up on the southeast ridge. We heaved on our loads again and moved 150 feet up the ridge to the dump made by Hunt two days previously. The ridge was quite steep, but the upward-sloping strata of the rocks gave us quite good footholds and the climbing was not technically difficult, although loose snow over the steep rocks demanded care. The dump was at 27,350 feet, but we considered that this was still far too low for an effective summit camp, so somewhat reluctantly we added all this extra gear to our already large loads. Gregory took some more oxygen, Lowe some food and fuel, and I tied on a tent. Apart from Ang Nyima, who was carrying just over forty pounds, we all had loads of from fifty to sixty-three pounds. We continued on up the ridge at a somewhat reduced rate.

Despite our great burdens we were moving steadily, though very slowly. The ridge steepened onto a slope of firm snow and Lowe chipped steps up it for fifty feet. By 2 P.M. we were beginning to tire and started looking for a camp site. The ridge appeared to have no relief at all and continued upward in one unbroken sweep. We plugged slowly on, looking for a ledge without success. Again and again we hopefully labored up to a prospective site only to find that it was still at a 45-degree angle. We were getting a little desperate until Tenzing, remembering the ground from the previous year, suggested a traverse over steep slopes to the left, which finally landed us onto a relatively flat spot beneath a rock bluff.

It was 2.30 and we decided to camp here. All day the magnificent peak of Lhotse had commanded our attention, but now its summit was just below us. We estimated our height at 27,900 feet. Lowe, Gregory, and Ang Nyima dropped their loads on the site with relief. They were tired but well satisfied with the height gained, and to them must go a great deal of the credit for the successful climb of the following day. Wasting no time, they hurried off back to the South Col.

It was with a certain feeling of loneliness that we watched our cheerful companions slowly descending the

ridge, but we had much to do. We removed our oxygen
sets in order to conserve our supplies and set to work with
our ice axes to clear the tiny platform. We scratched off
all the snow to reveal a rock slope at an angle of some 30
degrees. The rocks were well frozen in, but by the end of

a couple of hours' solid work we had managed to pry loose
sufficient stones to level out two strips of ground a yard
wide and six feet long, but almost a foot different in levels.
Even though not breathing oxygen, we could still work
quite hard, but rested every ten minutes or so in order to
regain our breath and energy.

We pitched our tent on this double level and tied it
down as best we could. There were no suitable rocks
around which to hitch our tent guys, and the snow was far

too soft to hold aluminum tent pegs. We sank several of our oxygen bottles in the soft snow and attached the guys to these as a somewhat unreliable anchor. Then while Tenzing began heating some soup I made a tally of our limited oxygen supplies. They were much less than we had hoped. For the assault we had only one and two-thirds bottles each. It was obvious that if we were to have sufficient endurance we would be unable to use the four liters per minute that we had originally planned, but I estimated that if we reduced our supplies to three liters per minute we might still have a chance. I prepared the sets and made the necessary adjustments. One thing in our favor was that Evans and Bourdillon had left two bottles of oxygen, still one-third full, some hundreds of feet above our camp. We were relying on this oxygen to get us back to the South Col.

As the sun set we crawled finally into our tent, put on all our warm clothing and wriggled into our sleeping bags. We drank vast quantities of liquid and had a satisfying meal out of our store of delicacies: sardines on biscuits, canned apricots, dates, and biscuits and jam and honey. The canned apricots were a great treat, but it was necessary first to thaw them out of their frozen state over our roaring Primus. In spite of the great height, our breathing was almost normal until a sudden exertion would cause us to pant a little. Tenzing laid his air mattress on the lower shelf half-overhanging the steep slope below and calmly settled down to sleep. I made myself as comfortable as possible half-sitting and half-reclining on the upper shelf with my feet braced on the lower shelf. This position, while not particularly comfortable, had decided advantages. We had been experiencing extremely strong gusts of wind every ten minutes, and whenever I received warning of the approach of such a gust by a shrilling whine high on the ridge above, I could brace my feet and shoulders and assist our meager anchors to hold the tent steady while it temporarily shook and flapped in a most alarming manner. We had sufficient oxygen for only four hours' sleep at one liter per minute. I decided to use this in two periods of two hours, from 9 to 11 P.M. and from 1 to 3 A.M. While wearing the oxygen we dozed and were reasonably comfortable, but as soon as the supply ran out we began to feel cold and miserable. During the night the thermometer read $-27°$ Centigrade, but fortunately the wind had dropped almost entirely.

At 4 A.M. it was very still. I opened the tent door and looked far out across the dark and sleeping valleys of Nepal. The icy peaks below us were glowing clearly in the early morning light and Tenzing pointed out the monastery of Thyangboche, faintly visible on its dominant spur 16,000 feet below us. It was an encouraging thought to realize that even at this early hour the lamas of Thyangboche would be offering up devotions to their Buddhist gods for our safety and well-being.

We started up our cooker and in a determined effort to prevent the weaknesses arising from dehydration we drank large quantities of lemon juice and sugar, and followed this with our last can of sardines on biscuits. I dragged our oxygen sets into the tent, cleaned the ice off them and then completely rechecked and tested them. I had removed my boots, which had become a little wet the day before, and they were now frozen solid. Drastic measures were called for, so I cooked them over the fierce flame of the Primus and despite the very strong smell of burning leather managed to soften them up. Over our down clothing we donned our windproofs and onto our hands we pulled three pairs of gloves—silk, woolen, and windproof.

At 6.30 A.M. we crawled out of our tent into the snow, hoisted our thirty pounds of oxygen gear onto our backs, connected up our masks and turned on the valves to bring life-giving oxygen into our lungs. A few good deep breaths and we were ready to go. Still a little worried about my cold feet, I asked Tenzing to move off and he kicked a deep line of steps away from the rock bluff which protected our tent, out onto the steep powder snow slope to the left of the main ridge. The ridge was now all bathed in sunlight and we could see our first objective, the south summit, far above us. Tenzing, moving purposefully, kicked steps in a long traverse back toward the ridge and we reached its crest just where it forms a great distinctive snow bump at about 28,000 feet. From here the ridge narrowed to a knife-edge and as my feet were now warm I took over the lead.

We were moving slowly but steadily and had no need to stop in order to regain our breath, and I felt that we had plenty in reserve. The soft unstable snow made a route on top of the ridge both difficult and dangerous, so I moved a little down on the steep left side where the wind had produced a thin crust which sometimes held my weight but more often than not gave way with a sudden knock that was disastrous to both balance and morale. After several hundred feet of this rather trying ridge, we came to a tiny hollow and found there the two oxygen bottles left on the earlier attempt by Evans and Bourdillon. I scraped the ice off the gauges and was greatly relieved to find that they still contained several hundred liters of oxygen—sufficient to get us down to the South Col if used very sparingly. With the comforting thought of these oxygen bottles behind us, I continued making the trail on up the ridge, which soon steepened and broadened into the very formidable snow face leading up for the last 400 feet to the southern summit.

The snow conditions on this face were, we felt, distinctly dangerous, but as no alternative route seemed available, we persisted in our strenuous and uncomfortable efforts to beat a trail up it. We made frequent changes of lead on this very trying section and on one occasion as I was stamping a trail in the deep snow a section around me gave way and I slipped back through three or four of my steps. I discussed with Tenzing the advisability of going on and he, although admitting that he felt very unhappy about the snow conditions, finished with his familiar phrase, "Just as you wish." I decided to go on.

It was with some relief that we finally reached some firmer snow higher up and then chipped steps up the

last steep slopes and cramponed on to the South Peak. It
was now 9 A.M. We looked with some interest at the virgin
ridge ahead. Both Bourdillon and Evans had been depress-
ingly definite about its problems and difficulties and we
realized that it could form an almost insuperable barrier.
At first glance it was certainly impressive and even rather
frightening. On the right, great contorted cornices, overhanging masses of snow and ice, stuck out like twisted
fingers over the 10,000-foot drop of the Kangshung Face.
Any move onto these cornices could only bring disaster.
From the cornices the ridge dropped steeply to the left
until the snow merged with the great rock face sweeping
up from the Western Cwm. Only one encouraging feature
was apparent. The steep snow slope between the cornices
and the rock precipices seemed to be composed of firm,
hard snow. If the snow proved soft and unstable, our
chances of getting along the ridge were few indeed. If we
could cut a trail of steps along this slope, we could make
some progress at least.

We cut a seat for ourselves just below the south summit and removed our oxygen. Once again I worked out
the mental arithmetic that was one of my main preoccu-
pations on the way up and down the mountain. As our
first partly full bottle of oxygen was now exhausted, we
had only one full bottle left. Eight hundred liters of oxygen at three liters per minute? How long could we last?
I estimated that this should give us four and a half hours
of going. Our apparatus was now much lighter, weighing
just over twenty pounds, and as I cut steps down off the

south summit I felt a distinct sense of freedom and well-being quite contrary to what I had expected at this great altitude.

As my ice ax bit into the first steep slope of the ridge, my highest hopes were realized. The snow was crystalline and firm. Two or three rhythmical blows of the ice ax produced a step large enough even for our oversized high-altitude boots and, the most encouraging feature of all, a firm thrust of the ice ax would sink it halfway up the shaft, giving a solid and comfortable belay. We moved one at a time. I realized that our margin of safety at this altitude was not great and that we must take every care and precaution. I would cut a forty-foot line of steps, Tenzing belaying me while I worked. Then in turn I would sink my shaft and put a few loops of the rope around it and Tenzing, protected against a breaking step, would move up to me. Then once again as he belayed me I would go on cutting. In a number of places the overhanging ice cornices were very large indeed and in order to escape them I cut a line of steps down to where the snow met the rocks on the west. It was a great thrill to look straight down this enormous rock face and to see, 8,000 feet below us, the tiny tents of Camp IV in the Western Cwm. Scrambling on the rocks and cutting handholds on the snow, we were able to shuffle past these difficult portions.

On one of these occasions I noted that Tenzing, who had been going quite well, had suddenly slowed up considerably and seemed to be breathing with difficulty. The Sherpas had little idea of the workings of an oxygen set and from past experience I immediately suspected his oxygen supply. I noticed that hanging from the exhaust tube of his oxygen mask were icicles, and on closer examination found that this tube, some two inches in diameter, was completely blocked with ice. I was able to clear it out and gave him much needed relief. On checking my own set I found that the same thing was occurring, though it had not reached the stage to have caused me any discomfort. From then on I kept a much closer check on this problem.

The weather for Everest seemed practically perfect. Insulated as we were in all our down clothing and windproofs, we suffered no discomfort from cold or wind. However, on one occasion I removed my sunglasses to examine more closely a difficult section of the ridge but was very soon blinded by the fine snow driven by the bitter wind and hastily replaced them. I went on cutting steps. To my surprise I was enjoying the climb as much as I had ever enjoyed a fine ridge in my own New Zealand Alps.

After an hour's steady going we reached the foot of the most formidable looking problem on the ridge—a rock step some forty feet high. We had known of the existence of this step from aerial photographs and had also seen it through our binoculars from Thyangboche. We realized that at this altitude it might well spell the difference between success and failure. The rock itself, smooth and almost holdless, might have been an interesting Sunday afternoon problem to a group of expert rock climbers in the Lake District, but here it was a barrier beyond our feeble strength to overcome.

I could see no way of turning it on the steep rock bluff on the west, but fortunately another possibility of tackling it still remained. On its east side was another great cornice and running up the full forty feet of the step was a narrow crack between the cornice and the rock. Leaving Tenzing to belay me as best he could, I jammed my way into this crack, then kicking backwards with my crampons I sank their spikes deep into the frozen snow behind me and levered myself off the ground. Taking advantage of every little rock hold and all the force of knee, shoulder, and arms I could muster, I literally cramponed backwards up the crack, with a fervent prayer that the cornice would remain attached to the rock. Despite the considerable effort involved, my progress although slow was steady, and as Tenzing payed out the rope I inched my way upward until I could finally reach over the top of the rock and drag myself out of the crack onto a wide ledge. For a few moments I lay regaining my breath and for the first time really felt the fierce determination that nothing now could stop our reaching the top. I took a firm stance on the ledge and signaled to Tenzing to come on up. As I heaved hard on the rope Tenzing wriggled his way up the crack and finally collapsed exhausted at the top like a giant fish when it has just been hauled from the sea after a terrible struggle.

I checked both our oxygen sets and roughly calculated our flow rates. Everything seemed to be going well. Probably owing to the strain imposed on him by the trouble with his oxygen set, Tenzing had been moving rather slowly but he was climbing safely, and this was the major consideration. His only comment on my inquiring of his condition was to smile and wave along the ridge. We were going so well at three liters per minute that I was determined now if necessary to cut down our flow rate to two liters per minute if the extra endurance was required.

The ridge continued as before. Giant cornices on the right, steep rock slopes on the left. I went on cutting steps on the narrow strip of snow. The ridge curved away to the right and we had no idea where the top was. As I cut around the back of one hump, another higher one would swing into view. Time was passing and the ridge seemed never-ending. In one place where the angle of the ridge had eased off, I tried cramponing without cutting steps, hoping this would save time, but I quickly realized that our margin of safety on these steep slopes at this altitude was too small, so I went on step cutting. I was beginning to tire a little now. I had been cutting steps continuously for two hours, and Tenzing, too, was moving very slowly. As I chipped steps around still another corner, I wondered rather dully just how long we could keep it up. Our original zest had now quite gone and it was turning more into a grim struggle.

I then realized that the ridge ahead, instead of still monotonously rising, now dropped sharply away, and far below I could see the North Col and the Rongbuk Glacier. I looked upward to see a narrow snow ridge running up to a snowy summit. A few more whacks of the ice ax in the firm snow and we stood on top.

My initial feelings were of relief—relief that there were no more steps to cut—no more ridges to traverse and no more humps to tantalize us with hopes of success. I looked at Tenzing and in spite of the balaclava, goggles, and oxygen mask all encrusted with long icicles that concealed his face, there was no disguising his infectious grin of pure delight as he looked all around him. We shook hands and then Tenzing threw his arm around my shoulders and we thumped each other on the back until we were almost breathless. It was 11.30 A.M. The ridge had taken us two and a half hours, but it seemed like a lifetime. I turned off the oxygen and removed my set. I had carried my camera, loaded with color film, inside my shirt to keep it warm, so I now produced it and got Tenzing to pose on top for me, waving his ax on which was a string of flags—British, Nepalese, United Nations, and Indian. Then I turned my attention to the great stretch of country lying below us in every direction.

To the east was our giant neighbor Makalu, unexplored and unclimbed, and even on top of Everest the mountaineering instinct was sufficiently strong to cause me to spend some moments conjecturing as to whether a route up that mountain might not exist. Far away across the clouds the great bulk of Kangchenjunga loomed on the horizon. To the west, Cho Oyu, our old adversary from 1952, dominated the scene and we could see the great unexplored

ranges of Nepal stretching off into the distance. The most important photograph, I felt, was a shot down the north ridge, showing the North Col and the old route which had been made famous by the struggles of those great climbers of the 1920s and 1930s. I had little hope of the results being particularly successful, as I had a lot of difficulty in holding the camera steady in my clumsy gloves, but I felt that they would at least serve as a record. After some ten minutes of this, I realized that I was becoming rather clumsy-fingered and slow-moving, so I quickly replaced my oxygen set and experienced once more the stimulating effect of even a few liters of oxygen. Meanwhile, Tenzing had made a little hole in the snow and in it he placed various small articles of food—a bar of chocolate, a packet of biscuits, and a handful of candies. Small offerings, indeed, but at least a token gift to the gods that all devout Buddhists believe have their home on this lofty summit. While we were together on the South Col two days before, Hunt had given me a small crucifix which he had asked me to take to the top. I, too, made a hole in the snow and placed the crucifix beside Tenzing's gifts.

I checked our oxygen once again and worked out our endurance. We would have to move fast in order to reach our life-saving reserve below the south summit. After fifteen minutes we turned to go. We had looked briefly for any signs of Mallory and Irvine, but had seen nothing. We both felt a little tired, for the reaction was setting in and we must get off the mountain quickly. I moved down off the summit onto our steps. Wasting no time, we cramponed along our tracks, spurred by the urgency of diminishing oxygen. Bump followed bump in rapid succession. In what seemed almost miraculous time, we reached the top of the rock step. Now, with the almost casual indifference of familiarity, we kicked and jammed our way down it again. We were tired, but not too tired to be careful. We scrambled cautiously over the rock traverse, moved one at a time over shaky snow sections and finally cramponed up our steps and back onto the South Peak.

Only one hour from the top! A swig of sweetened lemonade refreshed us and we turned down again. Throughout the climb we had a constant nagging fear of our return down the great snow slope, and as I led down I packed each step with as much care as if our lives depended on it, as well they might. The terrific impression of exposure as we looked straight down onto the Kangshung glacier, still 10,000 feet below us, made us move with the greatest caution, and every step down seemed a step nearer safety. When we finally moved off the slope onto the ridge below, we looked at each other and without speaking we both almost visibly shrugged off the sense of fear that had been with us all day.

We were now very tired but moved automatically down to the two reserve cylinders on the ridge. As we were only a short distance from camp and had a few liters of oxygen left in our own bottles, we carried the extra cylinders down our tracks and reached our tent on its crazy platform at 2 P.M. Already the moderate winds of the afternoon had wrenched the tent loose from some of its fastenings and it presented a forlorn sight. We had still to reach the South Col. While Tenzing lit the kerosene stove and began to make a lemonade drink heavily sweetened with sugar, I changed our oxygen sets onto the last partly filled bottles and cut down our flow rates to two liters per minute. In contrast to the previous day, when we were working vigorously without oxygen at this camp, we now felt very weak and exhausted. Far below on the South Col we could see minute figures moving and knew that Lowe and Noyce would be waiting for our descent. We had no extra sleeping bags and air mattresses on the South Col, so reluctantly tied our own onto our oxygen frames. Then with a last look at the camp that had served us so well we turned downward with dragging feet and set ourselves to the task of safely descending the ridge.

Our faculties seemed numbed and the time passed as in a dream, but finally we reached the site of the Swiss Ridge Camp and branched off on our last stage down onto the great couloir. There an unpleasant surprise greeted us. The strong wind which had been blowing in the latter part of our climb had completely wiped out all our steps and only a hard, steep, frozen slope lay before us. There was no alternative but to start cutting again. With a grunt of disgust I chipped steps laboriously downward for two hundred feet. Gusts of driving wind whirling down off the ridge tried to pluck us from our steps. Tenzing took over the lead and cut down another hundred feet, then moved into softer snow and kicked a track down the easier slopes at the bottom of the couloir. We cramponed wearily down the long slopes above the South Col.

A figure came toward us and met us a couple of hundred feet above the camp. It was George Lowe, laden with hot soup and emergency oxygen.

We were too tired to make any response to Lowe's enthusiastic acceptance of our news. We stumped down to the Col and slowly ground our way up the short rise to the camp. Just short of the tents my oxygen ran out. We had had enough to do the job, but by no means too much. We crawled into the tent and with a sigh of sheer delight collapsed into our sleeping bags, while the tents flapped and shook under the perpetual South Col gale. That night, our last on the South Col, was a restless one indeed. The bitter cold once again made any deep and restful sleep impossible and the stimulating effects of our success made us so mentally active that we lay there for half the night reliving all the exciting incidents and murmuring to each other between chattering teeth. Early the following morning we were all very weak and made slow but determined preparations for our departure.

The two-hundred-foot slope above the South Col was a great trial, and even when we commenced the long traverse down toward Camp VII we found it necessary to move very slowly and to have frequent rests. The upper part of the Lhotse glacier seemed very steep to us and as we came down the ice steps toward Camp VII our main wish was to rest. We were only thirty yards from the camp when a cheerful shout attracted our attention and there to greet us were Charles Wylie and several of the Sherpas, all looking fresh and strong and with the same question trembling on their lips. The hot drinks they pressed into our hands and their joyful acceptance of our news were a great stimulant in themselves and we continued on down the Lhotse glacier mentally if not physically refreshed.

As we approached Camp IV, tiny figures appeared from the tents and slowly drifted up the track. We made no signal to them but wearily moved down the track toward them. When only fifty yards away, Lowe with characteristic enthusiasm gave the "thumbs up" signal and waved his ice ax in the direction of the summit. Immediately the scene was galvanized into activity and our approaching companions, forgetting their weakness, ran up the snow toward us. As we greeted them all, perhaps a little emotionally, I felt more than ever before that very strong feeling of friendship and co-operation that had been the decisive factor throughout the expedition.

What a thrill it was to be able to tell them that all their efforts amongst the tottering chaos of the Icefall, the disheartening plunging up the snowy inferno of the Western Cwm, the difficult technical ice work on the Lhotse Face, and the grim and nerve-racking toil above the South Col had been fully rewarded and that we had reached the top.

To see the unashamed joy spread over the tired, strained face of our gallant and determined leader was to me reward enough in itself.